JAMES PATTERSON

THE MIDNIGHT CLUB

HarperCollins*Publishers*

HarperCollins*Publishers*
77–85 Fulham Palace Road,
Hammersmith, London W6 8JB

www.harpercollins.co.uk

This paperback edition 2006
10

First published in Great Britain by
Century in 1990

Published by HarperCollins in 1998

Copyright © James Patterson 1989

The Author asserts the moral right to
be identified as the author of this work

ISBN-13 978-0-00-722489-0
ISBN-10 0-00-722489-3

Set in Meridien

Printed and bound in Great Britain by
Clays Limited, St Ives plc

This is for J., for P., and for N.,
who told me what it's like to be in the Chair

It's for my father and mother
Charles and Isabelle

Night of
the Detective

1

Long Beach, New York
March 1986

The night that John Stefanovitch was shot couldn't have been colder, or the stars more dazzling in high winter skies.

Shortly past midnight, Stefanovitch tramped down the creaking, solidly frozen boardwalk at Long Beach. He was humming 'Surfer Girl,' one of those awful beach-town ditties that could usually bring a smile to his lips.

Stefanovitch's eyes stayed sharply focused. They very carefully swept the silent, gritty beachfront neighborhood.

The Grave Dancer was nearby. Stefanovitch felt it all through his body. It was a second sense he had sometimes, almost a paranormal gift. The scumbucket he had been tracking for almost two years was so close it made his skin crawl.

He finally arrived back on Florida Street, the desolate side lane where he and his detectives had agreed to gather. Actually, he'd been there ten minutes ago, then walked down to New York Avenue and the funkytown boardwalk to clear his head.

The full team of fourteen Narcotics detectives was assembled. This was a joint Nassau County and NYPD strike force, each of them handpicked to go after the Grave Dancer.

Stefanovitch said his hellos, patting the backs of down parkas, playing the crowd.

Stefanovitch fit in, which was unusual for a lieutenant. Maybe it was because he'd never seemed overly impressed with himself, never felt making 'Loo' meant that much anyway. Or maybe it was because he was more cynical, and funnier about his perspective on the world, than any of the detectives working under him.

True to form, he was wearing a weathered black leather coat, over a hooded gray sweatshirt. The outfit made his six feet two inches seem more compact, more physically impressive. Underneath a crushed black fedora, his hair was long and brown, and unruly. His eyes were a cool, dark brown, but could warm up once he got comfortable with someone. People said Stefanovitch looked like some kind of flaky film star, and he thought that wasn't all bad. Flaky film stars seemed to be running the world these days.

In the electrified darkness of Florida Street, car trunks sprung open with almost no sound. Out came .357 Magnums, twelve-gauge shotguns, NYPD- and Nassau County-issue guns. Also, full ammo pouches.

The beachfront neighborhood felt as if it were about to explode.

The dope raid was going to be bigger than the celebrated French Connection. As much as two hundred kilograms; over a million and a half fixes for New York's 250,000 addicts.

They were closing in on Alexandre St-Germain, the animal called the Grave Dancer; the man who had been Stefanovitch's obsession during the past twenty-two months. That was no accident either. Stefanovitch regularly got the most important narcotics cases in the NYPD. He was talented, and he thrived on challenges. For the past few years he'd been the department's 'big play man.' Nothing but the fast track for him.

Stefanovitch finally turned to his second in command, a 260-pound detective named Bear Kupchek. 'You all ready, Charlie Chan?' he asked.

'Ah. Wise man never ready to walk down dark alleyway at night.' Kupchek grinned like the portly Chinese detective.

'Fuck you, Charlie,' said Stefanovitch.

John and Anna Stefanovitch
Brooklyn Heights

Hours before, Stefanovitch and his wife, Anna, had gone out to dinner. He had taken her to the glittery River Cafe, tucked like an expensive tiara beneath the Brooklyn Bridge.

After dinner, they had gone back to their apartment in Brooklyn and snuck up to the indoor pool on the roof. It was closed after nine, but Stefanovitch had a key. He brought a tape deck, and they danced on the rooftop, first to Robert Cray and his blues, then to the romantic Brazilian Laurindo Almeida.

'We're breaking the law that you're sworn to uphold,' Anna whispered against his cheek. She was so soft and fine to hold; a great slow dancer, too. Elegant and totally desirable.

'Bad law. Unenforceable,' Stefanovitch whispered back.

'Some policeman you are. No respect for authority.'

'You bet. I know too many authority figures.'

He started to unbutton Anna's dress, which picked up the green of her eyes, the gold of her hair, and which felt like the smoothest silk under his fingers.

'You going to try for indecent exposure now?' Anna smiled softly.

'For starters maybe. I have some other felonies in mind, too.'

After they slipped out of their dinner clothes, they did a few slow laps; then they floated languorously in the moonlit pool, under the glass rooftop, the twinkling stars.

With Anna, Stefanovitch had a way of doing wonderfully romantic things. He'd become a master of the unexpected: a dozen American roses arriving at the grade school where Anna taught fourth grade; a weekend ski trip to Stowe, in Vermont; gold shell earrings he spent an hour at Saks picking out himself.

He reached out and pulled her body closer in the deep end of the pool. Her green eyes were warm and wise – spectacular eyes. Her body seemed glazed in the moonlight. She was a fantasy he'd had since he'd been a kid in school. The two of them fit together perfectly.

'Sometimes I can't believe how much I love you,' he whispered, his breath catching slightly on the words. 'Anna, I love you more than all the rest of my life put together. I'd be lost without you. Sad but true.'

'Not so sad, Stef.'

They made tender, then passionate love in the still, blue-green water of the swimming pool. In the middle of the coldest March in years.

At the moment, John Stefanovitch was sure he had everything he had ever wanted out of life. Getting St-Germain would be the icing on his cake.

The Grave Dancer
Long Beach

Until past midnight, Alexandre St-Germain had been at a black tie affair given at a Fifth Avenue penthouse in Manhattan. The party-goers were mostly investment bankers and other Wall Street power brokers; their wives; assorted young playthings. A very good black combo played, and seemed particularly out of place in the setting.

St-Germain himself fit in splendidly: he was sophisticated; wittier than any of the bankers; a wealthy and respected European investor with seemingly unlimited capital . . .

Now, the Grave Dancer was approaching Long Beach Island, cruising along in a dark sports car. He was feeling particularly sanguine about the past few weeks. He had been mapping out a strategy that would ultimately change the face of organized crime. He had financial backing, both in New York and abroad. He simply had to make certain nothing went wrong during the next few critical months.

One man has been interfering lately, St-Germain was thinking as he crossed the bridge onto Long Beach. A detective named Stefanovitch had taken it upon himself to make St-Germain's life in America difficult, if not impossible. He was a master at harassment. He was persistent, and cleverer than most policemen. He had already caused more trouble and embarrassment than St-Germain could allow.

Twice he had trailed St-Germain to Europe. He had conducted surveillance watches outside his apartment on Central Park West. One evening, he had followed St-Germain into Le Cirque, practically interviewing the restaurant's owner, Sirio Maccioni.

This desire to prevail against the odds, to tilt against windmills, seemed to be an American trait. St-Germain had watched it fail miserably in Southeast Asia during the early seventies; he would watch it fail again now in New York. Stefanovitch was challenging him, and that couldn't be permitted.

His sports car finally entered Long Beach, and he gunned it toward his rendezvous. An important lesson had to be taught tonight.

John Stefanovitch
Long Beach

Fourteen NYPD and Nassau County detectives walked single file, making uneven lines on either side of Ocean View Street in Long Beach.

They passed forty-year-old tract houses and a few Irish bars on the narrow street. Occasionally, there was a pizza stand or ramshackle novelty store, boarded up for the winter.

'I could use a slice of pizza,' Bear Kupchek cracked. 'Pepperoni and onions, extra cheese.'

'I could use a sane partner,' John Stefanovitch whispered back.

They continued walking until they reached an even narrower street, called Louisiana. Nothing but parked cars were visible there, dented and rusting like the dank beach cottages themselves.

At the far end of Louisiana, the detectives entered a sharp bend, which opened into a wide fork. Two large beach houses stood at either end, like sentinels.

Stefanovitch knew everything about Alexandre St-Germain: that he was the current drug star in Europe, the largest narcotics dealer in years; that he was also known as a businessman in parts of the world, a legitimate financier and investor – which made tripping him up that much more difficult. Stefanovitch knew that St-Germain and his organization were moving very impressively into the United States; that St-Germain had masterminded a Byzantine, highly effective system to control organized crime throughout Europe, known as the 'street law.'

This street law applied to criminals and to the police alike. There were strict rules, and they were known to everyone. Rival crime lords, but also policemen, prosecuting attorneys, even judges who came into conflict with St-Germain's system, were dealt with ruthlessly. Murder and sadistic torture were the usual forms of retribution. Revenge against friends and family members was common. Alexandre St-Germain said that he refused to live by the rules of the weak.

Tonight, Stefanovitch and his Narcotics detectives were breaking the street law. They were striking a major St-Germain drug factory inside the United States.

Stefanovitch's eyes were drawn suddenly to the far left of the cul-de-sac. The house lights there had blinked out.

'Uh-oh. The left. See that?' Bear Kupchek pointed.

Stefanovitch and everyone else stopped, their legs and feet suddenly frozen in step.

The wind from the ocean held a sibilant, almost ominous whistle in the background.

'What's that all about?' Kupchek whispered. 'I hope somebody's just going beddy-bye late.'

'I don't know. Hold tight.' Stefanovitch was slowly raising his Remington. He had a sick feeling, the beginning of an adrenal rush.

Through the trees the moon had cast everything in a pattern of strange black and white shapes.

'Hey, detectives! Big fucking surprise, huh?'

A voice suddenly boomed.

'Hey! . . . Over here!'

More gruff voices came from the opposite side of the narrow street. Several men were hiding in the darkness.

'No! Over here, cocksuckers!'

A row of blinding white floodlights went on. Bright crisscrossing lights bloomed in every direction.

Then heavy gunfire exploded from both sides of the street; a deadly commotion of noise and blazing light commenced on signal.

'*Get down. Everybody get down!*' Stefanovitch yelled as he pressed the safety, pumped his own shotgun, and felt his body shift into automatic.

'Get down!' he screamed as he fired at the beaming lights. 'Everybody, down!'

All over the street there was pandemonium. Detectives were screaming and cursing. Stefanovitch finally dropped on his stomach. He was gasping for breath. He had a flashing thought about Anna: the idea of never seeing her again.

He pressed his body against the freezing cold concrete. He didn't know whether he'd been hit or not. He genuinely didn't know. The odors of motor oil and gasoline stuffed his nose.

Down on his stomach, Stefanovitch wiggled until he was underneath the rear end of a parked car. He ripped his hands and knees as he struggled forward. Where the hell was the backup? What could he do now?

He made it to a second parked car. As he did, his head cracked against the undercarriage. He cursed. His lungs ached horribly. The submachine guns kept giving fire.

For a moment, he was hidden under a third parked car.

He wondered if he should stay there. The auto's body was so low that his face scraped the ground. His mind screamed.

A fourth car was parked up tightly against the third vehicle, cheek to cheek. He kept straining to hear the sound of approaching police sirens.

Nothing. No one in the neighborhood had called the police.

He kept moving from parked car to car. Away from the killers and the massacre. Did they know where he was? Had anyone seen him?

He stopped counting how many cars he'd gone under. He was numb all over from the cold.

The last parked car was anchored at the corner of Ocean View. The attackers' voices were fading down the street. He needed a breath, before he got up and tried to run.

Stefanovitch finally pushed himself from underneath the last car.

Then he ran as fast as he could, sprinting to his left.

He was numb and sweaty-cold, so otherworldly and out of it. He was running, though, and nobody was going to catch him. He zigzagged as he went, feeling like a ground missile released from its cramped vault.

Everything was unreal. His feet had never struck against the pavement quite like this before. His breathing was labored and very painful.

Just keep running.

It was a disembodied thought. It held him together.

Nothing else was important.

He finally saw the side street where he and his men had

parked their cars. The cars, Mustangs and Camaros, Sting-rays, BMWs, were sitting up ahead, silent and empty.

Stefanovitch rounded the corner onto Florida Street. He saw his black van. *Call for help*, his mind screamed.

He fumbled to get the keys out of his pocket as he ran. Finally, a siren screeched in the distance.

The wind and sweat-soaked clothes were biting cold against his skin. His hair threw off water.

Five yards from the van a shotgun thundered loudly in his ears. It went off directly behind him. The explosion reverberated against the bone of Stefanovitch's skull. It rattled his insides.

The first shotgun blast passed clearly through his right side. It seemed so simple to say, to think – *shot in the side*.

The first hit turned John Stefanovitch around, the way a caroming, speeding truck would have, the way a grown person can easily manhandle a small child.

The second shotgun blast exploded almost on top of the first brutal assault. The blast shattered the vertebrae on the left side of Stefanovitch's spinal column. A jagged shard of bone broke through the flesh, like antlers on a wall.

The bullet actually ricocheted inside his body, twisting, turning, like an oblong object under water. Then it burst out his side, leaving a huge hole.

Shot in the back.

Stefanovitch was lying facedown. He was half on, half off the gritty, iced sidewalk pavement.

His eyes were watering, so that he seemed to be crying. He wanted to crawl away, to do something, but he couldn't move an inch.

The hidden gunman finally appeared from the shadows. The gunman walked forward, stopping over the sprawled, spreadeagled body, staring down for a long silent moment.

Stefanovitch could hear the man's breathing, the inhu-man calmness . . . He could hear exactly what the gunman was doing. Suddenly everything was clear and distinct inside his mind. He was about to witness his own murder.

To hear the killer actually pump a third shell into the chamber. To hear him pause for a long, breathless second, then hear him fire again.

One final shot, point-blank into Stefanovitch's back.

Then the Grave Dancer walked away from his supposed pursuer.

Alexandre St-Germain
Brooklyn Heights

Alexandre St-Germain drove a Porsche Turbo Carrera, sleek and midnight blue. Nothing but black glove leather and dim red control lights were visible inside. The only sound was the racing tires against the pavement, a noise like tape being pulled away from an uneven surface.

Lessons, he thought to himself as he drove. The world needed object lessons, but especially the police detective who had come after him; who had stubbornly trailed him for two years.

The apartment building in front of which St-Germain finally parked seemed all wrong. It was faded red brick, rising maybe nineteen or twenty stories. It was the kind of place where mothers on the high floors throw change wrapped in tinfoil down to their kids for ice cream.

The Grave Dancer followed a black woman inside the apartment building, some kind of nurse from the look of the white spongies and stockings showing below her cloth coat.

The hallway of the floor where he got off the elevator was like all the others in the building. The night's stale cooking smells. A clicking in the heating system. Pale blue walls; a worn blue and black hallway runner.

Alexandre St-Germain rang the bell for 9B. He rang the doorbell insistently, seven times.

Finally, a woman's voice came from inside, sounding very hollow and distant.

'I'll be right there. I'm coming. Who is it?'

The dark blue door for 9B swung open. The look on Anna Stefanovitch's face instantly revealed her lack of comprehension.

'Something happened to Stef,' she said. A statement of fact, not a question.

'Yes. And now something is happening to you.'

There was no pain. Anna definitely *heard* the hollow, muffled shotgun blast from less than three feet away. She saw the bright streak of light illuminate the hallway, a little like a photographer's flash camera going off. Anna Stefanovitch was dead before she hit the floor inside the foyer.

Alexandre St-Germain, the Grave Dancer, left the apartment building as confidently as he had arrived.

PART ONE

The Grave Dancer

2

Isiah Parker
125th Street, June 1988

The Orange Julius stand tucked on the corner of 125th Street and Frederick Douglass Boulevard had at least one advantage over many of the other stores in the area – an open, lively view onto the street. A view of the changing, or rather, the decaying neighborhood: the sealed-off and abandoned buildings, like Blumstein's, Harlem's last department store, and the Loews Victoria, both shut down now. The Hotel Teresa, where Fidel Castro had once stayed while visiting New York, now an office building. The Apollo – where Basie, and Bessie Smith, Billy Eckstine and Ellington had played – closed, and now opened up again. Who knew for how long?

Isiah Parker stood behind the brightly colored counter of the Orange Julius stand. He was dutifully wiping it down, while he watched the fascinating panorama of 125th Street stretch out before him. He had the thought that squalor and misery had never been so interesting; he had no idea why that was so.

He heard his name being called by the juice-stand boss. 'Hey, man, you deaf or what? Two fucking banana Julius, man.'

Isiah Parker wasn't deaf. As far as his hearing went, he was discovering lately that he had rabbit ears. He was like the professional athletes whose hearing seemed to magnify personal insults and jeers from the grandstands. Parker thought briefly about making an Orange Julius concoction out of the juice-stand boss's face. He thought better of it, for the moment, anyway.

'Yes sir, two Julies on the way,' he muttered in a low growl directed at the boss.

'Two *banana* Julius.'

'Yes sir, two banana Julies coming up.'

All this time, he had kept his attention beaconed out onto the street. Specifically, he was watching the crumbling overpass that supported the ancient New York Central Railroad tracks.

He'd been waiting almost a week for this very moment . . . and now he wasn't sure what to look for. So he watched real closely, while he fixed the Julies: crushed ice, fresh banana, special surgary powder from the parent company, godawful sweet-and-sour taste, in his opinion.

Then suddenly, Isiah Parker was sure what he was watching. The two dealers got sloppy, and he saw the exchange. He saw the briefest flash of dollar green out on the street.

'Hey you, Parker. *Parker!*' he heard once again.

'Hey *you*, man,' Parker talked back. 'You shut the fuck up. Just shut your mouth, understand?'

Perhaps for the first time in his life, the bullying Orange Julius boss shut up. There was something about the look on Parker's face that said he was a lot more serious than any ordinary counter guy ought to be.

Suddenly, Isiah Parker vaulted up and over the counter. There was a powerful animal spring in his body.

The usual loiterers inside the juice stand looked up as he burst out of the scarred Plexiglas doors. He was holding a .22-caliber revolver up toward the sky and the molded stone rooftops of nearby buildings.

Across 125th Street, one of the cocaine dealers had already seen him coming.

Damn, Parker thought to himself.

The drug dealer and his buddy suddenly began to sprint down Frederick Douglass Boulevard. They went due east on 125th Street. Then south. And east again.

A cabbie honked at him angrily. Parker's hand whacked down hard on the yellow cab's hood. *Take absolutely nobody's shit on the street*. That was the lesson he'd learned a long time ago in Harlem.

Then Parker was running at full speed. He was running wildly, like yet another hyped-up junkie or thief. He was doing what he had once loved to do, in another time and place. Something he'd done well enough to get into a Texas college on a track scholarship. College, where he learned to deal with his anger a little, learned to mask it better, anyway, talk around it.

At thirty-five years old, he could still run. Maybe not any record-breaking hundred-yard dashes, but he could run faster than two pitiful drug pushers who had just tried to sell a slab of coke to fourteen-year-old kids on 125th.

Faster than two total scumbags who strolled the Harlem neighborhood with no respect for anybody or anything. Like the people here were nothing, and not a single thing mattered except their making money off the sadness, off the need for a little flash of hope and painless escape.

Parker started to smile as he ran. Wild sense of humor up in Harlem these days. One of the dope dealers must have pulled a muscle, because he started limping and grabbing at his left thigh. Now *that* was hilarious.

Isiah Parker flashed by him as if he were standing still on a relay block. He pistol-butted the drug dealer on the side of his head as he went by. The dealer went down in the gutter in a heap of flashy clothes.

Parker was almost sure the other dealer was named Pedro Cruz, a Colombian cowboy who had been slumming in the 125th Street neighborhood for the past few months. Pedro Cruz could really run.

As if to underscore that fact, Parker felt a fire exploding inside his chest. His thighs were starting to burn. His heart was slamming around, and things were getting congested and painful. Eight blocks already. C'mon, man, get tired.

Some people standing along 124th Street recognized Parker. Isiah Parker had been around the neighborhood for a long time. A lot of people knew Isiah. Even more of them had known his brother, Marcus.

Familiarity aside, nobody was going to stop the scum dealer he was chasing. You stopped some South American-looking guy in Harlem, you could wind up dead, or in even worse trouble.

Besides, chase scenes were fun to watch on a slow-moving summer afternoon, better than a Sylvester Stallone movie at the Loews Theatre.

One Hundred Twenty-fourth Street was like a grave-yard for old, busted-up Plymouths, Chevys, Fords. A few neighborhood dudes clapped for the footrace going down on the otherwise hot and boring afternoon. Nobody seemed to care why the chase had started.

Finally, Parker was running almost side by side with the Colombian drug pusher. He looked over at the other man – almost like he wanted to pass, instead of catch him.

The drug dealer was Pedro Cruz, all right. The bearded Colombian tough didn't even know how to look frightened. He was trying to figure how to go for his gun and keep running full speed at the same time.

His right hand was clawing furiously inside the flapping nylon vest, which he wore over the bare, brown skin of his chest.

Parker finally took a full-stride lead on Cruz.

Suddenly, Isiah Parker seemed to be floating *backward* in time and space . . .

His arm came up, his elbow bent, and it smashed full force into the drug dealer's chin.

Cruz toppled over in a complicated three-point cart-wheel. He ended up in a crumpled heap against a sagging cyclone fence that was full of holes, so that everybody in the neighborhood could get in and out of the yard as they wished.

Isiah Parker was pleased that he hadn't shot the drug dealer. He took out his .22 revolver and pointed it up at the hunched-over, snooping superintendent on a nearby brownstone porch. The superintendent cringed, and tried to slime away.

'I'm a police officer . . .,' Parker said between gasping breaths. 'Call the Nineteenth Precinct . . .'

The superintendent grinned as if he had just won on *Family Feud* or *Wheel of Fortune*. He shuffled back inside his building and called the police. He appreciated a good chase scene on *Miami Vice*, or on his front porch, for that matter. Harlem was still pretty good for that, at least.

At three in the afternoon, New York undercover detective Isiah Parker was still wearing the Orange Julius T-shirt and his stained juice-stand apron. He'd lost the leather hat somewhere, a nice chapeau, too.

The strange outfit made him seem like a regular New York workingman. It made him feel like part of the gritty neighborhood; it didn't matter which neighborhood.

This neighborhood was in southern Harlem, between Broadway and West End Avenue. Parker stood on the street corner, sucking on an orange Italian ice, checking out the scene. He was noting little things he would need to remember tonight, this night of revenge.

Finally, Isiah Parker headed back to the Nineteenth Precinct in Harlem, where he was still on duty until four-thirty.

3

West Ninty-ninth Street
Midnight

On the southernmost border of Harlem, the summer night had turned sticky-hot, almost fetid. A few blocks away, families were sleeping out on fire escapes and on tenement rooftops.

A battered black Ford Escort was parked halfway between Riverside Drive and West End Avenue on Ninety-ninth Street. Three men were cramped inside the car, waiting in the darkness.

At twenty past twelve they were rewarded for their diligence and patience.

'That's them now. They're here. Blue Mercedes.'

A man named Jimmy Burke spoke softly inside the Escort. He straightened himself behind the car's steering wheel. He gestured down Ninety-ninth Street, toward a town house known to the men in the Escort as Allure.

The four-story town house was overshadowed by the neighborhood's taller and more stately apartment buildings. Discreet and inconspicuous, its midblock location allowed visitors to slip in and out with a minimum of notice.

A dark blue Mercedes stretch limousine had eased to a stop in front of the elegant town house. A steep gray-stone stoop led the way to oak double doors, illuminated by antique gaslight lamps.

Two men in dark business suits stepped out of the limousine. The men carefully peered around the street before allowing a third passenger to follow them out into the night.

'Two soldiers . . . A driver. He sure as hell travels light.'

One of the men inside the Escort had been stretched across the length of the backseat. Isiah Parker leaned forward now. He had closely cropped black hair, and a smoothly handsome face. His rangy body strongly suggested professional athletics, though Parker would have said it was his skin color, not his body, that made some people think he might have been a basketball player once upon a time.

'We'll give the garbage an hour or so to relax and get comfortable,' Parker said, speaking calmly. 'Then we go in. Why don't you turn on the radio, Jimmy? Brothers on Ninety-ninth Street would be listening to a little music, you know. Ba-dah-dah-deet. Let's do it up right.'

Alexandre St-Germain
Allure

Alexandre St-Germain was sitting on top of the world, and he knew it. How many other men had succeeded in one business, much less two? How many had entrée into Wall Street boardrooms, but also the private homes of Anthony (Joe Batters) Accardo, of Carmine Persico?

St-Germain even understood the danger of personal vanity. He had seen the results again and again. And yet, he knew he was smarter than other men. He had read more; experienced far more. He had been educated at the Sorbonne: economics and biology. He preferred the school of hard knocks.

At twenty-two, he had been known in Marseilles as Mercedes. Just the single name, which everyone in the demimonde seemed to know. Even then, he had a special quality that allowed him to buy and sell narcotics on the docks, and then mingle with the rich on their priceless yachts. Alexandre St-Germain had style; he had exceptional good looks; plus the gift of charm. He had learned to use these qualities to unlock doors everywhere around the world.

In Tripoli, he was the Butcher – the chief contact for arms deals with Syria and Libya, for any murderers willing to pay for the highest quality and service.

Now he was known by police departments as the Grave Dancer. He was a man with many different faces, different names, different life-styles.

So this is Allure, St-Germain considered as he wandered through a spacious foyer, then the luxurious living room downstairs. He smiled as he observed the richly furnished surroundings inside the club on West Ninety-ninth Street . . . Elaborately carved double doors. Cold marble floors. A de Kooning, a Pissarro, a Klee. A piano room leading into a planted solarium.

It was mostly eclectic. Art Deco here and there. A hint of Italian Renaissance. Gallic touches such as a Louis XVI buffet in the hallway, some antique French prints.

There was a wet bar stocked with cut glass decanters, bottles of Taittinger, hock, fresh lime and lemons, ice that looked like assortments of diamonds. Fresh flowers: mossed roses and nosegays graced a long serving table.

And the most beautiful women and young boys were stationed everywhere. They reminded him of models at a Paris fashion show, gently mouthing their hellos, affecting their effete bows. A few wore body paint, their faces streaked like artful urban savages.

Some of the most respected men in the world were clients here, he knew. The overdone elegance was an attempt to pander to their wealth and supposed taste; to assuage middle-class American guilt, perhaps; to mask the reality that this was a highly expensive bordello, one of the finest in the world.

He was escorted by a tall black model, who took him arm in arm up mahogany stairs to the second floor. A painted runner distinguished the staircase. The model was slender and long-legged, superior in every way.

He was aware of a slight surge of anticipation. He wondered what surprises had been prepared for him tonight.

Alexandre St-Germain pushed open the heavy oak bedroom door on the second floor. The woman at his side had silently, very efficiently, vanished.

The two women inside the bedroom suite at Allure were exquisite, far surpassing his escort upstairs, or any of the courtesans he'd seen so far. Both were young; both call girls captured the essence of innocent, wide-eyed American beauty.

So far, so good. Very good, indeed.

'*Je m'appelle Kay,*' one of them said to him.

'*Bienvenu à Allure. On nous a choisies de vous saluer, de dire bonjour . . . Il y a d'autres jeunes filles, si vous desirez.*'

'No, I don't desire any other women,' St-Germain answered in English. 'The two of you are very beautiful.'

The woman who had spoken first, Kay, was dark-haired, but extremely fair-skinned. Her skin actually looked dusted with some kind of fine powder. Her eyes were delicately sketched. The powder accentuated her cheekbones. Her hair was combed to one side, softly pulled behind her ear.

She communicated expressively with slender hands. Her smile was brilliant, and seemed sincere. She was very good indeed. Even her French was polished.

'I'm Kimberly. Kim.' The second girl seemed shy, younger than the first. She was no more than eighteen, with long blond hair, flowing almost to the bottom of her spine.

The scent of expensive perfume reached St-Germain as he stood transfixed in the open doorway. The smell of flowers surrounded him. Things were done to perfection at Allure, just the way St-Germain demanded that they be.

The bedroom suite was a fantasy maze of cut glass, Italian marble, two-inch-thick carpeting, and mosaic tile. Music whispered from hidden speakers, a light tango-rock beat currently featured in the trendiest after-hours clubs. Drugs were laid out all over a chrome and glass coffee table. The atmosphere was undeniably sexy, but also romantic.

The dark-haired woman, Kay, wore a Hermes gown that was delicately split up the side. The dress revealed a tease of nylon stockings, with silver pendants that mysteriously spiraled upward. The dress made her appear liquid, accentuating every curve, every nuance of her body.

Kimberly was long-legged as well, with firm, sculpted breasts and a glowing tan. Her nipples were already erect. She also wore an evening gown, Givenchy or Yves St Laurent, along with spike-heeled slippers and sophisticated makeup.

Alexandre St-Germain smiled and bowed. This couldn't have been better if he had arranged each detail himself.

The three men from the Escort knew which buzzer to press once they entered the vestibule of Allure. One important question, which wasn't to be answered for some time, was how they were admitted into the front hall of the apartment itself.

The police theory was that they gained entry either through an open window that led into the garden, or by sneaking up from the cellar. Neither theory was correct.

They came in through the oak double doors in front.

They were wearing raincoats, ball caps, and high-top sneakers, yet they proceeded into the front hall as if they owned Allure.

They each carried an Uzi machine-gun pistol.

The two call girls had begun to undress Alexandre St-Germain. They worked slowly and sensually, like an improvisational dance troupe.

Their fingers played musical scales up and down his spine. Then, the same fingers were like delicate airbrushes on his thighs, biceps, and genitals. The elaborate ritual reminded him of the finest geishas in Kyoto.

Naked, he was impressive, well muscled and firm. He

worked on his physique with a private trainer, in New York, and had done the same for years in London. Like everything else in his control, his body was close to perfection.

Alexandre St-Germain stood up suddenly. He waved the girls away. Instantly, his eyes seemed flat and cold. He was somewhere back inside his own mind again. Who knew where he went in his private thoughts?

He hurried across the bedroom without saying a word, entering a bathroom connected to the suite. The door closed and the water ran full force inside.

The three men – Jimmy Burke, Aurelio Rodriquez, Isiah Parker – separated once they were inside the downstairs area of Allure.

The two bodyguards were watching television on the first floor, and were easily dispatched. In a way, it almost seemed too easy so far.

When Alexandre St-Germain returned, the two call girls understood that he was in complete control for the evening.

He was wearing a black leather mask, in keeping with the current trend of danger in the world of kinky sex in New York. The mask had zippers that looked like jagged scars running down both his cheeks. Polished metal studs jutted across his forehead and chin.

This was the Grave Dancer, just the way legend had him: exotic and mysterious.

The drugs consumed upon the Grave Dancer's arrival began to take effect. His slurred sentences dominated their attempts at conversation; jumbled words ran into and over more jumbled words.

Expensive oils were poured, then smeared over the muscular curves of Alexandre St-Germain's body. High overhead, a network of mirror images ebbed and flowed across the ceiling. Shadows danced and fused with one another. A warm, lubricated finger slid into his rectum. Another entered his mouth.

Then something was wrong. Suddenly, in the midst of all the pleasure, something was happening, something completely out of symmetry.

'What's that? The sound?'

They all heard it. Outside in the hallway. It began with a heavy footfall . . . Approaching footsteps that then seemed to trail away.

Voices were approaching upstairs. Several voices merged into a solid block of noise. Everything was happening too fast now.

St-Germain sat upright, fully alert, but also trapped in silk sheets and too many pillows, in the jumble of bare legs and arms, silk stockings and garters thrown everywhere on the bed.

Both women were on their knees, their lovely mouths open in surprise.

'Who is it? Who's out there?' St-Germain demanded.

The bedroom door was flung open. A man holding a machine-gun pistol rushed inside. A black billed cap was pulled over most of his face. He was in a professional shooting crouch.

'What? . . . Are you from the Midnight Club?' Alexandre St-Germain completely lost his composure as he spoke. A burst of words came tumbling out of his mouth in a voice that wasn't quite his own. '*Are you from Midnight?*' he screamed again.

'Get out of here. Both of you,' the man with the gun said to the two call girls.

The women frantically ran from the mirrored bedroom, tripping over one another as they tried to get into the hallway.

At that same instant, a submachine-gun blast nearly ripped off the head of Alexandre St-Germain. The shocked European crime boss was thrown back hard against the creamy white bedroom wall.

'*Midnight?*' came a final gargled scream.

4

John Stefanovitch
West Ninety-ninth Street; Two a.m.

Nightmares.

There were these recurring nightmares that suddenly came true in his waking hours, John Stefanovitch had begun to think. It was happening to him right now.

The back of his neck was soaked with sweat, and his khaki sport shirt was sticking. His heart raced underneath the plastered-down shirt. He felt sick to his stomach, as if at any moment he could completely lose it.

The tires of his van squealed as it accelerated, then curled down the hill, speeding onto West Ninety-ninth Street.

Less than forty minutes before, he'd been awakened by the anxious voice of his captain in Homicide . . .

'There's been a multiple homicide up on West Ninety-ninth Street. It looks like a professional hit. They used submachine guns, maybe Uzis . . . It's Alexandre St-Germain.'

'What about St-Germain? What are you saying?' Stefanovitch had asked. His voice was groggy, his brain only partially awake.

'He's dead. Somebody got the scumbag tonight. I thought you'd want to know, Stef.'

Once he was on Ninety-ninth Street, Stefanovitch easily spotted his partner, Bear Kupchek. He saw the Bear as his van slowly rolled down the steep hill toward Riverside Park. It would have been difficult *not* to notice the six-foot-four, 260-pound detective.

'I live all the way out in Ridgewood, New Jersey,' Kupchek said in greeting. The meaning of the remark

29

was that from almost thirty miles away, he had still beaten Stefanovitch to the Upper Manhattan crime scene.

Stefanovitch was too preoccupied to be insulted by the Bear. He was reaching and groping into the backseat of the van, making noises like someone searching through pots and pans in a cluttered kitchen.

'They didn't call me right away,' he said into the backseat. 'That figures, I guess.'

'You are some kind of paranoid asshole sometimes. I mean it, Stefanovitch. Stop thinking like that.'

'This isn't paranoia. They didn't call me until they found out they couldn't get somebody else to schlep up here. They didn't think I could handle this.'

Stefanovitch finally shoved open the van door. He nearly hurled the folded body of a specially designed twenty-two-pound wheelchair out onto West Ninety-ninth Street.

He then shimmied across the front seat, trying not to wince as a knife of pain pierced his lower spine.

Grasping the door with one arm, he pulled open the lightweight, foldaway wheelchair and sat down in it with a dull thud. The whole operation had taken a little less than twenty seconds. About average assembly time.

'Christ, you're actually getting slower at that. I'd have thought a former farmboy-jock like yourself would have that knocked cold by now.'

Kupchek was still nagging and complaining at him from the sidewalk. He was really wound up tonight, Stefanovitch could tell. Kupchek had been Stefanovitch's number two for nearly four years, since before the transfer to Homicide. He had learned not to help Stef unless the help was absolutely necessary, or explicitly requested.

Stefanovitch hit the sidewalk rolling, ignoring the stream of gibes from Kupchek. Both of his arms were pressed down hard against the rubber guards over the wheels of his chair. The tarnished silver vehicle seemed to fly, moving faster than it looked as if it ought to.

He aimed himself toward the general commotion, down

where the dome lights on half a dozen police cruisers were rotating, shining emergency red and blue. The riot of bright colors caused him to squint both eyes.

'How many dead inside, officer?' Stefanovitch finally stopped in front of a well-kept brownstone. He questioned a bleary-eyed patrolman posted at the foot of the stairs.

The young patrolman recognized Lieutenant Stefanovitch from Homicide. John Stefanovitch's controversial return to active duty had made newspaper and television reports around the city a year before. Since then, his reputation in the police department had shifted from 'hard-charging,' to 'tough and cranky,' to 'presuicidal.'

'Three, sir, I think. Two on the first floor. Throats cut. One's up on the second floor. The coroner himself's inside.'

'Big deal.' Bear Kupchek seemed to let the words slide out the side of his mouth. 'I'm here myself, aren't I? Lieutenant Stefanovitch is here himself.'

Kupchek suddenly lifted Stefanovitch out of the wheelchair. The sight was startling and completely unexpected, but the young patrolman didn't allow himself to blink, much less smile.

'Don't just stand there, bring along Lieutenant Stefanovitch's chair,' Kupchek snapped back at the patrolman, who immediately obliged.

'Easy with the merchandise,' Stefanovitch said as he was hoisted up the front stairs like a bulky sack of grain. No matter how much he tried to rationalize it, being carried was humiliating. It made him feel like a freak. That was the word; it was exactly the way he felt, the way a lot of people in wheelchairs were made to feel.

'All right, let the lieutenant through,' Kupchek called ahead in a loud, gruff voice.

Stefanovitch and Bear Kupchek passed through a crush of crime-scene regulars as they made their way into the brownstone. The familiar jangle of guns and handcuffs surrounded them.

Officers nodded and muttered their hellos. Everyone seemed to know Stefanovitch and Kupchek. Necks stretched to catch the sight anyway.

Kupchek put Stefanovitch back into his wheelchair on the second floor.

'Thanks for the ride,' Stefanovitch said.

'All in the line of duty. Anyway, it helps keep me svelte.'

'Bear, I want you to wake up the Fifth Homicide Zone.' Stefanovitch then said to Kupchek, 'Make it the Fifth and the Sixth Zone.'

'You want me to call *Good Morning America*, too?'

'Canvass every car between Ninetieth Street and One Hundred Tenth. We'll need all the license plate numbers. Find out who might have been parking a car on the street late tonight. Maybe somebody saw something. Have them wake up the supers in all the buildings along Ninety-ninth ... See if any garages are open late. Find me a witness, Bear. That'll keep you svelte.'

The two call girls who had been with Alexandre St-Germain were being held for questioning. They were waiting inside a formal parlor on the second floor.

From the hallway, Stefanovitch saw a young, extremely beautiful blond woman, a heartbreaker of the first magnitude. She was wrapped in an expensive-looking brocaded silk robe, sitting with her face hidden in both hands.

Even in shock, she was stunning. Her hair was pulled back, tied in a red satin ribbon. She didn't look as if she belonged at Allure. Maybe at some manicured estate in Westchester, or up on the Connecticut River.

'Her name's Kimberly Victoria Manion,' Kupchek confided. 'She does some modeling, some acting. She only does special numbers here at Allure. Calls them dates. That's what she said, Stef. Originally, she's from Lincoln, Nebraska.'

'She should have stayed out there in Nebraska,' Stefanovitch said.

'The other one is Kay Whitley.'

32

The second call girl waiting in the parlor was even more interesting to Stefanovitch. She had already changed into a yellow slip of a dress, with cream-colored stockings and expensive, conservative high heels.

'She's from Poughkeepsie originally. She tells everybody, all her clients, that she's from Boston. Very proper way of speaking. Lots of long *a*'s.'

Stefanovitch finally entered the parlor. His voice was quiet at first, almost soothing.

Both of the women looked up. They were obviously surprised by the wheelchair, but also by the good-looking and virile man sitting in it.

'My name is John Stefanovitch. I'm a lieutenant with the Homicide Division. The man in the clip-on tie is Senior Detective Kupchek. As you already know, there's been a murder here. Three murders, actually. Both of you are material witnesses.'

The girls nodded without saying anything. Kimberly Manion's cheeks were streaked with mascara. Stefanovitch felt sorry for her, but he figured she was probably tougher than she looked.

She was, he found out over the next two hours. Both girls were tough.

By the end of the question-and-answer session, it was four in the morning. Stefanovitch hadn't learned nearly enough. He didn't have a description of the hit team, not even agreement on their number. Or how they'd gotten inside Allure.

'I'd like to see where he was shot. Bear?'

Stefanovitch twisted his body around in the wheelchair, and spoke to Kupchek. He had been putting off the final step, but the time had come.

His partner nodded, but he didn't seem too happy about Stefanovitch's decision.

'The medical examiners are still there. The coroner's wagon is parked out on the street. I've already taken *beaucoup* notes in there, Stef. Leave it alone.'

'Go ask them to take ten. I have to see the bedroom. Just the way it is. Just the way *he* is.'

'Why do you want to go down there? I took enough notes for *Crime and Punishment II*. They're doing forensic sketches. Don't do this to yourself.'

John Stefanovitch pushed himself out of the parlor without saying anything else to Kupchek.

Once he was in the hallway, Stefanovitch realized that he felt more drained than he'd thought. His mouth was dry. A dead weight was pushing down on him, making his shoulders sag.

Stefanovitch passed inside the high-ceilinged master bedroom. He closed the paneled, heavy wooden door behind him.

Alexandre St-Germain was laid out alongside an unzipped gray body bag on the bed. *The Grave Dancer was right there*.

The shock of the brutal murder finally struck Stefanovitch with a physical jolt. Bile rose in his throat. *Someone had gotten to the Grave Dancer before he had*.

The attack had exposed jagged bone on both sides of St-Germain's chest. The mobster's head and most of his neck had been savaged by the machine-gun volley. The body looked desecrated, smaller than life, smaller than the grandiose reputation, certainly. Still intact on one of the gang leader's fingers was an immense diamond and onyx ring, easily fifteen carats, a marquise cut.

At the moment of death, Alexandre St-Germain seemed to have suffered intense pain. Stefanovitch knew the feeling. He'd experienced everything about the moment, except the release of death itself.

Stefanovitch moved closer to the bed, which was still draped in silver satin sheets. His mind was moving back and forth through time, flashing too many images for him to absorb.

Part of him was inside the West Side town house – but part of John Stefanovitch was in Long Beach, two years

34

ago. Another part of him was holding his wife, Anna, cradling her in his arms, sobbing his hopelessness. He could remember what Anna's touch had been like. The scent of Bal de Versailles, her favorite perfume. These memories never dimmed. Sometimes their intensity was a comfort and sometimes it was horrible torture.

All of the agony and physical suffering during the past two years seemed compressed into this moment. He felt an indescribable rage. A burning had settled in his chest.

Stefanovitch leaned forward in his wheelchair, careful not to topple it over and find himself in a state of helplessness. He stared at the remains of Alexandre St-Germain, the Grave Dancer, wearing his million-dollar diamond ring.

Then he made one final gesture he would remember long after everything else had faded.

John Stefanovitch leaned forward and he spit onto St-Germain's bloodied corpse. 'Welcome to hell,' he whispered, not even recognizing the sound of his own voice. *'Rot in fucking hell!'*

When he turned to leave, the Bear was standing in the doorway. The detective frowned and slowly shook his head. 'Yeah, you're just fine, Stef. See everything you needed to see?'

5

Sarah McGinniss
East Sixty-sixth Street

At four o'clock that morning, a successful writer named Sarah McGinniss had experienced an unmistakable ache gnawing into the tender walls of her stomach. It was the same dull pain she felt each time she dragged herself out of bed at that hour. She moaned and groaned, mocking herself like the Whiners on late-night TV.

Every morning between four and four-thirty, Sarah forced herself up to write, before her small son, Sam, was awake, besieging her for French toast, or maybe Belgian waffles, as if that sort of thing were the most common breakfast fare for every growing boy in America.

She was unusually tired this morning. Though she had tried, she hadn't slept at all.

As she brewed a second pot of coffee, she alternated glances at grainy black-and-white photographs she'd once taken of Alexandre St-Germain with vacant stares out the kitchen window, down onto deserted East Sixty-sixth Street.

Near the photographs on the kitchen counter was a draft of a seven-hundred-page manuscript on organized crime. The working title was *The Club*. The book featured Alexandre St-Germain, who had tried to usher the underworld into a new age. An hour before, she'd received a call from a friend at UP saying St-Germain was dead. One problem Sarah hadn't solved was how to reconcile the life of a man who was both a crime lord and a well-known businessman. Now she never would.

Sometimes, when she was having trouble getting going

with the early morning writing, she would scrawl *Be there* across the top of a page. It forced her to see and feel everything about the scene she was attempting to describe.

Somebody murdered Alexandre St-Germain, she thought now. *Be there.*

As Sarah moved around the kitchen, she couldn't help think about how very far she had come, and how quickly. It was difficult for her to imagine that less than five years ago she'd been a reporter, virtually a stringer on the *Times-Tribune* in Palo Alto, California.

She had moved to Palo Alto with her husband, Roger, from San Francisco, where she had written for the *Chronicle*. They had relocated because Roger had gotten a teaching job in creative writing at Stanford.

The notion of staying in San Francisco because she had a good job at the *Chronicle* hadn't even been a consideration for Roger. Sarah had finally agreed to move, mostly because she wanted to have a baby, and Palo Alto seemed like a beautiful place to raise a child.

In the spring of 1984, Sarah wrote her best work to date, a vitriolic, deeply felt nine-thousand-word piece about corruption in northern California hospitals. She had written the article because she was personally outraged by the payoffs she had discovered going on between hospital suppliers and some staff doctors.

A twenty-three-year-old nurse by the name of Jeanne Galetta read the three-part feature in the *Times-Tribune*. She liked something about the writing style, something in Sarah's ability to get the truth down in a straightforward way. The nurse decided to contact Sarah about a subject that was deeply troubling her.

Jeanne Galetta was employed by one of the private nursing services operating around Palo Alto. As recently as a month before, the nurse had been working at the Cavanaugh estate in nearby Woodside. During Jeanne Galetta's ten-month relationship with Agnes Cavanaugh, a bedridden woman in her early fifties, she had become convinced that the wealthy woman's two daughters were poisoning their mother.

Agnes Cavanaugh suffered a massive stroke and died soon after the nurse first talked to Sarah about her suspicions. An autopsy was requested, and performed. Traces of cyanide were found throughout Agnes Cavanaugh's body.

Because of the wealthy Cavanaugh family's notoriety, the series that Sarah wrote was carried in the *San Francisco Chronicle* and also picked up by the United Press. The two Cavanaugh daughters were indicted on first-degree murder charges. They were eventually convicted, right there in the downtown Palo Alto courthouse.

Because she'd understood the power of her story from the beginning, Sarah had been shaping the early interviews with family members and friends into a lengthy manuscript, which she decided to call *A Mother's Kindness*. She had finished all but the last two chapters by the end of the court trial.

A Mother's Kindness was published the following fall. It almost immediately exceeded the publisher's expectations, breaking out very big in California and all through the Far West. Ultimately, *A Mother's Kindness* became the number-one best-seller in nonfiction, and the book was turned into a successful television mini-series that was kindly reviewed.

Then, almost as abruptly as it had begun, the fairy-tale experience ended – crash-landed like a paper airplane in a wind tunnel. One month after she had been written up in *Time* and *People*, Roger left her.

He admitted he couldn't stomach being referred to as 'Sarah McGinniss's husband.' Roger also confessed that there was a twenty-three-year-old graduate student at the university who had been 'consoling' him. As Sarah later learned, the graduate student had been helping Roger 'cope' during her pregnancy with Sam as well.

The more she heard about Roger's girlfriend at Stanford, the angrier Sarah became. She had sacrificed, no strings attached, while he was getting his doctorate, and then when he decided they should leave San Francisco. Now he had shown that he couldn't give even a little of himself for her. He had been calling her 'the Shana Alexander of Palo Alto.' It was a pretty funny line, but damn him anyway.

She and Sam moved to New York City the next summer, partly because of research work she needed to do for her new book, but mostly because Sarah knew she had to be far away from everything that had happened in her marriage. She wanted no reminders.

More than anything now, she needed to write a very good book. She wanted to show that *A Mother's Kindness* hadn't been a one-shot. Sarah especially wanted to rub Roger's face in each and every page.

A cigarette with a long ash dangled from her hand that morning in mid-June. It had gotten that bad: cigarettes again; two pots of coffee before noon every day. Sarah quietly sat down and she stared at the blank sheet rolled into her old Smith-Corona.

On the very top of the bare white page she had written *Be there*. But today it was more complicated than that.

John Stefanovitch
Allure

Almost any automatic car can be fixed to accommodate a handicapped driver. In Stefanovitch's case, the mechanics were particularly simple, modifications he supervised himself.

A hand-operated throttle system was all that was necessary for him to drive again. The hard part was learning to ignore, then forget completely, the ingrained foot reflexes every time he had to hit the brakes, or accelerate. He was still working on that. The streets of New York were an interesting place to practice. As he turned down West Ninety-ninth Street in the daylight, Stefanovitch noticed that the four-story town house that held Allure was in mint condition. He sat in his car for a few minutes observing the street, but particularly the elegant, early-thirties building that housed Allure. He wanted all the turmoil in his mind to be manageable before he ventured inside again.

So far today he'd had his regular workout at the gym, then several hours of mental agony at Police Plaza, headquarters for the NYPD. He was baffled by almost everything about the St-Germain killing.

Around eleven o'clock, he had visited the autopsy room at Police Plaza. He'd wanted to see St-Germain one more time. He still didn't understand the motive for the shooting, and without a motive there couldn't be a solution.

The corpse was laid out among a host of other homicide victims from around New York. The Grave Dancer seemed less than imposing in the midst of rows of stainless steel trolleys, walls of refrigerator compartments, green-robed pathologists with sharpened blades and blasé expressions.

The Pathology chief, Thomas Yamada, had assigned himself to St-Germain. He was gutting his star cadaver, while a police stenographer dutifully took notes.

'His testes weigh thirty-three and a half grams,' Yamada said to Stefanovitch as he wheeled himself toward the trolley. 'Average.' He shrugged and seemed disappointed.

'That all you have for me, Tommy?' Stefanovitch asked. He wasn't in the mood for Yamada's dark humor.

'Vital stats have been checked with the Sûreté. ID by three "business associates." I'll let you know if anything else comes up. Not a neat job. Vengeance style. Somebody didn't like this buggerer a lot. Somebody besides you, Stef.'

When most of the confusion in his mind had subsided, Stefanovitch reached into his van's backseat for the Chair. 'Onward, Christian Soldiers' ran through his head. Onward, indeed.

Kay Whitley was being held in the same parlor where he had questioned her the night before, or rather, early in the morning. She had apparently 'forgotten' to tell him a few details, so they were meeting again.

Kupchek and another Homicide detective, Harold Lee Friedman, were mooning around the parlor when he arrived. They looked like uncomfortable mourners at a wake. Nobody was talking.

Kay Whitley looked even more startling without the exotic makeup she had been wearing with St-Germain. She had on a blue cardigan sweater, a chic Claude Montana T-shirt, tight faded jeans. She wore scuffed and stained black leather boots that reached up near her thighs. Sunlight from the windows behind wrapped around her nicely.

Stefanovitch wanted to talk to her alone this time. They had to reach some kind of understanding. He asked Bear Kupchek and the other detective to leave the room.

When they were alone, the expensive call girl did something that startled Stefanovitch. Without saying a word, she leaned forward and put her hand lightly over his wrist.

He could feel her softness, her body's warmth, and he had no idea what she was up to.

'Before we start, Lieutenant, I want to thank you for last night,' she said. 'I know you could have been a lot tougher on us. I feel badly about leaving some things out.'

'Maybe I should have been tougher,' was all that Stefanovitch said for now. He had to admit, though, she'd thrown him a beauty of a change-up curve, absolutely caught him leaning the wrong way in the batter's box.

'Anyway, I'm sorry.' She pulled back her hand, but held him with her eyes. Her cheeks were flushed a soft pink. If it was an act, it was a good one. 'I had to think a lot of things through first. I had to choose sides carefully.'

'Kupchek said you had something to show me?' Stefanovitch finally said. 'Anything you give me now might be considered a peace offering. We'll see.'

'All right, Lieutenant.' Kay pointed toward a mirror that took up half of one wall of the sitting room. 'We can start over there.'

She stood and walked to the mirror. She stooped down and pressed something metallic at the bottom of one pane of glass. Then, she straightened up and pushed on the upper-right corner of the glass.

The mirror opened outward like a free-swinging door. Stefanovitch craned his neck to see inside.

Kay flicked on fluorescent lights, and then he could see everything. It was a peace offering, all right.

A small compartment, about six by eight, was hidden behind the mirror. Stefanovitch followed her across the longer room and inside the smaller one. He whistled softly as he entered.

'They could make movies in any of three master bedrooms from here,' Kay said, answering two of his questions right away.

Stefanovitch nodded as he peered around the compact room. He had quick eyes in a new place, taking everything in, making connections and mental notes.

There were two sleek, black Sony videotape cameras. One wall was covered with stacks of videocassettes, hundreds of cassettes in black boxes. The blue-movie history of Allure? A complete library of tender and touching moments?

He asked the $64,000 question next. 'Was this room being used last night?' There was nothing like having a homicide filmed to help catch the murderer.

'I don't know, Lieutenant. I don't remember seeing Johnny around all last night. Johnny D's the guy who usually runs the cameras. He's one of the managers.'

'But last night *might* have been filmed by this guy Johnny D?'

'Sure . . . we've been filmed a lot. Sometimes they told us they were going to be in here. Sometimes they didn't. That was supposed to keep us in line, I guess. Actually it did, a little. You never knew who was watching, or why they were watching.'

Bear Kupchek had entered the parlor again. He was

standing in the doorway of the room, a huge shape looming behind Stefanovitch's chair, something like a big brother, something like a friendly gorilla.

'Hmmm? What have we here? Did they get last night on film?' he asked with a frown. '*Look* at all the home movies. What's this, the New York porn-film festival?'

Stefanovitch looked back over his shoulder. 'We don't know if they filmed last night or not. You'd better get the lab techs here again.'

'This might even be where the hitters hung out.'

'We'll check that, too. Let's get all the cassettes packed up and shipped down to Police Plaza in the meantime. We'll need a private screening room. I don't want word to get out until after we've looked at some of the tapes ourselves.'

Stefanovitch's gaze returned to Kay. He thought that she'd lost a little of her city-cool look, the confident slickness he'd seen the night before. She kept changing, and he couldn't figure her out.

'We owe you one,' he finally said to her. 'You can go home now. Like they say in the movies, though, don't try to leave town. We'll be in touch.'

John Stefanovitch and Bear Kupchek
West Ninety-ninth Street

After they left Allure later that afternoon, the Bear and Stefanovitch sat out in his van. They watched a bright red sun sinking over New Jersey. They shared a six-pack of Miller from a very pricey bodega on Broadway.

As they sat and talked, Stefanovitch was reminded of how much he depended on the Bear. If he was the head, the Bear was the body for the two of them. Only the Bear had a head on him, too. The Bear was street-smart, street-smart and a good friend.

Kupchek finally leaned across the front seat and he pounded Stefanovitch's arm. It was like being whacked by a ball peen hammer, but Stefanovitch didn't blink.

'You are some hump,' Kupchek frowned after delivering the lethal punch. Then he started to laugh. 'You like her, don't you?'

'I like who?' Stefanovitch asked. There was something about the Bear's round, homely face. He loved to tease that innocent face. He liked rearranging the parts. The Bear was his own personal Mr Potato Head.

'*Who?* That fat old lady waiting for the Riverside Drive bus over there . . . *Kay Whitley*. That's who!'

'Oh, come on. You think I'm having fantasies about some high-priced call girl? Just because she's one of the most beautiful women in New York. Twenty-five years old. Flawless body.'

Bear Kupchek proceeded to whack Stefanovitch's arm again. 'She's a very expensive, fucked-up hooker. She's one of our two witnesses so far.'

'No shit, Sherlock. Stop punching my arm. You'll hurt your hand.'

'You are pretty hard for a wimp in a wheelchair. I'm almost impressed.'

'My physical therapist would smile, for maybe three seconds, if she heard you say I was developing a little muscle tone. Her name's Beth Kelley. She has a flawless body, too.'

'Another significant other in your life? She pretty? This personal therapist of yours?'

Stefanovitch started to smile, then he laughed out loud. The Bear loved to gossip about anything.

'She's prettier than I am, for sure.'

'So what's the problem? You dating her? You seeing anybody, Stef? New York's most eligible wheelchair bachelor?'

'Don't start up. Go home to New Jersey. See JoAnne and the Bear cubs tonight, while you have the chance. Before this St-Germain mess heats up any more . . . *Hey!* Where the hell are you going? We're right in the middle of a beer! A conversation!'

44

'I'm going home to Jersey, to see JoAnne and the kids. You're absolutely right for once in your life. First time for everything. Good night, Stef.'

'Good night, Bear,' Stefanovitch called after the hulking figure already moving down Ninety-ninth Street, heading toward a familiar blue station wagon with Great Adventure stickers plastered all over the rear window.

Stefanovitch sat in his van and slowly finished his Miller . . . *It isn't going all that good, now that you ask,* he was thinking to himself. *I'm not seeing anybody, okay. I'm also uptight about this investigation.*

I've got to get somebody to talk to, or I'll blow up one of these days . . . Yes, I like the way Kay Whitley looks. No, I'm not going to get stupid over it. I don't think so, anyhow . . . If you want to know the truth, I don't have the nerve anymore.

How's that for being honest as I can be, Bear?

6

John Stefanovitch
Coney Island Amusement Park

For the past few months John Stefanovitch had been planning to take the rest of that day off. He wasn't going to allow anything, not even the St-Germain murder investigation, to get in the way. At four o'clock, he hurried home to his apartment, across the city on East Eighty-first Street. Tonight was his night.

After the Long Beach shooting, he'd been forced to find a place in midtown. That experience, more than anything else, had awakened him to the kind of fun times he was going to have in the Chair.

Stefanovitch had eventually located a modern high rise on the Upper East Side. It was a neighbourhood he'd never really liked. His being in a wheelchair had dictated the choice of apartments.

The wife of the man who owned the building had suffered a stroke and now had to face life in a wheelchair herself. The tragedy had sensitized her husband to the predicament of the wheelchair-bound in the city. The two of them had personally examined every walkway and building entrance from the point of view of someone coming or going in a chair.

Stefanovitch grabbed an hour-and-a-half nap at the apartment late that afternoon. Then he was back in the van, driving out to Coney Island, in Brooklyn.

At around seven o'clock, he arrived at one of the amusement park's sprawling parking lots. Several hundred people were already gathered in a blockaded area, which had been closed to regular traffic. Stefanovitch had never seen so many people in wheelchairs.

His own speed-racing chair had been customized by his father and his brother, Nelson, in Pennsylvania. They had given him the racer that past November. It weighed only twelve pounds. Unlike old-fashioned chairs, which made people *look* handicapped, the sports chair was sleek and jet black. It had twenty-eight-inch-high tires.

Stefanovitch's brother and his father had apparently seen the van heading into the lot. They came running as Stefanovitch was pulling his racer out of the back. They'd driven all the way from Pennsylvania to see him race.

'Look at this.' Nelson held up a wrinkled Day-Glo T-shirt, an obvious gift for the night's big event. The shirt said 'Mike's Submarines – Eat the Big One in Minersville.'

'What race you in, Stef?' his father asked as they started away from the van, headed toward the main-event area.

All around the crowded parking lot, Stefanovitch observed the victims of accidents, of crippling illness, and of wars, especially Vietnam. Everybody looked so pumped up tonight, excited as hell. Stefanovitch found that he was, too.

'I'm in the miracle mile. Maybe my stamina will make up for some technique and experience I'm missing. Some of these guys, and the women, are amazing.'

A handsome, outdoorsy-looking man with sun-bleached blond hair and a beard suddenly came up alongside them. Stefanovitch had met Pierce Oates at his first race, about five months back. Amazingly, John Stefanovitch had come in third in a field of ten, most of them racing vets. He had caught Pierce Oates's appraising eye right off.

'You going to give me some competition out there tonight, man?' Pierce had a broad, charismatic grin. His racer was fire-engine red and looked fast.

'I'll do my best. Pierce Oates, this is my father, Charles Stefanovitch. My big brother, Nelson. They came all the way from Pennsylvania. My whole family's nutty like that. The family is a big fan of the family. Same thing happens for a Pillsbury bake-off if my mother has her angel food cake entered.'

'That's terrific. I love it. Just to watch me whip your tail?' Pierce's smile seemed carefree, even after all that had happened to him.

'How are you, Pierce? Nice to meet you.' Charles Stefanovitch shook hands with the man in the wheelchair next to his son. 'You beat Stef, you get to wear the Mike's Subs T-shirt next race.'

'That's all the incentive I need.' Pierce Oates whooped loudly and laughed. The muscular, sun-bronzed man then veered off to mingle with the other racers.

'He's a little overexuberant, but he's great,' Stefanovitch said to his father and brother. 'Some of these guys are tremendous athletes. What they go through to be here is incomprehensible. You can't even imagine.'

Charles Stefanovitch leaned down close to his son and he spoke to him in confidence. Stefanovitch's father was a quiet man who had never in his life told Stef that he loved him, never actually used the words. Physically, he was tall and lean, almost noble in his bearing. His son John had once had a similar bearing.

'Just do the best you can, Stef. Nobody can ever ask for more than that . . . Win this one for Mike's Submarines.' The old man finally cracked a wry, country smile.

It took another twenty minutes to get the participants in the miracle mile ready at the start. Stefanovitch spotted Pierce a few places down the line. The two of them laughed and flashed victory signs. He could tell that Pierce was primed to kick his butt, ready to mop him up in the four-lap race.

He remembered two things Pierce had told him about racing the first time they'd met. One was to watch the lead racer, no one else. Otherwise you could get lost back in a slow pack and wind up completely out of the race.

The second thing was that the difference between first place and the middle of the pack was a matter of how you *stroked* your wheelchair. Stefanovitch had been working on his stroke almost every night in Gracie Square Park, even

48

out on the streets of New York while he was working.

The starter's pistol suddenly exploded, and the fifteen men in wheelchairs accelerated off the line with surprising quickness and agility.

This was his first really top-drawer competitive race, and he wanted to do respectably. Certainly, the torture sessions at his gym had given him a body that *looked* as if it could compete with the others. He'd know soon enough.

The lead racer for the first quarter-mile was a black guy in a fireplug-red T-shirt and white visor. He was burning up the track. Stefanovitch wondered if he could last at that pace. He doubted it, and he was right.

In the second quarter, the black racer dropped back to second. Then to third. Stefanovitch stayed in his position, about halfway back in the pack.

The new leader was in a low-slung racer that looked like a soapbox-derby special.

Pierce Oates was in third place now, stroking beautifully. Pierce looked as if he could race at that speed all day.

The third quarter was physically and mentally tougher, even in the middle of the cruising pack. Stefanovitch's arms began to tense up, becoming hard as rock, petrified from the biceps down into the finger joints.

He started to panic. He was losing steam, noticeably so. He wondered about the others. He was jerking the chair instead of stroking. The other racers all looked smooth and relaxed.

Another racer passed him, a balding, willowy man with 'Stoke-Mandeville Games' emblazoned in bright blue on his shirt. Stoke-Mandeville was the important international race held in England every year. If the willowy guy had competed there, he had to be good, and dedicated, too.

Stefanovitch didn't feel like he was *gliding* now. His arms were almost rock-hard; the pain was spreading like fire into his upper shoulders.

If he had anything left, he had to make a serious move soon. *If* he had anything left.

He went for it at the start of the fourth quarter. A strong shot of adrenaline kicked in. Second-wind time. Pride, fear, one or the other was working on him. Fingers of some powerful unseen hand were making him *stroke*.

He passed Stoke-Mandeville.

Then the bullet-headed black guy who had led the race in the beginning.

Pierce Oates was moving into the lead now. Pierce looked invincible. He was stroking, really stroking!

A fast final quarter would take about fifty-five seconds in a top wheelchair race. He'd done that well *in practice*. The average mile time might be anywhere from three minutes and forty-five seconds to four minutes.

The pain in his arms was excruciating – his biceps were numb. His chest was on fire.

The crowd was screaming at all the racers. They were really into it. That part of the feeling was great, exhilarating and completely unexpected.

Each breath Stefanovitch took roared through his lungs. He felt as if his chest were being torn apart.

He had to make his move. He had no idea what he had left inside, how much of the second wind remained.

He kept his eyes on Pierce Oates's golden yellow shirt, the sheath of his back muscles.

The *stroke* is everything, he reminded himself one more time. Nothing but the *stroke* mattered.

Faces flashed by, cheering wildly on either side. His eyes were glazed now, fixed on the golden shirt weaving a few yards in front of him.

Someone threw water all over him and the wetness felt wonderful. The dousing relieved the fire inside. Only for a few seconds, but that was okay. He still had his wind.

It was like he'd said to his father – he was coming back now. That was why the race was important. Stefanovitch was coming back from the dead.

Both his arms were petrified stone, but the lightweight chair was flying. His stroke couldn't have been better.

His arms and his stroke were one fluid motion. All the torturous sessions at the Sports Center were finally paying a dividend.

He had almost caught Pierce. Almost, but not quite.

It was exactly the way he'd dreamed about this race while he trained every night in New York. Except that he couldn't pull away from the other man.

He and Pierce were streaking toward the winner's line and the largest part of the cheering crowd. They were almost even. Both were yards ahead of the third and fourth racers.

He couldn't take Pierce, though. He couldn't get ahead of Pierce Oates. He couldn't do it.

He wouldn't let Pierce take him either. He couldn't let that happen now.

'Your hand . . . *Your goddamn hand!*' Pierce was suddenly screaming at him.

Stefanovitch didn't understand – then he did.

He reached out his hand, finally touching Pierce, connecting with him.

The two of them sailed across the finish line together, clutching each other's hands like teammates. Christ, they *were* teammates. The wheelchair boys.

Stefanovitch's brain was screaming. He hadn't felt anything like this since before Long Beach, before the shootings.

He saw his brother and father in the crowd. He spotted his father, and the old man was smiling, but he was crying, too. In their thirty-five years together, he'd never once seen his father cry, not for family weddings, christenings, or funerals. Not once before right now.

Pierce Oates was hugging him, too. Everything was going to be all right somehow. For one night, anyway, Stefanovitch was back.

7

Isiah Parker
The East Side

It was a little past nine-thirty and traffic on Third Avenue was getting noticeably lighter, moving at a steady pace. Isiah Parker and Jimmy Burke waited in front of a closed, darkened Doubleday bookstore on the corner of Fiftieth Street.

Both men were dressed in beige linen suits. They looked like any of the businessmen still slouching out of high-rise offices on the midtown avenue. Isiah Parker had often speculated that a mugger or thief who dressed like a successful businessman in Manhattan would probably never get caught, never be stopped and questioned by most street cops, anyway.

When he finally saw the Caddie limo approaching the fancy awning in front of the Smith & Wollensky Steak House on Third, his mind went blank. He concentrated on nothing except what had to be accomplished in the next ninety seconds.

'Let's walk,' he whispered to Burke, standing at his side. 'We're East Side businessmen. We've had a nice supper for ourselves. We do this right, nobody will remember us. We're *invisible men*.'

John Traficante and the *consiglière* James O'Toole were feeling full of the good life after two Steak Wollenskys and several cocktails inside the East Side restaurant. Traficante, a first underboss in the New York Mafia, was also known in the underworld as Johnny Angel, the Angel of Death. This presumably had to do with the number of murders he had committed since growing up in the mob-spawning grounds of Howard Beach and later Canarsie, in Brooklyn. Traficante had been the favored hit man inside the Lucchese family. He had remained 'hands-on' as he rose all the way up through the ranks. His murder victims included a federal judge, several New York policemen, a newspaper writer, and potential witnesses, including women, and two young children on Long Island.

O'Toole, the lawyer, pushed open the glass and mahogany doors as they left the steak house. They passed a couple waiting for a cab under the forest green canopy. Caesar DeCicco, their bodyguard-driver, was opening the front door of Traficante's limo.

'He's a good boy,' Traficante said of his forty-seven-year-old bodyguard. 'Loyal as a pet snake.'

Some jerk in a business suit wasn't looking where he was going out on the Third Avenue sidewalk. He bumped into O'Toole, then brushed against Traficante's Gucci suit.

'Hey . . . hey, easy. Whutcherrush?' the gangster bristled.

'I'm sorry. Excuse me, sir. Sorry,' Isiah Parker said.

The Uzi appeared out of nowhere.

A short burst followed, and the stocky bodyguard, DeCicco, was thrown bouncing up on the hood of the Cadillac.

The couple walking toward their cab dove to the ground, the woman shrieking. Patrons inside the restaurant suddenly stared at the scene in horror. The maître d' went down on the floor.

A Colt Magnum flashed against Traficante's mottled face.

'Cop killers,' Isiah Parker hissed at him. 'Scumbag.'

The Magnum fired twice under Traficante's chin. It lifted the mobster's head right off his shoulders.

Parker dropped the gun right there. He and Jimmy Burke quickly, but calmly, walked down East Fiftieth to a waiting Buick Skylark. The two NYPD detectives disappeared inside, and the nondescript sedan drove off.

Invisible men.

8

John Stefanovitch
One Police Plaza

At a little past eight in the morning, Stefanovitch propelled himself between the double-glazed front doors and into the main lobby of One Police Plaza. He had two newspapers, a *New York Times* and a *Post*, folded over his lap. The news was all bad. 'MAFIA HEAD SHOT DOWN! MOB WAR RAGES.' His high from Coney Island was definitely over.

A used and battered VCR had been set up by Audio-Visual in a cozy interrogation room near his office. By eight-fifteen, he was viewing the first of the videocassettes that had been discovered at Allure.

As he watched the tape, Stefanovitch kept thinking about St-Germain's words, the phrase the two call girls had heard him use. *'Are you from Midnight?'* For years, there had been stories about something called the Midnight Club. Supposedly, it was a small group of crime lords who controlled organized crime around the world. The precise makeup of the Club remained mysterious.

Had the secretive Club ordered the deaths of St-Germain and Traficante? Who inside the Midnight Club would be giving the orders? What might be on the sex tapes from Allure?

Stefanovitch had decided to watch the videotapes alone. He couldn't imagine what might be recorded on the tapes, but he didn't want anyone else there when he found out. Crime figures? Powerful New York businessmen? Entertainers? Politicians? Members of the Midnight Club?

The fewer people who knew what was on the tapes, the

less complicated and political the murder investigation was going to be.

Sarah McGinniss was hunched forward inside a Checker cab. She was trying to leaf through some of her files on Alexandre St-Germain as the taxi sped down the West Side Highway.

Much of the material in her St-Germain file had been compiled by an unusual researcher, a former Organized Crime Task Force member. According to the files, many of the women involved in high-level prostitution weren't professional hookers these days. They were more likely to be aspiring types in the glamour professions: models, actresses, women who worked at employment agencies, film-production houses.

According to her source, the super-rich didn't have to exert themselves much in order to obtain sex. If they were at a Mortimer's in New York, at Chasen's or Spago's in LA, the maître d' might have the names of available women, or men. The same was true at exclusive hotels. Bordellos like Allure operated in several cities around the country: Los Angeles, Miami, San Francisco, Las Vegas, Houston, Dallas, even Cincinnati and Cleveland, and much smaller cities as well.

Sarah finally shut the folder holding her notes. At eight-thirty, the Checker pulled up in front of its destination downtown. Sarah jumped out and hurried up the front steps, then across the pedestrian mall into Police Plaza.

She checked the name she'd scribbled in her notepad – *Lieutenant John Stefanovitch*.

'Shit. Christ Almighty, what? What is it, Bear?'

The first images had no sooner flashed onto the VCR monitor screen when Bear Kupchek entered the darkened office and interrupted the movies. Stefanovitch reached over and flicked off the set.

'I *told* you I wanted to screen these by myself.'

Kupchek's doughy face twisted itself into a frown. 'I heard you the first dozen times. I think I understand the situation. You want to be alone with the dirty movies.'

'So what's the problem? I have about a hundred hours of tapes to watch before lunch.'

Kupchek was jiggling change in the pockets of baggy gray trousers that looked like the pants of an old man. A plastic protector for pens stuck out from his white shirt pocket. Kupchek was about as stylish a dresser as the guys who hung out at the OTB betting parlor near Stefanovitch's apartment. All his clothes looked borrowed from someone who'd had his heyday in the Depression.

'I just took a message for you from reception down in the lobby. A Ms Sarah McGinniss is on her way up now. Ms McGinniss has the PC's permission to screen the home movies. She's a writer of note. Apparently, she traded favors for some inside things she knows about St-Germain. Make your day?'

'I heard something about that. The captain mentioned her to me. Listen, there's no way some investigative reporter, writer, whatever she claims to be –'

Stefanovitch stopped himself in midsentence. He had no choice. Someone – presumably Sarah McGinniss – had just entered the room.

'Good morning,' she said in a pleasant, very low-key voice. 'Lieutenant Stefanovitch, I'm Sarah McGinniss. The writer you were just mentioning?'

Somehow, Stefanovitch succeeded in masking his frustration. He managed to smile, and muttered hello to the slender, dark-haired woman at the door. She was no Kay Whitley, but she was attractive, certainly not what he'd expected when he heard a writer was coming around.

'Bear, could the two of us, Ms McGinniss and I, have a minute?' he asked.

His hands thrust deeply into his pockets, his tongue planted even deeper in his cheek, Kupchek slowly backed out of the room. He shut the door behind him, letting it click with great effect.

'May I say one thing before you start, Lieutenant?'

'I don't think so.' Stefanovitch sighed and shook his head. He understood that he had to be absolutely stubborn with her, maybe even unreasonable. 'Look, we're both busy people. You're writing your story, your book. I'm conducting a nasty, complicated murder investigation. One that's particularly difficult for me.'

'Lieutenant Stefanovitch, I think maybe –'

'I can't get involved in New York City politics right now. I won't. I like what I know about your work. I read *A Mother's Kindness*. But these videotapes are part of an ongoing homicide investigation. I don't care what you can tell me about Alexandre St-Germain. So, please leave.'

'I like the way you said all that, Lieutenant. The compliments about my book especially.' When Sarah finally got to say a few words, a disarming twinkle came into her eyes. 'The problem is, I'm not so sure it tracks.'

'I don't particularly care what –'

'I listened to you, Lieutenant. Play fair, please?' Sarah smiled. She seemed slightly amused by the outbreak between them. 'For one thing, the tapes are under the police commissioner's jurisdiction, not yours. Second, the PC *is* interested in the material I have on Alexandre St-Germain, and especially the Midnight Club. I promise not to get in your way, Lieutenant, as long as you don't get in mine.'

Sarah began to slip out of her jacket, an old electric-blue-and-pink windbreaker. Besides the cheery jacket, she wore a faded club shirt, khakis, and old running shoes. The outfit was comfortable, and it seemed appropriate for a long work session at Police Plaza.

'Hold on there. Hold up. Please don't get yourself comfortable.' John Stefanovitch was pushing his wheelchair toward her.

'Listen,' he said. 'Either I watch these tapes by myself, and this homicide investigation proceeds . . . or *you* watch the tapes, and the entire investigation shuts down until you're finished in here.'

'That's your choice.' Sarah shrugged. 'If you want to wait, that's fine with me.'

She sat down in one of the two hardwood chairs inside the cramped, musty, rather inhospitable office. The office was tiny, no more than seven by nine. She'd been in bigger clothes closets, nicer Port-O-Sans, classier phone booths.

Sarah suddenly stood up again. She walked over to a small wooden counter and poured herself a cup of coffee.

'Why don't you have some coffee?' Stefanovitch said from across the room.

'Thanks.' Sarah took a sip, her lips poised over the Styrofoam. 'My God, it's liquid ash. Do you make your own coffee? *Is* this coffee?'

'I make my own coffee, and I happen to like it strong. As my father used to say, "It puts hair on the chest." I wasn't expecting company. I didn't invite any company. All right, watch the videotapes.'

Stefanovitch hit the PLAY button of the VCR with the heel of his hand. Two naked bodies appeared on the television screen. An appropriate punctuation to the conversation.

'Great. Really terrific.' He couldn't remember the last time he had boiled over the top like this. The investigation definitely had him uptight. He couldn't stop baiting her, either.

'You usually watch your X-rated videotapes at home, I imagine?'

'Sometimes at home.' Sarah was beginning to enjoy herself. At least she was winning most of the skirmishes, she felt. 'Hotels with pay TV are great, too. Occasionally I catch a pornographic movie by myself, over on Ninth Avenue.'

John Stefanovitch's eyes bored into the flickering television screen. He tried his best to concentrate on the sequence of images.

The tapes from Allure were as explicit as anything shown on Ninth Avenue in New York, or Zeedijk Street in Amsterdam, or the Reeperbahn in Hamburg. But there was a subtle, important difference. Nobody seemed to be acting on these tapes.

On the television screen an exotic blond, who didn't look any older than eighteen or nineteen, posed seductively. She lolled on the edge of a double bed draped with silver lamé sheets. The young prostitute was slender and narrow-waisted, as entrancing as any *Vogue* or *Cosmopolitan* model.

A gauzy, cream white nightgown revealed the outlines of her breasts. Her large brown eyes were dusted with delicately applied eyeliner. Her hair was clipped back on one side, held by an exquisite ivory barrette. He thought of Kay Whitley and Kimberly Manion; of the perfection demanded at Allure.

Where did they get such beautiful women? Sarah McGinniss was also wondering. What did any of this have to do with the murder of Alexandre St-Germain? With some kind of gang war that might be erupting around the world? With the shooting of John Traficante on Third Avenue? With the Midnight Club?

Watching the glossy film, she thought that she understood what a high-budget pornographic movie might look like. Sarah also began to feel embarrassed. Then, a bit later, more than a little embarrassed.

A well-preserved, silver-haired man, probably in his early fifties, entered the scene from camera left. He sat beside the blond woman on the bed.

Sarah could tell that the man worked out. He also looked rich; there was something pampered about him. His silverish hair was still wet, combed straight back. He wore a puffy, white half-robe. She thought she ought to be writing some of this down.

'I haven't been with anyone for three weeks,' the blond woman said. Her voice was soft, melodic. Her smile was slightly crooked, even more appealing because of the imperfection. The nipples of her breasts poked and pointed against the nightgown.

'You look so good to me, but you always do. I love the way you dressed for me tonight. All over Chanterelle, men and women were staring at you. Did you happen to notice, Gerard?'

The older man smiled, and seemed taken in completely by her. His ego was obviously close to bursting. A pair of expensive Italian loafers lay turned on their sides near the bed.

'Where did you go on your little trip?' he asked.

'Oh, I was on St Bart's. Lazing out completely. A friend of mine owns a villa up in the hills.'

'A friend?'

'Oh, a girlfriend.' The young blond's movements were almost feline; she had a natural grace, a poise that suggested dance training, maybe even professional dancing. There was a faint rustle of her nightgown, silk against soft skin. Sarah imagined somebody paying for her dancing lessons once upon a time. It made her sad to think about that. What a waste.

The girl curled herself around the old man's back. She began to massage his furrowed temple with both hands. Her nails were bright vermilion. He sighed at her touch.

After several minutes of massage, she suddenly left the bedroom suite. The romantic music in the background was subdued and sensual. Every detail had been attended to. Had it been this way for Alexandre St-Germain? Was it always like this at Allure?

The young woman returned with a silver metal carton that looked like a pillbox. She and the silver-haired man each selected a different-colored pill from the many rolling around inside the box. They had obviously practiced this routine before. They were laughing now, giddy as children allowed to stay up too late.

Stefanovitch had heard about one or two highly expensive, very private bordellos in New York. So this was what they were like. 'He took a Quaalude,' he said. 'I don't know what she had in her hand.'

Standing in front of Silver Hair, the prostitute slowly stretched the straps of her gown down over slender, freckled shoulders. The silk gown was finally bunched at her waist, her breasts revealed to the man, but not to the camera.

Next, she reached forward, underneath the man's robe. Sarah felt that she finally understood the word 'courtesan.' Things she had only read about in police reports were coming to life.

'I really missed you, Gerard,' the blond woman said in a soft stage whisper.

'Touch yourself down there, too.' The older man suddenly seemed humble. He slowly began to stroke himself.

Touch yourself down there, Sarah silently mocked the scene. She was angry at the man for using the young girl. When she had heard about her husband Roger's lover in California, she'd felt betrayed and used herself. She had also felt that somehow she must have been at fault for losing him.

'You're such a beautiful, beautiful man. You're so elegant. You do everything with such style, Gerard. I'm not just saying it because . . . you know.'

Sarah could tell that the silver-haired man needed to believe the words he was hearing. She had an urge to talk back at the movie. The scene was powerfully moving. Across the small room, Stefanovitch self-consciously cleared his throat.

'I have some Halls Eucalyptus, Lieutenant,' Sarah said. He deserved every zinger she could come up with.

Stefanovitch felt his face flush. His neck and his chest were tingling. He nearly laughed, though. Sarah McGinniss was quick on her feet. 'The pills probably made their bodies more sensitive,' he finally said.

'Have you used Quaaludes yourself?'

'Once or twice,' Stefanovitch said. Then he frowned when he thought about his remark ending up in her book. *Many, if not most, New York City detectives use illegal drugs themselves.*

'Let me undress you all the way now.' Silver Hair's voice was a low, sibilant whisper.

'Not yet. Don't rush this . . . Gerard? . . . There's something even better we can do. Is that all right? . . . You trust me?'

'Of course. Whatever you want to do is fine.' Suddenly he was sounding closer to his age. Unsure of himself.

The call girl rose from the bed again. She moved two steps away.

Very sensually, she slid the straps of her gown back up onto her shoulders. She let her long nails slowly trail down her legs, making a long scratching sound.

Stefanovitch thought of a few steamy Hollywood movies he'd seen. *Body Heat.* A remake of *The Postman Always Rings Twice.* They were tame and prudish compared with this.

And nothing had even happened yet. Just some foreplay *. . . But the real stuff.* Not wooden-Indian actors and actresses playing make-believe.

Midnight? Stefanovitch wondered again. What was Midnight? If it was the Midnight Club, what was the connection? Had the Club come after Alexandre St-Germain?

Or was someone coming after members of the Club? There was a big difference right there. A huge difference for his investigation.

The blond hooker's profile was turned sharply to the camera now. Did she know the scene was being filmed? By her employers? By someone else? Her lips parted, and they were ruby red and moist; they opened like an exotic string bag.

Her breasts were erect. If she was faking everything, she was a brilliant actress, much too good to be doing this film. Her palms rubbed against her nipples, blood rushing into her breasts.

With one hand, she reached underneath the gauzy white

gown. Her knees were bent as far forward as possible. She was on her toes, her slender ankles arched.

Suddenly, the silver-haired man started to spasm. It was the first time he had lost control. Silver Hair looked as if he weren't used to losing control. Stefanovitch was almost certain the older man was somebody important, somebody he ought to recognize.

Did he know about Midnight? Did the blond call girl know? Did anyone who visited Allure know the answers he needed?

There was no other sound inside the small office, only what was coming from the VCR.

Stefanovitch hadn't looked over at Sarah McGinniss for the last several minutes.

'Two thousand dollars a night.' Stefanovitch finally spoke. He felt that he had to say something, to break the tension.

'She's very clever,' Sarah McGinniss said from the other side of the room. 'She never let him touch her.'

9

Sarah McGinniss
Kennedy International Airport

'Daddy! Daddy!' Sam hollered. His little-boy voice was light with joy and expectation.

At that instant, Sarah winced. Her pain was sharp and immediate, almost overwhelming. Roger the Dodger was striding toward them inside the streamlined, crimson and blue TWA terminal. He was straightening imaginary wrinkles in his corduroy sports jacket and trousers. Daddy was home.

His face, as usual, looked nervous and too thin. He finally smiled and waved at Sam, both arms crisscrossing high over his head.

Sarah had to reach inside herself for a deep breath. Roger's smile made her remember how the two of them had been in the very beginning, for almost six years, actually. She remembered how funny and charming Roger could be, when he was in the mood. Plus the undeniable fact that he had been a good father, a real daddy, right up until the time he had left them.

'Hello, pumpkin.' Roger immediately picked Sam up. In her mind's eye, Sarah could see him stooping and picking Sam up hundreds of times before that. She noticed how Sam was watching them both, still trying to understand what could have happened two years ago between his mom and dad. Sarah was still trying to understand that one herself.

'How are you, Sarah?' Roger finally acknowledged her. 'Looking all summer-brown and pretty,' he answered his own superficial question. 'You too, sport. Do you like your mom's beach house?'

'Sure, it's neat. Are you coming out there with us?' Sam asked, once again checking them out, both their reactions to his innocent-sounding question.

'Well, I don't know. We'll see, pal, but I think there will be enough other things for us to do for a while. I was thinking of taking Sam upstate to see my parents,' Roger announced to Sarah.

It was purely informational. He had Sam for two weeks during the summer, and two more weeks at Christmas, no strings attached. He could take him anywhere he liked. When he had called Sarah yesterday, Roger had even made a crack that this was a good time for Sam to be away – while she was working on such a potentially 'dangerous' story.

Sarah was conscious of the way Roger had used *pumpkin*, *pal*, and *sport* to address Sam. It was a little like the way she might avoid using the same word twice in a sentence in her writing, very self-conscious and uncomfortable. She was surprised at how hard these occasional meetings continued to be.

'Do you remember going up to Batavia?' Sarah asked Sam. She sensed that her voice was strained and sounded slightly unreal.

'Sure Sam remembers,' his father said.

'Of course. Grandpa and Grandma live there. The snow gets twenty feet high in the winter. Mom calls it Outer Bavaria.'

'She's quite the writer. Great imagination.'

Sarah didn't want to let Sam go, and the three of them continued to exchange cheery, if hollow-sounding, small talk in front of a flight insurance kiosk.

Both of them waved good-bye, their own zany two-handed wave. They smiled as if this were no big deal.

Sarah finally forced herself to turn away. She started to walk back toward the airport parking lot and her car.

She noticed that she was biting her lower lip, and then, finally, she was crying. Hot tears streamed down both her cheeks, her throat, and under the collar of her blouse. Her mascara streaked, but she didn't care. She coughed and began to choke as strangers stared.

A passing woman finally stopped and asked if she was all right, if she needed any help.

Sarah tried to explain that she was just being dumb – her ex-husband had two weeks of visiting rights with her little boy, and she missed Sam already.

The woman gave Sarah a sympathetic hug, and she kept lightly patting her arm while they talked. New Yorkers could perform such kind acts sometimes, Sarah knew, and it was especially touching when they did. She knew that she still loved Roger, in a strange, perplexing way. Sarah knew, too, at that moment, if not before, that she was over him. She had to move on with her life.

She felt so lonely, though. Sharing the moment with a stranger in Kennedy Airport, Sarah thought she had never been so alone in her life. All that she had was Sam, and now she didn't even have him.

Later that morning, she was unusually apprehensive from the moment she entered One Police Plaza. She didn't want to repeat the previous day's ordeal with Lieutenant Stefanovitch, but she needed to see some more of the videotapes, possibly all of them.

Fortunately, she was the first to arrive at the small interior office where the television monitor and VCR unit had been set up the day before.

An obliging secretary unlocked the inner office. Sarah then made herself as comfortable as possible in the enemy's camp. Over the next few minutes she developed a workable system for viewing the videotapes by herself.

Shortly past noon, the door to the office opened slowly. Sarah's eyes rose from the sheaf of log notes in her hands. Lieutenant Stefanovitch had arrived.

He hesitated before coming all the way into the room. Actually, he looked different today, almost like a real police-man. He was wearing a brown tweed sports jacket, green khaki shirt, semi-pressed trousers, and desert boots.

'I didn't know you were here.' He smiled. He was actually being moderately civil.

'I turn the volume down when I fast-forward.' Sarah offered an explanation for the silence.

'Anything interesting in the latest batch?' Stefanovitch asked.

She held up a pad that was full of the morning's notes. 'I'm keeping a log. What I've seen on the tapes is a mixture of organized crime figures, legitimate businessmen, an awful lot of show business celebrities, especially the Los Angeles-to-New York jet set.

'I made coffee,' Sarah said before she took another sip. She noticed that Stefanovitch was still being reasonably nice.

He was actually starting to laugh.

'You're laughing at me.' Sarah frowned. 'I'm playing by all of your rules, too.'

'I'm not laughing. It's just that you're so serious. The investigative reporter.'

It was Sarah's turn to smile.

Out of the corner of her eye, she could still see naked bodies dancing on the television screen.

'Lieutenant, I'm from Stockton, California. Do you know Stockton? Truck farms, migrant workers. My family grew up as onion toppers, lettuce thinners, pea pickers. I got out somehow. Got a newspaper job. As Red Smith used to say, "I make a living working a typewriter." The money, any notoriety, that just happened. I was lucky. I caught a very good story.'

'You also wrote a good book. That wasn't luck. That was you being super-serious again.'

John Stefanovitch found himself studying Sarah McGinniss a little more closely. There was hint of sweetness in her smile. Her cheeks were slightly flushed. She was embarrassed, and he was surprised that she would be so vulnerable.

'Listen, Sarah.' Stefanovitch looked contrite. 'I'm sorry for being a shit yesterday. That's the act *I've* had to play since all of this happened. Sometimes I overdo it just a little.'

'Maybe just a little.' Sarah smiled.

The small room was quiet for a few seconds. The pencil in Sarah's hand tapped lightly against the rigid spine of her log pad.

'Listen, are you hungry? Because I am. How about if we go around the corner for a bite? Do you know Forlini's? C'mon, Lieutenant. Might as well be hanged for a sheep as a lamb.'

On the way to the restaurant in Little Italy, Stefanovitch slipped a folded-up dollar to a street beggar, a wino wearing a heavy, black, tattered winter coat in June.

'Are you always so generous?' Sarah asked him.

Stefanovitch mumbled something about soup kitchens, about trying to do the right thing every once in a while. Sarah let it drop. Still, she was oddly touched. The image of this strangely charismatic man in a wheelchair helping out panhandlers stuck in her mind.

At Forlini's, the maître d' greeted Sarah with an effusive smile and a gallant, almost seductive handshake. 'Ah, *la bella signora,* so nice to see you always.'

Since she had been writing *The Club* and spending so much time downtown at Foley Square and Police Plaza, Forlini's had become one of her favorite lunchtime haunts. The maître d', and most of the waiters, knew her from several past visits. The maître d' took their drink order after escorting them to a corner table. He hurried away to the bar.

Sarah had brought other policemen there, and she always seemed to pay the check. Women paying for dinners in Little Italy was still unusual, highly suspect.

'So tell me about working on newspapers,' Stefanovitch said once the waiter had left them. 'I get to watch a few pretty good reporters occasionally. *Times* guys. *New York Daily News*. You broke into a tough club.'

'It's not quite so macho on the West Coast. Maybe a little bit where I started, in San Francisco. Certainly not in Palo Alto.'

Sarah had never really felt comfortable talking about herself, not even after her book had become successful. She didn't particularly want to talk about herself now, either.

'Why don't you go first?' she said across the small, intimate table. 'Tell me something about yourself, Lieutenant, anything you'd like. I'm going to have to write about you in the book. I've already written a little.'

'You wrote about yesterday?' Stefanovitch coughed and patted his chest.

'A little. Sure. I write every morning.' The look on her face was slightly impish, not so serious after all. Sarah McGinniss was actually much prettier than he had thought the other day. Her eyes had a nice sparkle.

'How did I come off in what you wrote this morning?'

'Just the way you were. Tough, pretty obnoxious. Remember, you're the one who told me not to act so serious.' They both laughed. Things were improving.

Their drinks came and the maître d' made the usual impassioned plea for several of the house specials. Stefanovitch chose the calamari, plus mozzarella and beefsteak tomatoes. He was still learning to curb his appetite, adjusting to life in the Chair. Sarah went with a linguine, clam, and shrimp dish; prosciutto and melon to start.

'My first impression was that you were pretty serious yourself,' Sarah said. She was talking with her head cocked to one side. The effect was captivating. 'Aren't you?'

Stefanovitch thought that she was working him a little bit, interviewing him. He found that interesting, a challenge to be dealt with.

'I don't know if I trust first impressions very much anymore,' he said. 'People are becoming too slick nowadays. There are too many good actors out in the world.'

'Now you sound like a cop again,' Sarah said.

'I am a cop. That was just my impression of one, though. Want to hear the Minersville, Pennsylvania, impression? The navy port-of-call impression? I do a few different voices, a few acts. Every street cop has to be a little bit of a con artist.'

Sarah decided to take a chance as she listened to John Stefanovitch become more human. Afterward, though – while they were heading back to Police Plaza – she would wonder if she'd had any right to ask the next few questions.

She leaned forward on her elbows, holding his eyes with her own. 'Tell me something about your life before the shooting, Lieutenant. Your wife's name was Anna, wasn't it? She was a teacher?'

Stefanovitch moved uncomfortably in his wheelchair. He raised his wineglass but didn't drink from it. His fingers lightly twirled the glass.

Sarah saw that he was uneasy with her questions.

'Yes, her name was Anna. Originally, she was Anna Maddalena. We met in Ashland, Pennsylvania, after I got out of the navy. I was in for four years.'

'Tell me about Anna.' Sarah's voice was quiet, confidential. Instinctively, she'd always been a good interviewer. She knew how to listen to people.

'I think that, uh . . . Let's see. When I was growing up, somewhere in between the usual bar-hopping stints, I guess I wondered what love was all about. Like how are you supposed to know when you're actually in love?'

He was much more open than she'd expected. It was almost as if Stefanovitch needed to talk.

'How do you know that this is it for your lifetime?' he continued. 'I was kind of lucky. Very lucky. For about four years, my priorities in life were very clear. Anna was first. Then came my job. In that order, and never a doubt about it in my mind.'

Sarah was noticing that Stefanovitch's hands had slid

together. He had workingman's hands. His fingers were clutched a little tightly, though, white at the tips.

'We just happened to fit very nicely together. I guess we completed each other. When I heard about Anna's death – I don't know how to describe what I felt. An emptiness, a sense of nothingness. Something shattered inside. I – I don't even know what to say to you.'

It was a small, subtle thing, but Sarah heard his voice catch on the last few words.

'End of interview,' he said. 'Okay?'

A terrible sorrow had been etched across his face. His brown eyes darted away, infinitely sad in that moment of truth, but then he forced them back to look at her.

Sarah felt ashamed. Something in his eyes had reached out and touched her unexpectedly, completely caught her off guard.

'I'm sorry. I haven't done that in a long time.' He offered a smile.

Sarah felt warmly toward him for the first time. She understood a lot more about who he was, and she regretted having intruded on his grief. She noticed that her own hands were clenched.

'No, no. I'm sorry. You probably haven't had somebody asking you personal questions like that. I feel bad. I'm so sorry. Really I am.'

Stefanovitch suddenly extended his hand across the table, carefully threading a path between the wineglasses. He was smiling again. A resilient man, Sarah thought.

'This is going to work out after all,' he said.

Sarah was still feeling embarrassed about her leading questions. She took Stefanovitch's offered hand and shook it.

She looked into his eyes, and knew she saw honesty there. Maybe he was right, maybe first impressions shouldn't be trusted anymore.

'So tell me what you saw at the dirty movies today,' he finally asked.

10

Isiah Parker
Cin-Cin

The only indication that 649 Spring Street wasn't just another greasy, somber warehouse facade was an inconspicuous blue neon sign. 'BAR' was all it said.

Neither the name of the after-hours spot – Cin-Cin – nor anything else that might attract attention was visible from the street. There was no clue that one of New York's hottest clubs was inside the dreary warehouse.

Isiah Parker leaned against a chain fence across the street from the club's entranceway.

He watched the usual doorman scene for a little more than an hour.

The caste system at Cin-Cin was based on money, looks, and what was described as 'who you know, who you blow.' The two punk-beautiful doormen were arrogant and cruel, contemporary racists, Parker couldn't help thinking as he watched them work, selecting one or two to be allowed inside, contemptuously rejecting others.

At three in the morning, Isiah Parker crossed the cobblestone street. Properly dressed, interesting enough, he was allowed inside Cin-Cin. He looked like he belonged, with his dark blue Paris blouse, loose black karate-gi trousers, black half boots, a diamond stud in his right ear.

Parker understood the scene at the Cin-Cin club. Friday night was *the* night here. Just as Monday was *the* night at Heartbreak, and Wednesday was *the* night at Area, and so on around the city.

Muscular bouncers were posted everywhere. They were

mostly nasty weightlifter types who weren't really all that tough.

The crowd milling around was the usual for a club of the moment. Commercial musicians and assorted SoHo artists. Uptown fashion models, designers, famous athletes, trash from Queens, undercover police detectives who were actually a recognized part of the scene.

Parker found himself wondering how these people could do the scene – starting to party at one or two, often continuing until eight or nine. Then maybe breakfast at the Moonlighter, or the Empire Diner. Then what?

There was the usual crush of bodies mingling around the large horseshoe-shaped bar. Most of the men and women were dressed in black – black boots, black shoes and socks, black leather and buckskin vests, black turtlenecks and pants. Some of these people would casually drop four hundred dollars for a pair of black combat boots at nearby Comme des Garçons.

A few adventures were outfitted in trash and vaudeville getups, pointy shoes from London, Betsey Johnson finery. Tattoos decorated an occasional cheek or forehead.

Isiah Parker's brother, Marcus, had once said that New York's night people were 'living rock 'n' roll.' Marcus had meant that they were actually *living* rock and roll lyrics, not faking it for show. This was their life.

As he drifted away from the central bar, Parker found his body beginning to respond to the music: European disco mainly, not recognizable songs. Groups from the Netherlands and West Germany, from Italy, Sweden, and Norway dominated. Occasionally an American or British tune would break through, by experimental groups like Husker Du, the Blow Monkeys, Fine Young Cannibals.

'You want to dance? Dance with me, okay?' A tall slender black woman had come up to Parker. She wore a molded-to-the-body black leather dress with zippers at the neck and across her breasts. A Pomes Segli veiled hat completed the outfit.

Pickups were made by both women and men, but more often by women at Cin-Cin. Parker wanted to be friendly, but not to stand out tonight.

'Sure, let's dance.'

They walked onto the dance floor and began to move.

'You're a good dancer. Smooth. Nice,' she whispered, smiling shyly after the song had ended. 'I have to go to the bathroom. Want to come *avec moi*?'

'Not right now. I'll see you later, maybe.'

'Okay then. Ciao. Thanks for the dance. I like your diamond, the earring. It suits you.'

'Ciao.'

Parker moved on. The girl was pretty, at least in these party lights, but he couldn't get connected tonight.

He passed into a smaller, more intimate chamber. Everything was glowing pink. Humorous, posturing flamingos were set into the walls.

Some of the club's owners, plus a few heavy hitters, were clustered in the pink room. A well-known tennis player was giving audience. So was a famous rock singer. His fashion-model wife was at his side.

Isiah Parker couldn't help thinking about his brother as he strolled around the room. He and Marcus had come to Cin-Cin in the glory days. He remembered a private room near the kitchen where crack was smoked in water pipes.

He noticed a clique of Oliver Barnwell's associates congregated in the room. Barnwell's group was the most territorial of New York's narcotics gangs. They controlled Harlem, Bedford-Stuyvesant, and most of SoHo. They were vicious about intrusions into their neighborhoods. Supposedly, Barnwell had been linked to Alexandre St-Germain, to the sprawling syndicate currently invading the US. To the Midnight Club.

Parker spotted Oliver Barnwell comfortably ensconced beside the bar. Worth two hundred million in his stocking feet, the mob overlord was outfitted in a brown suede sport coat, beige silk shirt, and tan slacks. Oliver Barnwell liked

74

white women, and Parker immediately thought back to Allure, the connection to sex.

Two spectacular-looking women were talking to him, whispering and posing. One of them toyed with the gold necklace around Barnwell's throat. She had long, nervous fingers. Isiah Parker thought that she was definitely drug-sick.

There were several possibilities. Parker carefully began to roll them around in his mind. Somehow, he had to get Barnwell out of the pink room.

He decided to work under the worst assumption: that the bodyguards had already noticed him. Maybe they remembered when he used to drop into Cin-Cin with his brother.

Suddenly, the small details didn't matter. Oliver Barnwell had separated himself from the group. He was heading out of the womblike room. Parker watched Barnwell discuss something with his bodyguards, then wave them away. He seemed to think of himself as the original macho man from central Harlem, the optimum smooth operator. He could solo if he wanted. Anywhere, anytime.

Isiah Parker followed the powerful drug dealer out of the barroom. It was easy to be unobtrusive in Cin-Cin, staying back fifteen or twenty feet.

Oliver Barnwell turned into a shiny black and white corridor leading to the bathrooms.

Isiah Parker followed behind. He tried not to think about what he had to do next. He couldn't deal with that now. He thought about being a soldier again, the times back in Cambodia and Vietnam.

He watched Barnwell's back disappear into one of the doorways along the corridor – the ladies' room, which usually had as many men as women inside.

The ladies' room at Cin-Cin was more crowded than the dance floor, or the main bar area. The musk of expensive colognes, mixed with liquor, created a fruity and exotic scent.

Oliver Barnwell sat on the edge of one of the shiny porcelain sinks, laughing with a couple of wild-looking ladies.

Parker's eyes took in the heavily made-up faces. Thin, pouty slashes for mouths. Oliver Barnwell tapping a Jamaican cigar against the table surface, lighting up.

Gloves were hot right now.

Azzedine Alaia fashions were, too.

Anything black and white.

Pomes Segli.

Armani still held his own with some of the more traditional men.

Cheap chic still had a following.

All kinds of sniffing and snorting were going on toward the rear of the cavernous bathroom. No sex seemed to be in progress, but Parker knew that sex wasn't unusual in the bathroom stalls of the ladies'. At three forty-five, it was still early; the night was full of promise.

Oliver Barnwell finally wandered back toward the smaller, interior room where all the toilet stalls and a few more sinks were located.

Parker moved smoothly now, edging up quickly from behind. All of his senses were alert. He was aware of almost everything that was going on in the bathroom.

For a moment, the two men could have been dancing a samba in the bathroom. It seemed as if the taller black man, Parker, simply needed to pass by to get to a toilet in a hurry.

'You piece of shit. Pusher,' he whispered. '*Pusherman!*'

At first, Oliver Barnwell thought that Parker had punched him in the pit of his stomach. The pain and surprise in his eyes were sudden and extreme.

When he looked down, he saw the stiletto stuck in his abdomen. An awful gush of blood was spurting. His eyes registered chaos and confusion. He seemed unable to believe he had been stabbed right there in the bathroom.

Isiah Parker hurried out of the crowded ladies' room.

76

Clutching his coat to his body, he let the knife drop as he walked.

Parker didn't feel much of anything as he pushed his way outside. Oliver Barnwell sold heroin and other drugs to thousands of men, women, and children on the streets of Harlem. That was all he wanted to think about right now. All he needed to know.

That, plus getting out of Cin-Cin as quickly as possible. Get to the elevator, get to the doorway, and out.

'Somebody's real sick in there. Hey, tell them somebody's sick. There's a bad overdose inside, man.' He spoke to anyone who would listen.

The usual sickies in the crowd wolf-whistled and clapped. Everybody else seemed to take it calmly. The word was passed around, messengered along routinely. Someone had overdosed in the ladies' room. A man was dead in there.

Parker waited for the freight elevator going down. He was trying to look like part of a group of seven or eight leaving the club. The rock music thundering inside was deafening.

He felt nothing as he finally descended to the street. Maybe a coldness in his stomach.

Out on Spring Street again, in the blue and black shadows across from Cin-Cin, Isiah Parker doubled over. He threw up against the cyclone fence. He held the thought inside – *murderer*.

Less than thirty minutes later, John Stefanovitch was riding up in the same groaning warehouse elevator to view the remains of Oliver Barnwell.

Invisible men.

11

John Stefanovitch
One Police Plaza

Stefanovitch spent all day Saturday working by himself at One Police Plaza. He enjoyed the relative quiet and the solitude.

The Organized Crime Task Force now included more than sixty detectives cooperating in all the boroughs of New York. There were briefings every day, including a progress review with the commissioner and several precinct captains.

On Monday, visitors from Interpol, Scotland Yard, and the French Sûreté would arrive in New York. During the past week, related killings had occurred in Palermo, Amsterdam, and London, where police officials maintained that organized crime wasn't the problem.

On Sunday morning, John Stefanovitch's black van entered the Queens Midtown Tunnel at six-fifteen. At the end of the long, gray tunnel, beyond the sleepy rows of tollbooths, he began his ride east on the Long Island Expressway. The sky overhead was pink, rolling up into a crisp blue that was peaceful and gorgeous.

For an hour and a half, everything was right with Stefanovitch's world. He could feel a slight tingle, an overall pleasant sensation sweeping through his body, even down into his legs.

He arrived at the outskirts of East Hampton, Long Island, at seven-fifteen. He ate a homemade sausage and cheddar cheese omelet at Gilly's Wharfside, where he also performed his Sunday ritual of reading the *Times*: news, sports, theater, 'The Week in Review,' books, and the magazine.

When he had been recuperating from his gunshot wounds

in New York Hospital, he had read the *Times* cover to cover for forty-five straight Sundays. He had also read books, hundreds of them: fiction and nonfiction, more than he had read during the first thirty years of his life combined. One of his favorites, *A Fan's Notes*, by Frederick Exley, was about a screwed-up high school teacher who wound up with nothing in his life except reading the Sunday *Times* and watching the Giants play football. Every Saturday the guy would drive forty or fifty miles away from his hometown and go on a rip-roaring toot. On Sunday it would be even more drinking, plus the *Times*, and the pitiful 'Jints' on TV. Always in some anonymous, down-and-out tavern where nobody knew who he was. Then it was home again, home again, to teach school on Monday morning.

After his breakfast, Stefanovitch entered East Hampton proper. Soon, he was passing comfortable old houses of no great distinction, sighting the broad fairways and monster greens of the Maidstone Club Golf Course, which flanked the road on the right. The imposing bulk of the clubhouse faced the ocean like a fortress-castle.

Three quarters of a mile beyond the golf course, entrances to impressive summer estates began to appear. Long, curling driveways led to improbably small sand dunes. Behind them, sprawling beach houses were quietly settled into the earth.

The short stretch along the beach road was exhilarating. He turned up the car radio, letting it blare and become an almost physical presence. He sang along with a Tina Turner song called 'Private Dancer.' He opened both front windows, and the sea breeze whipped his brown hair around his ears and across his forehead.

The house he was looking for had a modest driveway that curved gracefully at the end, to begin a turnaround. The turnaround broadened into a circle for parking cars. The house itself was dominated by weathered gray shingles with white latticing. All the window frames on the two-story house were neatly trimmed in white. Glossy, bright blue shutters were already catching sparkles of sunlight.

Stefanovitch was a little in awe. He hadn't been properly prepared for Sarah McGinniss's *beach cottage*.

She was sitting out on the back porch, waiting for him to arrive, or maybe just sitting on the porch for no reason at all.

They agreed to meet and spend Sunday wading through her confidential notes, the files on Alexandre St-Germain, Oliver Barnwell, and John Traficante. They would try to connect the murdered crime figures with somebody on the videotapes, or perhaps someone in Sarah's files. The change of venue to the beach house seemed like a good idea. Stefanovitch figured it was like playing a home-and-home series in sports.

A steaming mug was cradled in the lap of Sarah's bright yellow sundress. She looked different again. Prettier, but also more carefree.

'Good morning, Lieutenant.' Sarah rose and came walking toward his car. Her bare, bony feet balanced on the driveway's shiny white gravel and broken shells. The yellow sundress ballooned slightly with the sea breeze. He caught every detail.

'Morning, ma'am.' Stefanovitch smiled like a local Johnny Law. 'Which way to the servants' entrance?'

'Don't be a wise guy, Lieutenant. After the book hit, I had a few choices – investing in shopping centers in places like Bloomington, Indiana. Or maybe something like this house. I thought the house might be a little more fun than the Stop and Shops.'

Stefanovitch nodded. His eyes continued to survey the beachfront house and property.

'I'll show you where we're going to work. C'mon.'

He followed her along a bleached slat walkway that led toward the oceanfront.

It was a luminous day. The air was clear, thick with salt, and the sky was the brightest blue. Gray and off-white seagulls were flapping overhead, as if someone had thrown them handfuls of bread crumbs. Somewhere down the beach, a halyard rang softly against a sailboat mast.

Sarah had set up a long wooden worktable on the first extension of the front porch. It was covered with papers, shaded by a navy blue awning.

Stefanovitch could imagine her sitting out there, writing her books.

'Where would you like to set up shop?' She spoke over the hiss of the wind. 'I thought maybe that porch over there.'

'The porch looks great to me. It beats Police Plaza on a day like today. All kidding aside, this is very special.'

'All kidding aside, thank you.'

He had read somewhere, in one of the magazine interviews, that Sarah McGinniss was an extremely hard worker. She was supposed to be dedicated to her small son and to her writing, and she wouldn't let anything get in the way of either.

By two o'clock on Sunday afternoon, Stefanovitch absolutely believed what he had read about her. His eyes were burning and he had a throbbing headache. His shoulders ached from too much sitting in one place.

She showed no signs of tiring, though. She had mentioned lunch once, and he feigned indifference. She had then plunged on for another hour and a half of note taking, reading lengthy court transcripts, searching through as much original background material as Stefanovitch had seen in all his past homicide investigations put together.

The street law . . . the crushing reality of organized crime around the world in the middle 1980s . . . Sarah McGinniss had done exhaustive research on all of it.

Alexandre St-Germain was mentioned everywhere in the files:

> In his early years, but as recently as the previous spring, the Grave Dancer had proven to be the

most violent and vengeful of the crime lords. Behind the veneer of his good looks, his charm, St-Germain had been a psychopath. Was that why he had been murdered? Had his methods been too extreme? Had he embarrassed or worried someone? But who? Who was calling the shots in the Midnight Club? Who had gotten more powerful than St-Germain?

The Grave Dancer had enjoyed 'wet work,' performing many of the nasty murders himself. He had taught his horrifying 'lessons' all over the world:

A drug dealer, but also his two girlfriends, beheaded in Morocco. Their faces ruined. Their genitals slashed with razor blades.

Five young policemen blown to bits during their weekly card game in Los Angeles.

The two daughters of a judge in Rome kidnapped from private school, then raped and murdered. A twelve- and a fourteen-year-old.

A West German hospital bombed to get to a trial lawyer.

A nightclub bombed in London, fourteen dead, eleven of them young women.

So many lessons; all of them vivid and horrible and premeditated.

That was why the street law had been so effective.

But now somebody didn't want or need the old laws.

Who could that be?

What had changed so dramatically?

Solve the murder of the Grave Dancer, and all the other mysteries would solve themselves. Stefanovitch was almost certain of it.

Meanwhile, Sarah McGinniss's files went on and on.

When the French/Marseilles Connection had been temporarily broken, the Sicilian Mafia headed up the flow of most heroin trade into the United States. There had been incredible violence against the Italian judiciary and members of Parliament who interfered with the mob. The street law.

More than a hundred policemen, but also magistrates, had been murdered in Sicily during the past decade alone. Italy continued to have the world's largest black economy, the *economia sommersa*, or submerged economy.

In recent years, the Midnight Club had opened up negotiations between the Sicilians and the Marseilles group. The Club had connected the mobs with legitimate businesses in France and Italy. An Italian labor official announced on television that it was becoming impossible to tell the good guys from the bad guys.

Stefanovitch read on through the source material:

By agreement of the international crime leadership, presumably the Club, the Colombians had cornered the cocaine pipeline into the United States. A justice minister and twelve judges were murdered in 1985 for their efforts to help control drug traffic in Colombia and Peru. Another dozen drug policemen, trained by Americans, were murdered up-country.

In November of 1985, a band of Colombian assassins had actually assaulted the Palace of Justice in Bogotá. They went to the fourth floor, where judges were hearing requests for extradition of drug traffickers to the United States. The assassins killed a dozen of the judges right there. In total, 95 people were killed during the bloody siege. The street law once again . . .

The Yakuza, in Japan, had recently joined with the international cartel, working outside of their own country. Alexandre St-Germain had been

involved in effecting the negotiations. It represented the first time the Yakuza had ever worked
with outsiders. At the same time, the Midnight
Club had become heavily involved with buying
and trading in the Tokyo Stock Exchange.

According to page after page of Sarah's notes, crime was
truly organizing this time.

Taiwan's United Bamboo gang was currently
operating successfully in Houston, Miami, Los
Angeles, San Francisco, New York, the Philippines,
Saudi Arabia, Syria, Hong Kong, and Japan. United
Bamboo had reportedly completed an agreement
with Alexandre St-Germain, just before his death.

At about three o'clock, Stefanovitch checked his wristwatch. He finally collapsed against the back of his chair.

Sarah saw him, and she laughed. 'I'm *really* sorry. Some
hostess, right? I'm conditioned to grunt work behind a desk.
Reading tomes of stuff like this. I'll bet you're starving. I've
got deli food hidden away in the kitchen. Bought for just
such an occasion. Where would you like to eat?'

Stefanovitch stared up at the thin streak of ocean blue,
visible just over the luminous white of the sand dune.

'How about on the deck there? That looks pretty good
to me. I'll help with the food.'

'All right, sure. That'll be great. If you're interested, there
are extra bathing suits, towels and things inside the house.
I'm going to change into something myself.'

Sarah smiled at Stefanovitch.

'Please make yourself at home. Okay, Lieutenant? End
of amenities.'

She went off to change and to fix lunch. As instructed,
Stefanovitch showed himself around the spacious and open
downstairs of the beach house.

He found a changing area with a selection of cabana
jackets and swimsuits, a couple of them obviously for

Sarah's little boy, Sam. He appreciated the way Sarah hadn't found it necessary to show him around, or to tend to him too much. The single largest complaint about being 'handicapped' was people always trying to 'help' – except when you really needed it.

Fifteen minutes after he went inside, Stefanovitch had commandeered a pair of loose gray sweatpants and a well-worn, kelly green T-shirt that said 'Boston Celtics.' He imagined he looked like a typical New York cop, summering on the Irish Riviera. Well, not exactly typical.

He came down the walkway to the deck overlooking the sand dunes. For a couple of minutes, he just watched the surf gently rise and fall in the distance. Then he went back to the house and returned to the deck with plates and silver for lunch. He was making himself useful, which had always been his way, but which since the shooting had become a psychological necessity.

Eventually, he heard Sarah coming from the house. He swung around to see her carrying a tray with lunch.

Sarah had a slender, very sexy body. She was wearing a simple black one-piece. She'd let her hair down, combed it out, and pinned it behind one ear with a cherry red barrette.

'That's a pretty suit' was as far as he would let himself go. Intense confusion clouded his mind.

The two of them were comfortable enough with one another to be fairly quiet as they ate their lunch. Eventually, Sarah talked about her little boy. Listening to her, Stefanovitch got the sense that everything wasn't quite resolved between Sarah and her former husband. He didn't push her on it. He didn't have a book to write, after all. He didn't have an excuse to ask a lot of personal questions.

As he finished off an overstuffed crabmeat salad sandwich, he noticed that Sarah was gazing out to sea, momentarily off in her own private world.

'What are you thinking about?' he asked her. 'You're not already working again, are you?'

Sarah shifted her face out of profile. There was a softness that appeared sometimes; it understated her intelligence, and made her very approachable.

'Not really. No. Can I ask you a serious question? . . . There I go again. Another one of my famous probing questions.'

'No, it's all right.'

Sarah set down the last portion of her salad. 'Will you tell me about your legs? Only if you feel comfortable talking about it. You still have some feeling in them, don't you?'

'More than I want to sometimes,' Stefanovitch said and smiled faintly. 'There's an operation I could try. I've been told the chances are eight in ten I'd wind up paralyzed from the neck down. I don't think I like the odds. My doctor, actually about three different specialists, doesn't like the odds at all. It's not a real-world possibility. But I do have some feeling, yes.'

They were both quiet for a moment, perched amid the dunes under the clear, blue sky. Sarah looked over at Stefanovitch again. He was so different from what she'd sensed that first morning at Police Plaza. He had this aura about him, something special. If anything, his being in the wheelchair increased it.

She had the intuitive feeling that she had crossed some barrier he'd set up between himself and the outer world. She was becoming curious about what he'd been like before the accident.

'It's as hot as the Mets were last year,' Sarah finally said. It was the kind of silly thing she might have remarked to Sam. It made her think that maybe she hadn't been spending enough time around adults lately.

Her eyes traveled down toward the water, which looked cold and inviting.

'The ocean's something I don't think I could handle,' Stefanovitch said. 'I couldn't get this chair down there through all that sand. You go ahead. I'll amuse myself up here.'

'Mr Self-sufficient,' she lightly mocked him. She stood up on the creaking wooden deck. Finally, Sarah began to trot down toward the shimmering blue sea.

She provides a nice view from the back, Stefanovitch thought as she bobbed away. California girls. The little touch with the red barrette was the best part. Well, one of the best parts.

He would have been lying to himself not to admit that he was captivated. He was. But he cut if off there. Fantasies in that direction were too painful and ridiculous. He cursed softly, but he let it go.

He kept his eyes on her all the way down to the sea, every step.

The sun created millions of perfect jewels on the ocean surface. The line of surf was like a delicate white lace collar.

Sarah broke the white lace with a nearly perfect dive. It made his heart grab in spite of his commonsense resolve just a moment before. She was so 'regular' and just plain good to be around. He couldn't imagine anybody leaving her, as her husband apparently had done.

Around four-thirty, the two of them got back to work. They agreed to cover the remaining files before calling it a day.

As he watched her jot down several notes, Stefanovitch began to understand why Sarah McGinniss had become a successful journalist and author. She was single-minded, and absolutely driven by her work, at least by the writing of *The Club*. Sarah also seemed immune to the danger attached to writing her book.

Late afternoon breezes off the ocean arrived in refreshing swells for the next hour or so. Stefanovitch thought that he hadn't felt so sandy, so windblown, so good, in years.

He had completely lost track of time, and was surprised to look up and see that night had fallen. His watch said nine.

'You've really got yourself a beautiful spot here.' He

finally spoke. He moved away from the worktable, up closer to the porch railing with its view of the sea.

Sarah came over and sat on the whitewashed rail beside him. Her profile, difficult to ignore in any lighting, was alluring against the moon and the night sky.

'I still can't get it into my head that this is actually my place. The house. This little vantage point on sun and sea.'

Stop staring at her, Stefanovitch was thinking as he listened to Sarah. *You're acting like you've never been around a beautiful woman before*.

Odd things were happening to him. A sense of excitement; of imminent adventure; a feeling that something strange and shining was going to take place.

'Listen, Stef, I have some lobsters in the fridge. It's getting kind of late. Should we knock off? Will you have dinner with me?'

'If you let me cook something, I'd consider that invitation very seriously.'

'We can do a tag-team act in the kitchen.' Sarah smiled and gave a thumbs-up sign.

Stefanovitch wasn't really sure what happened next. Whether it was he or Sarah, or a little of both? Or *if* it really happened at all.

He was leaning forward at the same time that Sarah was slipping down from the rail. They were closer than either had intended. Their lips met. They were kissing as uncertainly as children trying it for the first time.

Sarah pulled away first, stepping back awkwardly toward the porch railing.

'I'm sorry. That was a . . . I'm sorry, Stef,' she stammered.

She was obviously as confused as he was, and he was very confused.

'Yeah. No problem. Just the moon working its magic,' Stefanovitch managed.

He followed Sarah inside to the kitchen. For a moment,

everything was uncomfortable between them, very quiet. Slowly they found some balance again, a comfort level. They had both made a mistake. That was all. It happened sometimes.

The preparations for the lobster dinner were interrupted by the telephone's ringing.

The call was for Stefanovitch. It was Bear Kupchek with news about the investigation.

It was an unusually excited Bear, Stefanovitch discovered as he took the call. He could see Sarah in the kitchen as he listened to New York. He thought he could still feel her kiss on his lips.

'Stef? *You there?* Anybody home?' Kupchek asked.

'Yeah, I'm here.' He tuned in to the phone conversation.

'Stef, I think we've caught a break.'

He concentrated on the Bear's gruff, excited voice over the phone.

'We've found somebody who was at Allure the night Alexandre St-Germain was shot. He says he can identify one of the hit men, maybe the people behind it. Says we're in for a big surprise. Big shockeroo. I'm going to meet him tonight, then I'll come by your place. Say by eleven, at the latest. I've got a feeling it's important.'

Stefanovitch calculated how long the drive back to Manhattan would take. He told the Bear that he would be at his apartment by ten-thirty.

'Well, that settles that.' He shrugged as he returned to the kitchen. His heart was still pounding from the phone call.

'Who was it?' Sarah had two-pound lobsters in either hand.

'Duty calls, Sarah. That was my partner. He has a lead on the St-Germain murder, finally. It's important. I've got to go back to the city.'

As soon as he was out on Dune Road, a sharp pain struck Stefanovitch. He had let Sarah McGinniss get to him, he realized. For someone who prided himself on common sense, he didn't seem to be using a lot of it.

During the hour-and-a-half ride back into New York, he couldn't stop thinking about Sarah. She was surprisingly down-to-earth. Even the way she talked about her little boy Sam had charmed him. Then there was the kiss on the porch.

Finally, as John Stefanovitch saw the cold, electric Manhattan skyline, he got his head back into the search for the Midnight Club, whatever that was going to turn out to be.

He wondered what Bear Kupchek had been able to find. A real shocker about the St-Germain murder, he'd promised. Well, he would know soon enough. The Bear always delivered.

12

Bear Kupchek
Central Park

Bear Kupchek entered Central Park at the black stone gates that lead to the pass-through at Sixty-third Street. He had seen other complex murder cases break open simply and suddenly. He hoped this would be one of those cases. And that it would crack open tonight.

The broad-shouldered, heavyset detective slumped toward the Wollman skating rink, where he was to meet the secretive witness from the murder scene at Allure. Kupchek checked his wristwatch as he entered a tunnel running underneath the ring road. Twenty feet above, cabs and private cars were streaming north through Manhattan.

It was 10:11 P.M., so he had four minutes to make it to his appointment. The detective whistled lightly, some half-familiar rhythm and blues tune. He'd been confident about their chances of catching some kind of break in the investigation. But in the middle of Central Park? At night?

Kupchek had been born in Manhattan, forty-two years before. Michael Christopher Kupchek, of West End Avenue and 106th Street. He remembered Central Park in times when nobody would have walked there at night – not even a hefty detective with a Colt Magnum in his shoulder holster. These days, people routinely jogged and bicycled through the park at night. Ironically, it had been the ineffectual John Lindsay who'd made the park safe. Lindsay had put in sodium yellow street lamps, probably because they looked pretty from the penthouses on Fifth and Park avenues.

Kupchek was about halfway through the tunnel when he heard a voice up ahead.

'Kupchek?'

'Who are you?' Bear Kupchek stopped walking immediately.

His right hand instinctively went to his shoulder holster and the Magnum. His eyes strained to locate an upright shape in the darkness.

'I'm looking for Kupchek,' the voice came again. It was muffled and hollow-sounding. It echoed against the damp stone walls.

This time, Kupchek reached inside his shoulder holster. He carefully withdrew his revolver.

'I guess you've found him,' he called back into the darkness. 'I'm Kupchek.'

Then Kupchek saw movement. He heard a rustle of leaves, maybe papers, to his left. The sound was about ten feet farther up the tunnel.

'Don't be jumping around,' he called ahead. 'Now who are *you*? What's up? Come on out so we can talk.'

A revolver suddenly flashed inside the tunnel. Not his revolver, either. The gun made a hollow pop, the kind a dum-dum can produce. The revolver flashed a second time.

Kupchek grabbed his chest. He nearly toppled over. *Oh Jesus*, he thought. *Sweet Mother of God.*

He'd never felt this kind of pain before. He'd been shot twice, up in Bedford-Stuyvesant and at Long Beach. It was nothing like this.

His chest felt caved in, brutally crushed. He felt a cold wetness. The sensation of air whistling through his lungs.

It hurt terribly. Intense shooting pains were knifing through his chest and arms. He felt woozy. He thought he might be going down, right there in the pitch-black tunnel.

The second shot exploded inside him – a punishing dum-dum round.

The power of being hit was sickening, physically nauseating. He was victim to the ability of a small metal projectile to so easily penetrate flesh and bone.

Bear Kupchek did the unexpected. He was working on instinct, nothing else. Survival was his only conscious thought. The handgun fired again, shot number three. The gunman missed.

Suddenly Kupchek ran straight at the man. Except that he swerved past him, out of the tunnel in a low, hurdling crouch.

And in that confused instant, Kupchek recognized the gunman. The man was a cop. Someone he knew. A detective. He'd been set up and shot by another policeman.

His mind was reeling, completely out of control as he rumbled up a steep hill that seemed all thorny branches and protruding rocks.

His lungs were sloshing liquid, filling up much too quickly with blood. Run. Just run, he told himself.

He made it to a bus-stop bench out on Central Park South. He barely made it.

He had to sit. It didn't matter how dangerous, how exposed he was. *He'd been shot by another cop.*

Bright lights were spinning every which way around him. He wanted to yell out to somebody.

But no. They couldn't help him, not these people innocently walking around the perimeter of the park: Plaza Hotel guests, tourists, a few neighborhood women walking their dogs. Then Bear Kupchek was angry, mostly with himself. He struggled to his feet. He began to weave away.

He shuffled toward the street and the bright, splintering lights of streaming traffic.

He flagged down a Checker cab, stepping in front of the off-duty taxi. Brakes shrieked up and down Central Park South. Drivers shouted through their open windows.

Kupchek waved his detective's shield at the driver; otherwise the cabbie might have run him down.

'Drive where I tell you. Police business, let's go.'

He was slurring his words. Blood was dripping onto his sport coat, his shoes, the inside of the cab.

John Stefanovitch
East Eighty-first Street

Stefanovitch had arrived home at his apartment a little earlier than he'd expected.

He could work out for twenty minutes or so. Maybe do a few Nautilus exercises; something he'd been neglecting since the investigation began.

Stefanovitch was fumbling for his keys when the elevator doors opened. He started out into the hallway.

He stopped the wheelchair. Dear God, no . . . no. His mind was a shrill scream.

The Bear!

He was slumped like a sack against Stefanovitch's front door. Blood had soaked through his work shirt and was visible from thirty feet away.

Kupchek spread his arms and tried to smile when he saw Stefanovitch coming. His eyes were glassy, and they started to roll up into his head. Kupchek looked so *weak*.

Stefanovitch pushed himself furiously down the hallway. His stomach was falling through empty space.

When he got a few feet away, he saw how bad it was. Right then he knew.

'Worse than I thought,' Bear Kupchek whispered.

Stefanovitch slid down out of the wheelchair. He sat on the floor with his body pressed against the Bear. *Oh please*, a voice whispered inside him.

'Don't try to talk. I'm going to get you help. Just lie still,' Stefanovitch said.

Bear Kupchek closed his eyes for several seconds. He opened them and began to speak – at least he tried to. A hoarse whisper came out.

'I love you, Stefanovitch . . .,' he managed. That was all.

Right then, it seemed as if Stefanovitch's friend could go no further, that he had to let go of everything. Bear Kupchek lay very still. His breathing faltered badly, then it stopped. Just like that.

Oh please, don't let this be happening, Stefanovitch's brain screamed. *Oh God, please.*

He whispered to the body in his arms.

'I love you, Bear. Oh Christ, Bear. Don't do this.'

Then Stefanovitch was all alone.

PART TWO

The Sixth Estate

13

Isiah Parker
Harlem

Isiah Parker walked the streets of Harlem without fear. This was his neighborhood. He tried to be optimistic, even though he heard voices and whispers in the darkness: teenagers delivering drugs in Suzuki Samurais, the current vehicle of choice for young dealers; a baby wailing in a tenement building with shiny metal sheets for windows; crack deals going down on every street corner.

As he walked, he remembered his brother: the year and a half when Marcus had been champion; the shocking murder; then self-righteous editorials about the tragedy in every newspaper.

A memorial service had been held in Harlem. That had been on December 30, six months ago. It seemed even longer to Parker, as he thought of it now.

Inside the cavernous Morningside Chapel, he had waited for the noise from his brother's mourners to quiet down. As he did, Isiah Parker felt that he was standing outside of himself, able to watch the unreal scene from some other dimension.

His voice finally rose, softly at first, then clear and powerful, without any musical accompaniment. He had sung like this at his brother's championship fight in Madison Square Garden. Bill Cosby and Ali had been there; so had Don King, Dustin Hoffman, Jesse Jackson. The closeness of Marcus and Isiah Parker had been publicized before the fight. Isiah Parker's baritone singing voice was a discovery, though. In a strange way, it was more emotional than the championship fight itself.

In Morningside Chapel that December, Parker's voice brought tears. His singing had never been more lilting and beautiful. Grown men and women wept inside the chapel. Cynical observers of the fight game wept; also thousands out on Morningside Drive, many of them in flowing Muslim gowns.

There was something so unjust about this death. Marcus Parker had been twenty-four years old when he died. Marcus had represented so many hopes, so many dreams buried inside the Harlem neighborhood . . . Someone is going to pay, Isiah Parker had promised himself at those last rites in Morningside Chapel. And someone *was* beginning to pay. Just beginning.

Two days after the murder of Oliver Barnwell, Parker stopped at a vacant telephone booth on the corner of 125th Street. He had to be sure about what he was doing next.

'This is Isiah Parker,' he said when someone came on the line. There was a hesitation on the other end. It wasn't quite six A.M. He had woken the Man up.

Finally, he heard a voice. 'I was going to get in touch with you. Let's not talk over the phone, Isiah. Where can we meet?'

'Take your regular New York Central train to work,' Parker said. 'But this morning, get off at the One Hundred Twenty-fifth Street station. I'll be waiting. Don't worry, nobody up here knows you. Nobody will see us together. At least, not anybody who matters to you.'

Parker hung up the pay telephone. He walked on, proceeding west along 125th, past more steel-gated storefronts, past the Apollo Theatre.

As he walked, he thought he liked the idea, meeting the Man up here in Harlem this time. Twice before, they had met – at large, crowded hotel bars in midtown.

Another time, they'd had a rendezvous in the town where the Man lived, Mamaroneck.

At seven-thirty, Parker was pacing the ancient wooden train platform at 125th Street. He watched several commuter trains arrive at the station, journeying from suburban Connecticut and Westchester, heading toward Grand Central Station. The tracks were built over an ornate waiting room that dated back to the early part of the century.

The platform overlooked central Harlem, with a view to the Hudson River and the New Jersey Palisades. The sun was bright that morning, casting a glow over the desolate buildings and the streets down below.

Isiah Parker had great affection for the beautiful and imposing railroad station. When he had been growing up, his mother and father had brought him and his brother there to embark on day trips – upstate to Bear Mountain, West Point, Newburgh, sometimes New Paltz, or the Catskill Game Farm.

A commuter train steaming south from Westchester finally rumbled into the station. A few desperate-looking merchants climbed out of the silver and blue cars.

Most of the passengers didn't bother to look out at the desolation of Harlem. They didn't want to deal with black mothers and their kids sleeping on the streets; with eleven- and twelve-year-old drug addicts; with failed urban renewal projects. Especially not at seven-thirty in the morning.

The man Isiah Parker needed to see finally stepped from one of the cars. He gazed up and down the dark wood platform, looking confused. He was neatly dressed in a dark blue suit that was formal for 125th Street.

Isiah Parker let the Man see him. He stepped out from behind a utility pole with a theater ad aimed at the train riders. '"The Mystery of Edwin Drood" Is a Musical,' it said.

Parker waved.

Isiah Parker walked down a flight of rickety stairs. He stayed thirty yards ahead of the Man. The soot-blackened stairs led to the main railroad station, a Victorian waiting room that had changed little over several decades.

The same old iron railing still went along the grimy walls, the same ornate moldings loomed sixteen to eighteen feet overhead. Probably the same dust was collecting on the walls and a line of faded red telephone booths. Every phone was out of order.

A blue door to the left of the newsstand said 'MEN'S.' Parker approached the door, pushing the heavy silver bar forward.

The bathroom looming beyond the door was empty, even at the height of rush hour.

Parker checked the foul-smelling stalls anyway. He found no early morning junkies shooting up, no street bums sleeping one off on a toilet.

The Man entered the bathroom a few seconds behind Parker. He stepped up to one of the cracked urinals and began to use it. He was a good manager of his own time. White men were excellent at that, Parker had learned over the years.

'How are you, Isiah?' He was matter-of-fact. For a moment, it almost made Parker angry enough to show his feelings. The Man was humoring him by coming here. He'd found a new way to be condescending. *Go and talk to Parker. Calm that nigger down.*

'This has been a hard time.' Parker tried to control his anger, any sign of what he was really thinking.

'I know it has been.' The Man was the deputy police commissioner of New York. His name was Charles Mackey. He had originally met Parker when the detective was being honored for having the most narcotics arrests in Manhattan. That was three years ago.

'If it's any consolation,' he said now, 'we're almost home. This next one is important, though, very important to us, Isiah. Then our little private war will be over. After that, they'll be doing the job for us. We're seeing it happen around the world already.'

'When you approached me,' Parker interrupted, 'you

said it wouldn't be much different from regular undercover police work. Well, it's different. It disorients you. You're not sure which side you're on.'

The deputy police commissioner listened and he nodded. Parker remembered that Mackey had always been a good listener, a rabbi inside the department.

'You're on the right side of the law. You're still on the side of the angels. Don't worry about that, Isiah. What the hell choice did we have? What choice did they give us? . . . They were practicing their goddamn street law. The Colombians had their own brand of the same thing. So did the Italians, the Cosa Nostra. What were we allowed to do in retaliation? *What were we supposed to do?*

'We could bring them to court, and not even get a grand jury to hear a murder case. Nine New York cops were killed last year. The street law was working perfectly. We had to do *something*. There were no alternatives left. You know that.'

Parker stared into Charles Mackey's large and moist blue eyes. He was a white man, a fish-belly, but for some reason, Parker had always trusted him. Something was bothering him now, though.

He couldn't figure out what it was. Something about the Man was wrong. Something about this undercover work was wrong. The side of the angels? He didn't know anymore.

'Do you know who murdered your brother, Marcus? Do you know who mutilated your brother's body?' Charles Mackey continued in an angry and almost self-righteous tone. 'Do you know the answer to that?'

'Yes, *I know* who murdered my brother.'

'Are you sure? Are you positive beyond a reasonable doubt? Is there *any* doubt in your mind?'

'I'm sure.'

'And do you see any case coming up before the grand jury? . . . I'll answer that for you – you don't! For the past ten years, the New York Police Department has been fighting a suicidal gang war. Nearly a hundred officers have been killed in the line of duty. Only we haven't been allowed to fight back until now. *Our job* was to *begin* to fight back.'

Charles Mackey placed a hand on Isiah Parker's shoulder. The older man seemed weary and drained suddenly. 'You have my word that this is going to stop soon. That means you have the commissioner's word. This is the last time. Alexandre St-Germain. Traficante. Oliver Barnwell. One more, then we're out of it. We dissolve your team.'

Parker shook his head. Finally, he smiled. He had no choice but to trust Mackey. 'You'll let me know the details? Who it is? When we go again?'

Charles Mackey seemed to be retreating into prayer. After a moment, he reached out and shook Parker's hand. 'What other choice did we have?' he whispered.

Deputy Commissioner Mackey left the subterranean bathroom. He hurried back upstairs, where he caught another commuter train downtown.

Parker didn't follow him out of the train station bathroom right away. He waited another few minutes down in the basement. One more time, he thought as he stood in the desolate public bathroom. Then we're out of it.

14

John Stefanovitch
Ridgewood, New Jersey

Bear Kupchek died in the emergency room at Lenox Hill Hospital, one of the city's best facilities. Stefanovitch had gone there with his unconscious friend, traveling in the back of a speeding EMS ambulance. He'd watched as the Bear was finally pronounced dead.

When a policeman or fireman arrives in critical condition at a New York hospital, the best doctors and nurses usually assist, trying everything to save the injured officer. There was nothing any of them could do this time. The shock and sadness of the emergency room staff was obvious, both touching and maddening to Stefanovitch.

On June 28, he drove north out of New York on the crumbling West Side Highway, then across the split-level expanse of the George Washington Bridge. The world was feeling fuzzy at the edges, unfamiliar and unreal to him.

Why Kupchek? What had the Bear found out? What was the missing clue? The words were being shouted inside his head. Everything but cymbals were crashing, creating a powerful effect, like the end of Hitchcock's *The Man Who Knew Too Much* . . . except that Stefanovitch didn't know too much.

He was headed toward Ridgewood, New Jersey, where he would attend Kupchek's funeral. He couldn't imagine anything worse that he'd have to do for the rest of his life.

As he reached Route 17, he remembered happier times, when the Bear and his wife, JoAnne, had used their combined incomes to buy a home in Jersey. It was during Kupchek's third or fourth year with the force. Recently, he'd told Stef that the value of their house had gone from under sixty thousand to almost four hundred thousand. The manager of the Yankees lived in the same neighborhood. Stefanovitch had been out there to visit in May. There'd been humongous steaks grilled on the Weber, a closely contested NBA play-off game, too many Coronas for him to drive home that night. He loved Bear's family. They loved Stef back. *This was so goddamn hard, so bad*.

As he drove past the shopping malls of northern Jersey, Stefanovitch began to think about another kind of small-town life, back in Pennsylvania, where he had grown up. All kinds of bittersweet memories were sweeping through his mind on the morning of Bear's funeral. His parents' farm. A soup kitchen they ran for poor people. A flood of images.

His grandfather had been a route driver for a regional bread company out near Minersville. For many years, George Stefanovitch had driven a beaten-up truck over the Catawissa Mountains to his territory, a nest of tiny villages.

He had given his grandson some free advice on careers one morning when Stef was helping out with the deliveries. His grandfather had been a god-awful singer who nonetheless loved to sing as he went over the Catawissas to work each morning. He'd told Stef that he didn't care whether he became the president of the United States or a ditchdigger when he grew up. Only one thing was important: 'When you go over the mountain to work every morning, make sure you're singing, make sure you're happy to be going on that trip every day. The same way I am in this broken-down bread truck. I am happy, Stef.'

Stefanovitch had never forgotten the advice, and somehow, through luck or good management, he found that he usually went to work singing, or at least humming along with the car radio. For whatever crazy reasons, he loved the job.

And if he could get through this particular day, he figured, he could get through any of them.

As he exited off Route 17, Stefanovitch could see crisp white church steeples silhouetted against the backdrop of Ridgewood. Majestic elms and oaks and lindens towered along both sides of the country road. At the church itself, dark blue dress uniforms were everywhere: hundreds of police uniforms dotted across a bright green patch of beautifully maintained lawn. Everything was so perfect that it made Stefanovitch feel ill, nauseated for a moment.

The funerals of police officers were usually part pageant, part small-town parade, part Greek tragedy. Perspiration bubbled on his forehead, and on the back of his neck. He braced himself for the act of getting out of the van, putting together his chair.

He could hear the motorcycle contingent approaching for the funeral. It was such a foreign and otherworldly sound. He thought that, had there been any way, the Bear would have carried him inside the church.

Finally, he began to push himself across the macadam lot toward the chapel. The sun over the high spires looked like a shattered bulb. His body felt numb.

Along the way, Stefanovitch was recognized by several police officers. Most shook his hand and muttered kind words. Then they continued on in their own private funks. A few shared quick Bear Kupchek anecdotes.

Blue dress uniforms were everywhere, like a graduation at some kind of military academy. A loudspeaker voice was asking that people proceed inside the church for the service.

Once he was in the vestibule, Stefanovitch was disturbed that he couldn't see the altar. That made him feel even worse than he had outside.

There was a light tap on his shoulder.

He swiveled in his chair and was surprised to see Sarah McGinniss beside him at the rear of the church. She had come out to New Jersey for the funeral. Somehow that buoyed his spirits.

Sarah bent forward and spoke to him. The lightest hint

of her perfume reached his nose. The physical closeness reminded Stefanovitch of their day working together at the beach house on Long Island.

'I'm sorry, Stef,' she said in a church whisper. 'I'm so sorry you had to lose your friend.'

Some of the emotional unrest, the chaos of bereavement, seemed to stop for an instant. Stefanovitch felt a quiet acceptance of Kupchek's death at that moment, as much as he was going to, anyway. 'Thank you for coming. It means something that you bothered to make the trip.'

Sarah craned her neck, watching things in the church he obviously couldn't see. He was feeling as helpless as a child. He remembered being a little boy back in Pennsylvania, unable to see inside some mysterious, incense-filled church.

'Listen, you have a pretty bad spot picked out for yourself here.' Sarah leaned down close to him again. 'Can I help out a little?'

'Yeah, I guess you could. I think I'd like to have box seats, down a little closer, for this one.'

Sarah began to push his chair up through the thick and somewhat resistant jam of police officers. The fact that it was John Stefanovitch, Kupchek's partner, helped to part the waves of blue. Then, Stefanovitch could finally see the main altar.

'This works pretty good at airports, too.' He smiled and said, 'It's one of the few benefits of the wheelchair, which I'm not afraid to play up.' Sarah had found them a spot closer to the front. They settled near the side entrance, where heavy oak doors with metal rings sealed off the vestry.

The back of Stefanovitch's shirt was already soaked. Air-conditioning was blowing down on his neck and shoulders. None of it really mattered.

He wasn't going to see the Bear again. *That* mattered. How many real friends did you get in your lifetime? Four or five at the most? If you were lucky. Now one of his was gone.

After a few minutes, a trumpet struck the first familiar and dreaded notes of taps. Bear Kupchek's funeral was beginning.

After the service, Stefanovitch and Sarah McGinniss left the church together. They went over to the Kupcheks' house in his van. Sarah had come out to Ridgewood with a representative from the police commissioner's office. She needed a ride anyway.

The Bear's oldest son, Mike, Jr, was only fifteen, but he already resembled a football middle linebacker at the college level. He was a junior Bear in almost every way, lumbering and cuddly at the same time. Stefanovitch didn't know whether to laugh or cry as he hugged Mike, Jr, as he talked to the boy about nothing, mostly, desperately needing to communicate affection to the Bear's son.

Later on, Stefanovitch and JoAnne Kupchek talked in the kitchen for over an hour. They drank Glenlivet from the same water glass. They held each other, trying to find comfort, eventually singing an old Polish love song from JoAnne and the Bear's wedding. They were both missing him terribly.

Stefanovitch had promised Sarah that he'd drive her back to New York. It was past five when they finally got onto Route 17 again, heading toward the George Washington Bridge.

They were stalled in heavy commuter traffic at the bridge. Cars were backed up a mile from the tollbooths. For the first time that day, they talked about the murder investigations; what Kupchek might have found out the night he was killed; whom he might have seen. Neither of them really had the heart for the talk.

Back in the city, Stefanovitch turned onto Fifth Avenue. Sarah asked him to make a left on Sixty-sixth. Her apartment was between Park and Madison.

'That's the place. The green canopy,' she said a few moments later.

Stefanovitch stopped the van in front of a prewar building with a forest green canopy. A spiffy doorman was there, Johnny-on-the-spot. A huge directory desk was visible through the open door into the lobby. Fancy place.

'Please come in for a minute. Don't play the hard-nosed New York City cop. Not right now, not tonight. Have one drink with me, Stef? Please?'

Sarah didn't give Stefanovitch a chance to answer. She called out the open window to the doorman, who was already approaching, cleaning his wire-rimmed eyeglasses as he lumbered forward.

'Mr McGoey, will you take care of Detective Stefanovitch's car? Find a spot for it?'

'Of course, ma'am. No trouble at all.'

A rustic fieldstone fireplace dominated the living room of Sarah's apartment. She started a modest blaze, and it seemed peculiar at first – the warm, crackling fire with the air conditioner on – but the aromatic smells of oak and pine quickly permeated the room and made it special.

The two of them began talking. They shared ironic perceptions and stories much more comfortably than they had at the beach house.

Stefanovitch eventually told her about growing up in coal-mining country, about his three years of globe-trotting, and finally finding himself in the navy, then his four-year marriage to Anna. For her part, Sarah finally told some stories about Stockton, California. Her humor about growing up was mostly self-effacing, and Stefanovitch liked her for it. Putting herself through school, she'd been an onion topper, cherry picker, Mexican-café hash slinger, McDonald's girl, Baskin-Robbins ice cream girl, plus a door-to-door encyclopedia salesperson for one day in Oakland, actually for four and a half hours.

Stefanovitch suddenly realized that he wasn't used to having a woman as a friend. He thought that most men still weren't ready for that – no matter how many claimed that they were. The new male was emerging, but he wasn't quite there.

Sarah brought him another Irish whiskey, his second or third, or maybe it was his fourth. Stefanovitch glanced at his watch, and he couldn't believe the time. It was twenty past ten. He'd been at her apartment drinking and talking for almost four hours.

Sarah noticed him checking his wristwatch. It was suddenly too quiet in the living room.

'I did need to talk to somebody tonight,' Stefanovitch said. 'You were right about that.'

He lightly fingered his drink, hearing the cubes clink. He was nervous, and he knew Sarah could probably see that. He couldn't talk about what he was feeling, though. Not yet, not right now. Not tonight especially.

'Sarah, thank you. I have to go home and sleep some,' he said finally. 'I have to go home.'

15

Isiah Parker
Harlem

Isiah Parker was dressed so that he wouldn't stand out on the street. He had on an old Lee sweater, faded black corduroys, worn high-top sneakers. He was a contemporary version of Ralph Ellison's *Invisible Man*.

He hadn't been able to sleep inside his walk-up apartment on 116th Street. There were too many random thoughts speeding through his head. He felt nervous and paranoid. Was he really on the side of the angels? The more he thought about it, the less certain he was.

He could visualize a single face so clearly now, every detail. He could *see* his brother inside a sleazy SRO hotel on the Bowery – the Edmonds. He remembered everything about that day.

The incident had occurred six months ago. It had been his RDO, his regular day off. When he received the news, Parker had hurried downtown to the Fifth Precinct, an old, traditional station house on Elizabeth Street. From the Fifth, he had gone by squad car to the Bowery.

At least a dozen leather-jacketed policemen were loitering outside the seedy Edmonds Hotel. Up and down Grand Street, vagrants and bums were sleeping it off. They congregated on crumbling doorsteps, on cast-iron grates where minimal heat came up from the subway tunnels.

One mange-haired black man wobbled around at the corner. He was trying to wash the windshields of cars stopped at the traffic light. Somehow, he made the glass grimier than it was before he used his paper towel.

Parker finally lowered his head, and he walked toward

the transients' hotel. What had Marcus been doing at a place like this? How had he wound up here, at the very end of the earth? How could this have happened to his brother?

He had to step over the depleted bodies of two men sleeping on the stairs outside the hotel. He stopped again, on a gritty stairwell inside.

Isiah Parker sat down hard on the stairs. His legs felt like rubber, and he was beginning to choke away tears. His hands started to claw uncontrollably at his jaw. He couldn't catch his breath . . . *because he knew.*

Parker finally tucked his head down low and away from his trousers. The single cup of coffee he'd had that morning began to spill onto the broken tile-and-stone steps . . . *He knew.*

His brother, Marcus, was upstairs.

Somehow, his brother had died up these broken stairs – in some mysterious way, the middleweight boxing champion had died inside this transients' hotel in the Bowery. How could that be? How could it have happened?

Parker struggled to his feet, and he began to slowly climb the last stairs. There were two more flights, but the odor was already indescribable.

At the top of the stairs, a policeman in a gas mask came up to Parker. 'You better put one of these on before you go in,' he said.

Isiah Parker was already entering the open door, ignoring the warning. He peered at the soiled, dismal living room. Black grit was on everything, like foul little bug eggs ready to hatch.

He walked inside a soot-covered bathroom. A fingerprint technician and a photographer from Police Plaza were working there. Both policemen wore gas masks and plastic gloves that went to their elbows.

His brother's naked body, bruised and broken, was slumped faceup in the bathtub. The color of Marcus's skin was dark in places, purple in others. His brother was ghostly pale from the neck up.

'They fed him a ton of junk,' one of the police technicians said. 'Must have been shooting him up with smack for a couple of days. Like they wanted to make him some kind of example.'

The medical examiner was an insensitive man whom Parker knew by sight. He spoke in a muffled drone. 'He OD'd on junk. His heart went pop. Couldn't take the strain.'

A broken heart, Parker thought. His brother, Marcus, who had always been so proud and strong, had died in the Bowery of a broken heart.

Now, standing on Ninety-sixth Street, Parker was remembering the scene at the Edmonds Hotel. Sometimes he would be walking somewhere, anywhere, and the images just came to him, flew at him like attacking birds. Would he ever be able to forget the Edmonds? The sights and smells in that horrifying bathroom?

Isiah Parker stared south down the wide, deserted promenade of Broadway. He finally saw the men he had been waiting for on the street corner.

Jimmy Burke and Aurelio Rodriquez were just stepping out of a black sedan parked in front of McDonald's and Dunkin Donuts. The three detectives had to talk about next steps; about a final hit, the most important one of all.

The side of the angels? Parker wondered once again.

16

John Stefanovitch
One Police Plaza

Stefanovitch wasn't just being paranoid – a lot of people *were* chasing him. The furor about the videotapes from Allure had become intense. Heavy rumors implicating government officials and prominent businessmen were appearing in the leading newsmagazines. Articles about sex clubs in Miami, Detroit, Los Angeles, and San Francisco filled the newspapers in those cities.

Finally Stefanovitch contacted a young film editor from NYU. He enlisted the editor to help him make a condensation of the videotapes, to get them down to a watchable couple of hours.

Stefanovitch had originally met Gregory Weinschenker while the filmmaker was researching a documentary about the street life of cops in the West Village. He had liked Weinschenker immediately. Unlike many of his university cohorts, Weinschenker had reached the radical conclusion that the average police officer was neither a sadist nor a new centurion. Weinschenker knew better from personal experience. His brother and father were cops. They happened to be honest, hardworking men, doing a difficult job that not too many other qualified New Yorkers wanted to do.

Stefanovitch and Weinschenker holed up in a room in the basement of Police Plaza. During the day, Weinschenker screened the videotapes by himself. He compiled tapes that included each new client and bits of dialogue that were relevant to the ongoing investigation.

More important to Stefanovitch was getting a better

understanding of the Midnight Club. Police files held evidence of the Club's existence, but no one had identified the membership – especially those rumored to be business leaders and government officials.

More questions than answers had been raised, which was typical of most police investigations. Who could be murdering crime chiefs around the world? Why?

Were the killings actually connected to the Club at all? How could he begin to make sense of something so secretive? In particular, why had St-Germain been murdered? Who might be next? Who was controlling the death lists?

At six each night, Stefanovitch arrived downstairs at the screening room. He studied the edited tapes over coffee and deli sandwiches. Usually, he worked with Weinschenker into the early morning.

He and Weinschenker had divided the clients at Allure into four categories: Entertainment Celebrities, Organized Crime, Business and Political, and Unidentified.

Very late one night, Weinschenker came and sat next to Stefanovitch.

'Hey, when this is over, can I tell my old man and my brother that I was deputized by the NYPD? How I was holed up in the basement of Police Plaza for three weeks? They'll freak. Not to mention my friends at film school, who'll label me as a member of the Fourth Reich.'

'You shouldn't tell *anybody* what's on these tapes. Remember what happened to Bear Kupchek. We can laugh about it down here, it helps the time pass, but this isn't a funny business. Especially not to the people on the tapes.'

Weinschenker slumped back into his director's chair. Stefanovitch felt bad, but knew he'd feel worse if Weinschenker was ever hurt because of what he'd seen.

Stefanovitch suddenly sat forward. 'Hold it, Greg . . . Can you go back there?' he asked. 'Just run it back until I tell you.'

'You want me to mark something for the catalogue?'

'Not yet. Just run it back. There. Let's watch it from here.'

Stefanovitch's eyes strained to capture each detail as the picture played again. The call girl on screen was beautiful, as they all were – professional models, aspiring film actresses, Broadway would-be's.

'What the hell is this, Stef? Give me a clue, kemo sabe.'

'Just watch for a minute. It's coming up again, right around here. Okay, that's it. We're close.'

The client was still dressed. He was sitting on the edge of the bed, wearing an expensive business suit. Stefanovitch knew who he was.

'Even I know who that is. He's Nicky Wilson,' Weinschenker said with a lopsided grin.

'That's right. And you're going to forget you ever saw Wilson on any of these tapes.'

'Yes, sir. Who's Nicky Wilson, anyhow?'

'All right, a little more volume.'

'Yes, sir. And a little less volume from me?'

Stefanovitch could feel his heart pushing against his chest. The back of his neck felt warm. What he was searching for was coming up on the tape.

'Listen to this, Greg. Right about here.'

'And then forget that I ever heard it.'

'Yeah, that's right.'

'*You're beautiful, which I'm sure isn't any great revelation to you. You're a little haughty about it.*' The man in the film spoke. Nicky Wilson. Wilson had run Harlem's narcotics and most of the prostitution until the district attorney had finally put him away nine months before. Oliver Barnwell had then inherited Harlem.

'*A lot of people say the same thing about you, Nicky,*' the girl said back to him.

Wilson laughed. '*Yeah? I guess a little arrogance is good for the soul.*'

'*This is the part where I get to undress you,*' she whispered. '*It's time to play . . . Very, very slowly.*'

'This is the Academy Award performance of the year,' Greg Weinschenker cracked.

'What does "slowly" mean? Exactly what are you planning?' Wilson asked.

'It might take an hour . . . just to get you undressed.'

'You have any other diversions in mind? Any other fun and games while we're getting undressed? I'm always ready to learn something new.'

The prostitute slid open a shallow drawer in a lucite night table. The table was attached to the bed. She produced a small black leather case that looked expensive and important.

Weinschenker glanced over at Stefanovitch. He hummed the theme from *Dragnet*. They had seen the same black Halliburton case on other videotapes. The leather case contained the works for a homemade cocaine cookout.

Wilson's voice level was an octave lower. It was slightly muffled on the tape. Stefanovitch had to listen more closely. He moved himself closer to the machine.

This was the place in the tape he'd been looking for.

'They think of everything, don't they . . . the Midnight Club . . . They really do think of everything.'

'Bingo.' Weinschenker grinned rather proudly. He reached over and pounded Stefanovitch's shoulder.

'Play it again. Just that little piece, Greg. Play it a couple of times for me.'

'. . . any other diversions . . . ? Any other fun and games . . . ? . . . They think of everything, don't they . . . the Midnight Club . . . They really do think of everything.'

Someone else at Allure was talking about the Midnight Club.

'Keep playing it, Greg. Just that one goddamn piece.'

17

Sarah McGinniss
Danbury Federal Prison

Late on July 1, Sarah McGinniss took an unexpected trip up into Connecticut. She traveled at night, and she traveled alone.

Everything continued to be in flux. The unfolding mystery had something to do with illicit sex; and it revolved around wealthy and powerful men: men and the age-old games they loved to play.

Sarah was seeing a side of men most women weren't allowed to observe. She was privy to their secret societies – the police, business, the government, the military, organized crime. For years, men had controlled White Houses, Pentagons, palaces, bordellos. The bottom line was always the same. They were in it for the power; for the visceral thrill; because of some lurid and primal fascination with violence. And now Sarah McGinniss was involved, too.

Sarah left New York City around quarter to twelve. She drove her Land Rover north on the nearly deserted West Side Highway, which became even lonelier beyond the twinkling lights of the George Washington Bridge. Sarah figured she would be at Danbury Federal Prison by a little past one.

Sarah had recognized Nicky Wilson the moment Stefanovitch showed her the videotape. She had already interviewed Wilson several times for *The Club*. Wilson had done business with Alexandre St-Germain; Wilson had once been the most powerful black crime boss in New York.

One of the interviews had been conducted at Danbury, so Warden Glen Thomas remembered her when she called.

Because of the earlier book interviews, the PC felt that she was the right choice to see Wilson now, the least likely to create unwanted attention. Sarah also happened to be the one Wilson consented to talk with.

The monolithic outline of Danbury Prison finally appeared against the backdrop of deep blue and moonlit sky. Bright searchlights glared out from the complex, pinpointing trees and dirt roads surrounding the prison. The silence in the night air was palpable.

Sarah had visited the federal prison twice before, but never late at night, and certainly not under the current circumstances. Massive stone gateposts, with elegant bronze plaques, flanked the entrance drive. A thick, stubby row of evergreens served as a wall between the road and the sweeping acres of lawn that rose behind. Cyclone fences appeared left and right as the Land Rover proceeded up the otherwise gracious drive. Then came decorative split-rail fences. Finally a turnaround unfolded in the driveway. Official parking stalls were labeled against a cement wall.

It was nearly impossible to prepare herself for the isolation and eerie sterility inside the prison at night. Nicky Wilson had insisted that their meeting be after lights-out. That way, none of the other prisoners would see his visitor.

Warden Thomas escorted her to the visitors' area, which was deep inside the cream masonry central building. Sarah took out a notepad with a list of prepared questions. She heard steel bolts sliding open, then slamming shut again.

Her eyes returned for a check of the questions she hoped to ask Nicky Wilson. Then Wilson was standing before her inside the visitors' cell.

There was no Plexiglas divider. No bars separating the two of them. There was no protection for Sarah.

Ironically, Wilson wasn't considered a dangerous prisoner. Hardly anyone at Danbury was, including mob bosses who had ordered scores of murders.

'You're always prepared, aren't you, babe?' A smile

touched the black man's lips. He gestured toward Sarah's notepad.

The past few months of prison had changed him dramatically. Wilson was gaunt now, with patches of silver shot through his wiry black hair. He was wearing a loose-fitting African-style shirt over light gray trousers, and fashionable European slipper-loafers. Nicky Wilson no longer looked like a drug overlord of New York and most of the East Coast.

When she had first met him, Wilson had been on trial for murder. He'd chosen Sarah as one of the reporters he would talk to. By the end of the trial, she had written two long articles about him.

'Hello, Nicky. I thought I did okay the last time we talked, but yes, I'm always prepared. I've got my questions ready.'

Wilson laughed. 'Write *this* down, then. The white media wanted a black man to atone for the sins of drugged-up America. They wanted to show how organized crime was dead. So, you tell me, is organized crime dead now that Nicky Wilson has been put away?'

Wilson smiled as he hunched down in the metal chair across from Sarah. He was close enough to reach out and grab her. One of the things he liked about her: she had never shown any fear of him.

During his trial at Foley Square, in New York, Sarah had attended the court sessions each day, trying to study and understand Wilson. He was articulate, impressively so for a man who hadn't been inside a schoolroom since the seventh grade. He had even considered defending himself at the trial.

He had always been polite to her, soft-spoken. His style was part of the reason he'd become the darling of the New York press – a killer and drug trafficker who regularly appeared at exclusive Manhattan parties and the best restaurants.

Sarah thought of the 'blue list' tapes again; the curious

mismatching of criminals with the crème de la crème of high society. Why was that? What did it mean?

'So what brings you up here, to my big house in the country? Why are we having meetings in the middle of the night?'

'Why do you think I'm here?' Sarah asked.

Nicky Wilson smiled again. He had always liked to play mind games with Sarah. His fingers made elegant steeples in front of his face.

'Well, all right . . . The warden leaves the room, which means you want to talk serious business. That's one observation.

'. . . There's nasty violence raging all over the place. New York, Detroit, LA, over in Europe. I know about these gang wars, but not too much. Not too much anymore. I just finished a real book, Sarah . . . *The Unbearable Lightness of Being*. Am I rehabilitated now?'

Sarah remained patient, always the good listener. The reporter. She'd reread all of Nicky Wilson's prison files before meeting with him again.

'No, I don't know anything more than you do about the mob war, the assassinations that are going down,' Wilson finally went on.

'One of the guinea families, the old-line guineas around New Jersey, has a million-dollar reward out for whoever hit the Grave Dancer. Alexandre St-Germain was immortal, Sarah. He was supposed to be untouchable. The bosses are nervous.'

'I hadn't heard about that,' Sarah said. 'You see, you do still get good information. You were right earlier, though – that I wanted to talk about something serious. I have some questions.'

Nicky Wilson lit up an English cigarette, a Silk Cut. 'I always enjoyed our talks. Even the one we had up here. I have all the time in the world. What kind of questions?' Wilson used a Cartier lighter, which seemed out of place in the austere visiting cell.

'The first question is whether you still have your nerve.'

Wilson's eyes were beacons. They searched into Sarah's eyes. 'If you've got something on your mind, say it.'

'I can help you get out of here. We can make a trade. If you're willing to cooperate with the investigation into the murders of Alexandre St-Germain and Oliver Barnwell.'

A physical shock traveled through Wilson's body. His hands curled into stiff clubs. Sarah realized that she was looking at the real Nicky Wilson.

'We want you to look at some videotapes,' she said. 'A lot of films were shot at Allure. I don't think many of the customers knew they were being filmed.'

Wilson said nothing; the corners of his jaw quivered. He was good at not giving away too much.

'We need identification, but most of all, connections. We know about federal judges, important politicians who went to parties at Allure. Entertainers, wise guys, went there regularly. Influential businessmen visited Allure. You were there yourself, Nicky.'

'No, I was never at Allure,' Nicky Wilson said. A hard tone had come into his voice.

'You were on one of the videotapes, Nicky. I watched the tape several times.'

Nicky Wilson stared at Sarah. To be sitting eighteen inches away from a murderer was such a strange, chilling experience. To stare into eyes that were tiny mirrors. Watching her. Revealing nothing.

Finally, Wilson spoke again. 'You better leave now. If that's what you wanted, you wasted a long trip.'

Sarah decided to keep pushing, although the look on Nicky Wilson's face told her to back off.

'I can help, Nicky. What is the Midnight Club? *They think of everything, don't they . . . the Midnight Club.* That's what you said at Allure. Who is in the Midnight Club, Nicky? What's happening? Who's killing who?'

Nicky Wilson suddenly rose. He called down the hallway to where the warden was waiting.

'I want to go back to my cell. Let's go. C'mon, man, let's go.'

Sarah wanted to stop Nicky Wilson. He knew something about Midnight. He could point them in a direction at least.

'You can call me in Manhattan. I'll come back up here. People are ready to help you,' Sarah said.

Nicky Wilson was peering down toward the warden. Finally, his head turned back. The smile, all familiarity, had vanished from his eyes.

'You think about something, babe. Think about why they sent *you*. Because they knew I'd talk to you? Maybe so. What kind of story does somebody want you to write? . . . C'mon, man, take me back to my cell,' Wilson said to the warden. 'I don't want to see her again under any circumstances.'

18

The Midnight Club
Kyoto, London, West Berlin . . .

There had never been anything quite like it.

The Club.

A secret society that stretched across the world.

In Kyoto, Japan, a powerful Yakuza member dutifully sat through an exotic and beautiful ancient tea ceremony. One of the geishas gently whirled an elegant bamboo whisk through waves of murky green tea. She moved the stirrer at just the right tempo to produce the tiny bubbles whose appearance separated master from apprentice at the task.

The geisha finally bowed twice and presented a small china bowl to the tall, silver-haired Japanese man. As he lifted the crisp rice cake it contained, he once again read a note that had reached him at this private garden. On the index finger of his right hand was an expensive black onyx and diamond ring, identical to the one worn by Alexandre St-Germain at Allure.

The powerful Yakuza leader finally rose from the table and went inside for a massage, and other ministrations from the geisha. The Midnight Club was to meet again.

In London, a respected House member was inside the mahoganied bedroom of a magnificent apartment overlooking Parliament and the Thames. He pondered the difficult times. He was recalling Alexandre St-Germain, the several months the Grave Dancer had spent living at Number 5 Newman Passage, taking control of the rackets all through England. St-Germain had reminded him of the most vicious American gangsters from the thirties. He had attempted to be larger than life, and had nearly succeeded.

The House member had his own idea about who was responsible for the lurid shootings in New York, and why the Club was being assembled for a rare emergency meeting. His source of information, the former number two to St-Germain in Europe, would soon be arriving in New York on Concorde. If all went well in the States, they would know everything by the same time tomorrow.

In West Berlin, a police commissioner read the urgent message from America a final time. He wiped his silver-rimmed spectacles on a handkerchief pulled from the lapel pocket of his dark business suit. '*Schmutzig*,' he muttered. '*Sehr schmutzig.*' It was not immediately clear whether he was referring to the wire-rimmed glasses, or the important message from the Club.

In all, twenty of the members received the news and made plans to come immediately to New York ... then on to another, still undisclosed location.

None of the wealthy and powerful men understood yet, but all of them would come. All had in their possession the onyx and diamond ring that signified membership in the Club.

19

Sarah McGinniss
East Sixty-sixth Street

Sarah's Manhattan apartment had seemed unbearably large and empty since Sam had gone off with his father.

She found that she missed their elaborately disorganized breakfasts together; then the chatty walks around the neighborhood each morning; and planning dinners; and movies like the *Star Wars* trilogy; and which ridiculous board game to play at the end of the day. Chutes and Ladders? Mousetrap? Monopoly? Whichever game lit up Sam's eyes the most.

She was constantly delighted at how much she liked being a mother, at least being Sam's mother. She had tried to deny traditional maternal feelings, but she was learning to treasure the experience.

Her heart ached for Sam whenever she had a free moment to think, so Sarah tried to have as few as possible. That was easy, with the Midnight Club investigation starting to boil over.

On the night of July 3, Sarah's part in the investigation was further solidified. The phone in her office rang at a little past ten. She'd been expecting a call from Sam and Roger.

'Hello. Yes. Speaking. This is Sarah McGinniss . . . All right. Yes, I can do that . . . That would be fine . . . Would you give him this message,' she went on. 'It's simple. Everything that he wants can be taken care of.'

Sarah hung up the telephone. Almost immediately, she picked it up again.

She called Stefanovitch. It was possible he would still be working down at Police Plaza.

He finally came on the line in his office: 'Stefanovitch.'

'McGinniss . . . I thought I might catch you. Listen, I have some good news for a change.'

'I think I'm ready for a little good news. I just had Kimberly Manion in here. She got a high-fashion commercial shoot because she worked at Allure. Great, huh?'

'Nicky Wilson wants to see me again, Stef. He wants to talk tonight, in fact. He's called for another meeting.'

'How did that happen? When? I thought he chased you out of Connecticut.'

'He did. But now he's apparently willing to make some kind of deal, to talk at least. I'm not exactly sure what it is yet.'

There was silence on the phone line; then Stefanovitch spoke. 'Do you want some company? I'm offering, if you do.'

'I write about true crime, Marshal Dillon. I've been doing it for about six years now,' Sarah answered back. 'I'll be all right.'

'Listen, Sarah, Bear Kupchek had been doing this kind of thing for a lot of years, too. At least he thought so. This is different. Nobody knows the rules.'

Sarah said nothing to that. She was thinking over what Stefanovitch had said.

'Let me ride up there to Danbury with you. Humor me. We'll sing overnight camping songs in the car.'

'Stef . . . I . . . All right. I'll be down there in about twenty minutes.'

Half an hour later, the two of them were heading up the West Side Highway, then onto the Saw Mill. During the ride, Sarah noticed that she was incredibly jumpy. She caught herself glancing into the rearview mirror.

She was looking for headlights – for cars that might be following them. *She was watching for – pursuers.* That was how absurd and out of hand it had gotten. She had the recurring thought that they were going to find Nicky Wilson murdered at Danbury.

She had never been a big fan of melodramas, and she wasn't keen on them now. Still . . . the violence surrounding the Midnight Club had been completely unpredictable so far: the grisly murders of Alexandre St-Germain, Traficante, and Barnwell; the unfortunate killing of Bear Kupchek. Why had Nicky Wilson suddenly changed his mind about talking to her?

Warden Thomas met them in the same building where Sarah had visited Wilson. Thomas looked like a gawky high school science teacher. He was too tall and thin, dressed in a brown tweed suit that was at least a size too large. The part in his grayish blond hair would have been perfect, except that most of his hair was gone.

'We're going over to the hospital,' he informed Sarah and Stefanovitch as they exchanged handshakes.

Sarah's breath caught. 'What happened to him?' she asked.

Warden Thomas shook his head. 'Nothing happened. We moved him into the hospital at his request. He claimed he was having chest pains. I think he wanted to be in a more secure area for your visit.'

The inside of the prison infirmary consisted of a few small rooms, almost like emergency room cubicles, which were evenly placed down the hallway from a nurses' station. The station itself was encased in protective Plexiglas.

The environment was sparkling clean, and looked organized and neat. It was also surprisingly upscale. Danbury was a country club compared with most prisons. Among inmates around the federal system, it was known as 'the Plaza Hotel.'

Stefanovitch was asked by Thomas to wait at the nurses' station. Sarah and the warden then went down to a room at the end of the corridor.

A tensor reading light was the only illumination inside the infirmary room. Nicky Wilson was seated in a cone of light streaming from the lamp.

'The chest pains are real,' he said when he saw Sarah standing in the doorway.

'No pain, no gain.' Her smile was slightly forced.

'I'll be right outside,' Warden Thomas said. He glanced at Sarah, then walked away, though only a few yards down the corridor.

'Who have you talked to about our meeting?' Wilson immediately asked her. He turned the tensor light away, and his face dropped into shadows.

'The police commissioner knows. The governor's office.' Sarah sat in the only chair inside the tiny room.

'Don't talk to anyone else.'

Sarah nodded. She wasn't going to argue with Nicky Wilson about anything right now.

'You'll understand why by the time I finish talking. Maybe you'll understand more than you want to. You might even know why I finally decided to talk to you instead of somebody else.' It was the second time Wilson had alluded specifically to *her* coming to the prison.

For the next forty-five minutes, she listened to Wilson talk. And Nicky Wilson was absolutely right, part of her wished that she wasn't hearing any of what the powerful underboss had to tell her.

'I am on the periphery of a group that makes up the most influential crime syndicate in the world. I don't kid myself about that; I'm on the outside looking in. I work for them. This syndicate is sometimes called the Midnight Club,' Nicky Wilson said.

'It's called Midnight because their meetings are always very secretive and held late at night. After midnight. The members are mostly unknown to the public, even to the underbosses. These are very private individuals. Some of the old-line bosses like their women, sometimes a little gambling, and they demand that kind of action at the meetings.

'Somehow it all works. For the past ten years, this syndicate has been responsible for running the major organized crime activity around the world. I mean the crime that is organized, not the small stuff, the wise-guy operations on the street.

'The syndicate has settled disputes and arbitrated between groups from different countries. It's made decisions about who should get a piece of the action, particularly as the Third World is divided up. That alone could have caused gang wars all through the late nineteen seventies. It didn't. The syndicate is the reason why.

'The profit – not the earnings – the *profit* per year is in the area of *sixty-five billion dollars*. The number has been rising steadily for the past ten years. If you think about how the world really works, about that much money at stake, you begin to understand the power of the syndicate. You also understand the paranoia operating right now. Some kind of a coup has been set in motion. A major coup that none of them understands.

'An emergency meeting was called during the past day or two. Word went out everywhere around the world. They want to talk about the killings. They're conducting their own investigation. *They're using police departments* around the world to investigate for them. You understand what I'm saying?'

Sarah understood, at least she thought that she did. Wilson was telling her that the syndicate had the full use of certain police forces, maybe even of governments. How was that possible, though?

'I can tell you where the emergency meeting will take place. I know the location. I can lead you to them. I'm willing to give you that, but you have to give me something in return. You have to get me out of here. *Because they won't. They've refused me.*'

Sarah stared back at Nicky Wilson. Neither of them spoke for several seconds. She finally told him that she could do what she'd promised at their first meeting. She could get him out of Danbury; she had assurances that this would happen. He just had to tell her everything he knew about the Midnight Club.

20

Stefanovitch
Atlantic City, New Jersey

As he steered his van south on the Garden State, Stefanovitch had two and a half hours to be alone with his thoughts. He needed the time to sort through the information he'd been exposed to during the two-week investigation. His mind kept rebelling against the overwhelming organizational task.

Something important was happening. The Midnight Club was meeting, and he knew where. More than a dozen international crime figures had already arrived in the United States.

That afternoon was beautiful, an autumnal breeze blessing the day. Features of the rolling green scenery of southern Jersey captured his attention again and again. It made him seriously question his New York City life-style, also his life's work.

For some reason, Atlantic City had always made Stefanovitch anxious and uncomfortable. There was something so sleazy and desperate about the New Jersey resort. He was having visions of the nervous glitz already; garish lobbies with too much Italian-restaurant red and gold; fake crystal chandeliers everywhere, including in the bathrooms; Christmas-tree-tinsel decor, even in summertime.

Flashy billboards began to float by on both sides of the Garden State. Messages tried to convince him that the odds were somehow better at Harrah's on the Marina. No, at the Golden Nugget. No, at the Sands. Free parking was offered as an enticement to gamble away hundreds, even thousands, of dollars.

Bally's had a sleek, continental-style restaurant, another slick poster screamed. The Golden Nugget boasted Steve Wynn and Frank Sinatra. Caesar's had Slotbusters!

Stefanovitch knew that there were two types of players in Atlantic City and Vegas. He'd learned that much from another cop, a sad, habitual gambler himself. There was the escapist, who wandered into casinos to get away from the boardwalk, the heat, maybe a complaining spouse; and there was the recognition gambler, who actually thrived on the crowds and glamor.

The main prey of the casinos was definitely recognition gamblers, mostly self-made men and women who owned cash businesses. These folks had lots of money in their hot little hands – and were willing to lose incredible sums just to be recognized as players. The logic of the recognition gambler was mind-boggling to Stefanovitch, but it was all documented by the successful casino owners. Atlantic City existed to service the recognition gambler.

The neighborhood leading to the beachfront was desolate, a maze of empty lots, boarded-up buildings, seedy rooming houses and tenements. A chorus line of frisky if bedraggled prostitutes waited near the Atlantic City bus station on Arctic Avenue. They waved good-naturedly at Stefanovitch's passing van. He waved back.

He was thinking that once upon a time, the state and city names on the street signs must have made tourists feel kind of comfortable and secure. I'm from the South, and here's good old Kentucky, or Tennessee Avenue, way up north in Atlantic City, home of the Miss America contest with Bert Parks. Only now, Tennessee Avenue, Delaware Avenue, Illinois Avenue, seemed like the absolute armpit of the world. The scene was as bad as Times Square, except that Times Square couldn't advertise itself as a beach resort.

Pacific and Atlantic avenues were a little different, definitely more upscale. Well-heeled tourists in pastel leisure and running suits dominated the street scene.

The Tropicana Hotel finally loomed on the horizon.

Then came Bally's Park Place.

And Caesar's, home away from home for all the lowballers in town.

Harrah's Boardwalk.

Steve Wynn's Golden Nugget.

Trump Plaza, which proved to Stefanovitch that Donald Trump believed in losers.

Farther down the boardwalk was Resorts International, which hosted a lot of shabby prizefights shown on ESPN and ABC's *Wide World of Sports*.

Caesar's Boardwalk Regency.

Spade's Boardwalk.

There were older hotels as well, and rooming houses set back a few blocks from the boardwalk. There were still a few originals, small hotels with half-block-long porches; and green wooden rocking chairs with lives of their own; and throwback families that seemed to have been there since the early 1900s.

Now the Midnight Club was in Atlantic City. The syndicate is meeting inside Trump Plaza, Stefanovitch thought as he approached the boardwalk in a slow-moving stream of late afternoon traffic.

Stefanovitch drove up in front of the Tropicana. He handed the car-park kid ten bucks, and asked him to keep the van handy. He had no intention of showing his shield to get special attention. No one could know that the New York police and the FBI were in Atlantic City.

'You get this chit validated inside the casino, sir. Then your parking's free. I'm on until two to get your car, sir.'

'Thanks. Hope this is my lucky night,' Stefanovitch said. He smiled at the hustling kid, who'd already spotted the wheelchair in the back.

'Any help with that, sir?'

'I'm fine. Thanks anyway.'

'You get it in Nam, sir?'

'Nope. Supply store on Fourteenth Street.'

The FBI and the police had taken adjoining suites on the

134

nineteenth floor of the Tropicana. They were registered as business executives at a sales conference for Thomson Electronics, the company that now owned RCA.

David Wilkes of the FBI ambled toward the door as Stefanovitch entered. There must have been forty officers and agents inside already. Telex machines and IBM PCs were working as fast as the slots downstairs.

'Jesus Christ,' Stefanovitch muttered as he rolled inside the crowded hotel suite. 'This is worse than the casinos.'

He and Wilkes shook hands. Wilkes was a friend of the New York police, and a real pro. He was buttoned up, very thorough, and basically nonterritorial. Wilkes also had an irreverent sense of humor, which was unusual for an FBI man.

'Do you feel like you've got enough help here?' Stefanovitch looked around the packed suite. His smile dripped irony as thick as any syrupy concoction from the boardwalk.

'I don't have enough of my own men, and too many of everybody else's.' Wilkes was a Virginian with a soft, easy drawl. 'I've got lots of Atlantic City PD, which is like getting help from a police auxiliary unit,' he went on. 'There are New Jersey state troopers, which would be fine and dandy if this were a Bruce Springsteen concert.'

John Stefanovitch was already peering out a row of glazed picture windows that faced Trump Plaza.

'What about our friends staying over at Trump's? Who've you seen go in there so far? Nice crowd?'

'Oh, sure. About a dozen of the dream-teamers so far. There are maybe three times that number in soldiers. We're keeping a log, running the list through the mainframe down in Washington. Computer connectivity, Stef, nothing like it. A ton of pretty women are cruising in and out of the penthouse. Some very pretty ladies over there.'

'Yeah, there's been some kind of connection to the ladies from the start. I doubt it's coincidence that this all started at Allure.'

'Sex still makes the world go round. You know, I used to fantasize about a bust like this. You ever?'

Stefanovitch continued to stare down the Atlantic City boardwalk – at Trump Plaza, at something off in the distance.

'Not since about two years ago,' he finally answered. 'A place called Long Beach. That was my big fantasy bust. It's not everything it's cracked up to be.'

'We don't believe the official meetings have actually begun yet. The dons, some of the bosses, are still arriving. It's pretty sobering – to watch all of the big guys roll in, to see them all together in one place.'

'Yeah. And it's only going to get better. All of them over there. All of us over here. Reminds me of Catholic school dances I used to go to.'

21

Isiah Parker
Atlantic City

Isiah Parker had registered under a false name at Trump Plaza. Detectives Jimmy Burke and Aurelio Rodriquez were at separate hotels along the boardwalk: Burke was at Bally's; Rodriquez was up at Resorts International. They were waiting for the final assignment; for a *name*, or *names*.

Inside his ocean-view room at Trump's, Parker unpacked a black leather duffel bag, which held his work clothes and supplies. He checked and cleaned his .22, an NYPD-issue revolver. Late in the afternoon, he strapped a lightweight shoulder holster over his shirt. A tan corduroy sports jacket would keep the gun out of sight while he was working downstairs in the hotel.

He was going undercover for one more hit. Who the hell was it supposed to be? Why this secrecy right up to the last minute?

Charles Mackey had promised to contact him after eleven that evening. A dozen high-ranking mob heads were already inside Trump Plaza. *They* were there because of the recent murders in New York, but also in Palermo, in London, in Hong Kong. Why was *he* there?

It was easy to blend with the meandering crowd on the glitzy main floor of Trump's. Parker showed a casual interest in the slots, where he quickly lost a palmful of quarters and dollar slugs. He drifted toward the craps and blackjack tables. Parker stomped around casually, as if he had no place to go, just some guy on a busman's holiday.

He was pretty sure nobody was paying attention to him.

Meanwhile, he had spotted several of Trump's security detectives. It was a challenge picking them out, one by one, then memorizing the faces.

Parker saw a Hispanic waiter enter a small private elevator on the mezzanine floor. When the empty elevator returned, he stepped inside and took it to the basement.

He knew that the secret to being where you weren't supposed to be was looking like you belonged. As he roamed past the hotel kitchen, a cart piled with food rattled out of the swinging doors. Parker walked alongside an elderly black waiter, a large, overweight man who swayed from side to side with every step.

'Men's exercise gym down here somewhere?' he asked the waiter, whose eyes seemed dazed.

'Yes, sir. Men's and women's gyms. Keep heading the way you going now. Be on your right.'

'That must be some kind of party upstairs in the penthouse,' Parker continued in a casual tone.

The waiter glanced away from Parker. He stayed quiet for a few shuffling steps, then he started to talk.

'Those gentlemen are spenders, tell you that. Every one of 'em on the comp. You know the comp? Free ride? You better believe they players.'

'The whole place seems to be jumpin' this weekend.'

'Every day in the summertime. Hey, I got to scoot, man. Don't look like you need too much exercise.'

Parker laughed, and he stayed alongside the waiter at the service elevators. Now he was pushing his luck a little. He lit up a cigarette.

'Real players upstairs, huh. They frisk you and everything? When you go into that suite? Hey, man, I was in a big game like that one time myself. In Las Vegas. While I was in the army. I was stationed at Fort Sills, Oklahoma.'

'Fort Sills, yeah. They don't frisk me. They not afraid some old fat man like me. Tip pretty good. Even the guys work for 'em tip good. You ain't been in no games like this one.'

The elevator finally arrived and the elderly waiter stepped inside with his food cart. Parker waved nonchalantly. The waiter didn't bother to wave back.

Isiah Parker turned away from the elevator. He walked down one of several tunnels that ran underneath the hotel. He considered the things he'd already learned walking around Trump's, and asking questions.

The penthouse suite had its own private elevator, for one thing. The elevators were guarded. The shift change was every two hours, which kept the men fresh. The next change was at twelve. The penthouse had its own wet bar, restocked twice a day. The floor could also be reached by the fire-escape stairway, which was heavily guarded, but might be taken easier than the elevator.

Trump's was definitely full. Donald Trump had originally bought the Plaza from Harrah's. He had remodeled for one reason only: to capture the five thousand known heavy rollers who were shared by the Golden Nugget and Caesar's. The entertainment schedule was upgraded from Norm Crosby / Mitzi Gaynor to Diana Ross / Frank Sinatra. Sixty-five easy-living suites were installed for the high rollers, who expected to be comped and treated like visiting movie stars at the casino-hotel. The syndicate members were high rollers, of course.

Hotel waiters, teams of waiters, had gone up to service the penthouse suite half a dozen times in the last eight hours. What Parker needed to know now was *who he was supposed to go after*. Which one of the mob overlords was the target?

He wondered who was making the final decision, maybe making it right now.

Just past ten o'clock, Isiah Parker finally ducked out of the hotel. He strolled north along the crowded boardwalk toward where the famous Steel Pier used to be.

He stayed tucked inside the main body of the crowd. Just to be safe. The moon sitting over the ocean was the creamy yellow of butter. It was glowing brightly. The steel gray ripple on the water was beautiful, but he had trouble enjoying the view tonight.

A glossy poster at Bally's proudly announced that Diana Ross was appearing there on Saturday night. Parker had once idolized her. He'd had the biggest crush on Prissy Miss Diana Ross. Things like that hadn't mattered to him for a while, though.

The underground police assignment mattered. Parker knew he had been given the job specifically because of his brother's murder. Charles Mackey and the police commissioner were using him, but at least they were up-front about it.

And now, several important crime lords were gathering in Atlantic City. He was supposed to hit one of them in the next twenty-four hours.

But which one?

And how was he supposed to pull it off?

By the time Parker made it to Resorts International, the last old-fashioned hotel on the boardwalk, his body was beginning to feel numb. He yawned and his jaw creaked, echoing inside his head.

He was about to head back toward Trump's when Isiah Parker saw something that shook him.

He ducked inside a video game arcade. His body shuddered, and he assumed the worst.

A man he knew by sight, another New York policeman, was heading down the boardwalk from the direction of Trump's. The man was propped up in a wheelchair, but he was still coming at a pretty good clip.

Lieutenant John Stefanovitch of Homicide was on the boardwalk of Atlantic City. The man investigating the St-Germain and Oliver Barnwell murders was down here for the weekend. Isiah Parker didn't think he'd come for the swimming.

22

John Stefanovitch
The Tropicana

Stefanovitch had taken a half-hour sanity break from the surveillance watch inside the Tropicana. He'd gone out on the boardwalk to clear his head, but also to satisfy his curiosity about what the new Atlantic City looked like.

Twenty minutes after his trip down the boardwalk, Stefanovitch was back inside the Tropicana. He was moderately refreshed, ready to wait and watch nothing happen some more. He changed into a fresh shirt, spritzed on some cologne, and waited. Always the waiting.

The hotel suite in the Tropicana resembled a political headquarters after either a disastrous election result, or an equally problematic celebration. The regular furniture had all been pushed back away from the windows. A lot of real functional stuff like chrome *torchère* lamps, sectional couches, glass cocktail tables, was stacked against two of the walls.

FBI men with high-powered binoculars and opera glasses were slumped in a row of dining room chairs, observing the penthouse across the way at Trump's. Used coffee cups and greasy sandwich wrappers were thrown everywhere, mostly just dropped on the floor near chairs.

The FBI men weren't just idly observing the penthouse suites at Trump's. Motion-picture and still cameras, but also sensitive directional microphones, were being used to record the syndicate meeting from every angle. None of the really important business had begun. A group of high crime overlords wasn't expected until the following morning, including the heir apparent from Europe, and the King of Kings in the Orient, who lived in Macao.

Stefanovitch had returned to his spot behind one of the gray-tinted picture windows. He slipped on a pair of bulky black earphones, and began to listen to more gangster conversation over in the penthouse.

Stakeouts are among the worst experiences in police life, he was thinking as he listened to overlapping electronic blips and snippets of conversation. You sat, and you waited. You began to feel as if you were physically turning into some kind of cold stone pillar. Only this time – maybe – it was going to be a little different.

In theory at least, the Atlantic City stakeout was a dream come true for the police. It was as if the situation had been set up for them, just for the purpose of listening in at the very top of the criminal underworld.

In a way, it was too good, and that worried Stefanovitch. It concerned David Wilkes of the FBI, too. It probably disturbed every tuned-in agent or officer in the surveillance room.

The Midnight Club was meeting across Texas Avenue. They were eighty, maybe a hundred yards away. It was almost as if it had been set up for the police to come and listen. Why, though? It didn't track.

Stefanovitch listened with his eyes shut. There was the sound of all these strange, guttural voices drifting over to him. Weird.

Finally, he pulled the earphones off, letting them rest around his neck.

Something was bothering him a lot. He couldn't figure out what. Something about the setup in Atlantic City didn't feel right to him.

Maybe because it seemed like such a perfect setup. The thing with Nicky Wilson at Danbury? It was too good, too neat, like prearranged fighting in a police academy class.

And then Stefanovitch realized when he had felt something like this before. Just one time. The same uncomfortable intuitions – with his pulse seeming to beat right through his skin.

He had felt almost exactly like this. That freezing March night at Long Beach, minutes before the ambush.

23

Sarah McGinniss
The Tropicana

Sarah rode by herself in the lumpy backseat of a police department sedan. The car was a light blue Buick, and it was transporting her from Manhattan down to Atlantic City. She had to see the end, to witness Appalachia II, as the operation was called at Police Plaza.

Around ten-thirty P.M., the sedan entered the boardwalk area of Atlantic City. The car headed up glittery Pacific Avenue.

There was a quick turnoff past Brighton; then the sedan maneuvered around concrete pillars at very close quarters. It stopped at a littered, dingy service and delivery entrance behind the Tropicana.

One of the detectives in the front seat jumped out. He dashed around to open the door for Sarah. Chivalry was still alive in the NYPD.

'I'm really sorry about this unnecessary bullshit. The service entrance.' He shrugged and shook his head. 'They're afraid somebody might recognize you.'

'I understand, Frank,' she said. 'This isn't the first time I've used the service entrance at a hotel. It probably won't be the last. Thanks for the ride, and the company.'

Sarah was hurried upstairs in a service elevator. She didn't mind bypassing the potted palm trees and artificial blue waterfall in the lobby of the Tropicana. Maybe some other visit.

David Wilkes left a clique of gray-suits to greet her as she entered the surveillance suite. As she shook hands with the FBI man, Sarah spotted Stefanovitch.

144

He was wearing a set of black earphones, watching Trump's like a knowledgeable player at the racetrack. He really looked in his element.

Sarah had met David Wilkes twice before, while she was researching *The Club*. She'd written two chapters about his Crimes Committee, and she liked Wilkes. He had absolutely no bullshit about him.

As she talked to Wilkes, Sarah checked out the scene. Across the street, inside Trump's, she could make out movement. It was almost as if the two groups were preparing to meet for some as yet unexplained reason.

'The windows are made of reflective glass in the suites here. That's one reason we picked this place. They can't see us. We're using high-powered directional mikes, so they won't find any bugs over there either. So far, so good.'

'It's eerie being allowed to watch something you know you shouldn't be watching.'

'So far, everything's working out better than I would have expected. We were able to get the best listening equipment. Everything's *too* good.'

Sarah finally pointed across the room. 'I see somebody I know over there. A friend of mine. I'm going to say hello to the lieutenant.'

'All right. I wouldn't admit to knowing that deadbeat character, though.'

A moment later, Sarah came up behind Stefanovitch. She lifted the earphones off his head.

'Are you the one who got me the personal invite down here to see this? If you are, I just wanted to thank you.'

Stefanovitch slowly swiveled around. He was smiling, for a change.

'The scribe has arrived. I guess we can start now. Pull up a card table chair. You can sit here and watch the Midnight Club in action. This is the way it really is on a stakeout.'

Sarah picked up one of the nearby chairs. She brought it over next to Stefanovitch.

'This is the real thing, huh?'

'Well, they're all here. This must be the Club. Tino Deluna from Miami. Ten Hsu-shire from Hong Kong. Daniel Steinberg from London and Paris. All the biggies in the mob. What comes next, I do not know.'

Sarah quickly discovered that 'surveillance' was just another word for Chinese water torture. For the first time, she understood what a police stakeout was about. After three and a half hours of sitting, occasionally listening in on the most banal and disgusting conversations at Trump's, she couldn't take any more.

She wandered around the Tropicana suite. Sarah went and talked to David Wilkes again. She came back to Stef and discussed everything from real-life godfathers to the night he'd seen the diving horse on the old Steel Pier, one of the unforgettable moments of his youth. 'Family entertainment, back when there used to be families,' Stefanovitch said.

Sarah got better at surveillance – at listening, at concentrating – but a little past three, she decided to put her head down on one of the cots in the adjoining suite. Stefanovitch had taken another two-hour turn. He seemed to be getting nourishment out of what he was hearing over at Trump's. He was an insomniac, anyway, at least he had been since the night of the shootings at Long Beach.

As he sat behind the reflective picture windows in the Tropicana, Stefanovitch pointed the directional mike this way and that. The bosses didn't seem to be talking about anything worth recording. His attention went wandering again. Something was still bothering him about the meeting.

Around four in the morning, Sarah reappeared. She touched Stefanovitch's shoulder, and he turned.

She was wrapped in a brown hotel blanket, looking lazy and comfortable. Images from her beach house filtered back.

'Don't you ever sleep?' she asked. Her eyes were still glassy and damp from her nap.

Stefanovitch shook his head. 'Not tonight.'

'I don't know. Everything looks so quiet over there now.'

'Most of the gentlemen who run organized crime around the world are there. How quiet can it be?'

Over in the penthouse, a session was developing among four or five of the bosses. They had traveled from different time zones, and apparently needed to stay awake to avoid jet lag.

Stefanovitch shuffled through a deck of photographs. Each picture was marked on the back with a name and brief profile.

One of the soldiers at Trump's crossed in front of a window. The man stopped walking suddenly. He had an oversized walrus mustache, a little like the TV host Gene Shalit's, only the soldier's deeply pocked face wasn't particularly friendly.

Walrusman seemed to be staring directly across at the Tropicana. He was looking right about where Stefanovitch and Sarah sat.

'He can't see us,' Stefanovitch whispered. Still, the soldier did seem to be staring at them.

'He sees *something*. I wonder what's going on inside all their heads? They're the ones being shot at.'

'I can't work up too much sympathy.'

Stefanovitch yawned, and he shook his head. Now he was getting tired. Right at the start of his watch.

'Why don't you go lie down?' Sarah said. 'I'll sit out here for you. Go ahead. I'm up now.'

'Looks like they're pulling all-nighters, too. They ordered more food,' Stefanovitch said and yawned again. 'My grandfather used to call men like that crumb-bums. Now they rule the world. The crumb-bums.'

Over inside the penthouse, a couple of hotel waiters in white half jackets appeared. They carried the usual silver trays, which helped keep room-service food so consistently soggy.

The waiters were followed by the same soldier who had been standing at the picture window. The return of Walrusman.

'It's funny the way you begin to feel a kind of identification with people you watch on surveillance.' Stefanovitch grinned.

'Yeah, I could really identify with some breakfast right now. I missed dinner. Ham and eggs! Mmm-mmm good. What is that other stuff there? Lox? That looks so-o-o good.'

The hotel waiters were efficiently setting out the contents from their trays. Room-service guys loved to do that. Tray tops off. Little red rose in a vase.

Stefanovitch remembered that he hadn't eaten himself. Crime did pay. A scene from *The French Connection* flashed through his mind – Gene Hackman, standing outside in the cold, watching some fancy French restaurant in Manhattan, while Frog One and his pal sat inside, eating everything in sight.

One of the waiters walked over to the row of picture windows. The waiter did seem to be looking across at the Tropicana. Was there something about the predawn light that made it possible for him to see inside the Tropicana's windows?

'Do you think they found out something?' Sarah asked.

'I don't think –'

Stefanovitch was suddenly sitting up in his chair. 'No. Hey! Don't do that, shit-for-brains. Hey. *Hey!*'

The waiter inside Trump Plaza was pulling the curtains.

'Damn it,' Stefanovitch muttered.

He switched his earphones up.

'Get away from those drapes, you creep.' Sarah had moved close to the picture window. Her nose was against the glass. 'What are they saying now? How good their nova and omelets look?'

Stefanovitch listened on his earphones. They *were* talking about the food.

Suddenly, someone screamed inside the penthouse. A horrible sound came over the earphones.

'What the –' Stefanovitch blurted.

Somebody in the penthouse yelled, *'Oh God, no! No!'*

The unmistakable roar of gunfire followed. Loud screams echoed over the headphones.

Stefanovitch pulled the earphones away. 'Somebody's attacking the penthouse. They just hit Trump's!' he yelled.

Sarah ran to get David Wilkes.

Stefanovitch hadn't moved so quickly in the last couple of years. His heart pounded. Spasms of incomprehension flickered.

He made it inside the first elevator. FBI men with shocked expressions were strapping on their revolvers. David Wilkes was there, his eyes still glazed. His button-down shirt was unbuttoned.

The elevator touched down and the FBI men ran across the Tropicana lobby. Stefanovitch was left on his own. His wheelchair nearly lifted off the floor as he burst forward.

Once he was outside the hotel, a cool ocean breeze slapped his face. He was soaking wet: his neck, hair, the back of his shirt. As he reached the far side of Texas Avenue, he remembered the walkie-talkie.

'This is Stefanovitch. What the hell's happening?'

No answer came back.

Stefanovitch reached the glass side doors into Trump's. Two security guards were body-blocking the way.

'You can't come in here!' one of them shouted.

'Police!' Stefanovitch flashed his shield.

Even more confused, they let him inside.

A blur of terrified faces, bodies in bathrobes and pajamas, swarmed across the lobby. Bizarre language punctuated the scene: 'There was a shooting upstairs!' 'No, it's a fire.' 'I tell you, it's a fire in the goddamn kitchen!'

Stefanovitch located the express elevator to the penthouse. Inside the elevator, he tried the walkie-talkie again. 'David? *David?'*

No answer came from Wilkes. What had he found in the penthouse? Why wasn't he answering? What had happened up there?

The padded elevator doors opened. Stefanovitch recognized the acrid odor of gunfire. He proceeded through the open door of the suite. Bodies were sprawled everywhere in the living room. A horrifying scene met his eyes.

The Midnight Club.

24

Isiah Parker
Trump Plaza

The telephone on Isiah Parker's bed stand started to ring. His eyes slid open and he reached for the jangling phone.

'Isiah! Somebody hit the penthouse at Trump's,' he heard, recognizing the voice of Jimmy Burke.

'Say again?'

'They went in with submachine guns. FBI agents and cops are all over the hotel,' Burke continued.

'Who went where with machine guns? What are you saying?'

'We have to get out of Atlantic City. We ought to leave separately, like we came in. I'll take care of Aurelio.'

'All right. I hear you,' Parker said. He thought Burke was making sense, though he wasn't sure.

Parker finally jumped out of bed. He lunged into the hotel bathroom, where he stuck his head under the tap, letting the cold water revive him.

All his worst fears and suspicions rose to the surface again. Why hadn't Charles Mackey called him? What about Burke and Aurelio Rodriquez? How could someone else have hit Trump's? Who?

Ten minutes later, Parker was one of several hundred spectators in a crowd outside Trump Plaza. Many of the people were still in their nightclothes. Some wore shoes or slippers, some were in bare feet. All the faces seemed in shock.

Police cars and EMS ambulances were crowded four and five deep across Mississippi and Arkansas avenues. Police cruisers were parked up and down all the other narrow side streets.

Parker stared at the blockaded lobby entrance to Trump's. He gazed toward the top floor, where entire picture windows had been blown out by the shooting.

He desperately tried to sort out what had happened. It struck him that he had never been told his target in Atlantic City. Deputy Commissioner Mackey hadn't called after eleven, as he'd promised to several times.

Undertones of terror and black humor circulated through the boardwalk crowd. The comedy was part high-roller irony, part *Saturday Night Live* tastelessness.

'Who the hell got shot?' a fat man in a garish bathrobe asked. 'Wayne fucking Newton?'

'Wayne Newton? He deserved to be shot, show he did last night at Caesar's.'

Parker finally began to inch away from the restless, milling crowd. As he did, he saw Lieutenant John Stefanovitch. Stefanovitch was leaving Trump's, pushing his wheelchair forward with grim determination. He looked numb and drained.

What was happening?

Parker finally walked down the steep stone steps dropping away from the boardwalk. He had to think in straight lines. Nothing but straight lines of logic.

Parker heard a soft cry . . . low, obviously uttered in fear and confusion. It took him a few seconds to realize that the sound had been his own voice.

He touched the .22 revolver concealed under his sports jacket. Then Parker continued down the eerie, darkened street, which was filled with obscure, almost solid black shapes. He could sort out street-sign poles, hydrants, garbage cans, the hulks of parked cars, the serrated outlines of trees.

He found that he couldn't get past the wall of his own shock. Not right now, anyway.

He had been undercover. He'd been waiting for special orders from New York, directly from Police Plaza. Somebody had hit Trump's. Who? The shock was still reverberating through his nervous system, building up force, adrenaline surging. He played back Detective Jimmy Burke's phone call, over and over, in his head.

Somebody hit the penthouse at Trump's! . . .

A hollow pain was knotting his stomach. Parker felt wasted, almost out of control. After he walked another block down Indiana Avenue, Parker stepped into one of the dark alleyways between tenement buildings. The alley smelled of urine and spoiled garbage. He took out his pocket recorder. He needed to get some of this down.

His voice was shaky, more than a little uncertain, as he finally spoke. He was feeling so paranoid. But was it paranoia? Why hadn't Mackey called?

'This is a surveillance log. The time is oh-four-hundred-thirty hours. This is Detective Isiah Parker . . . Someone just attacked Trump Plaza. It happened about thirty minutes ago.

'New York policemen and FBI agents entered Trump Plaza at about four in the morning. How the hell did they get there so fast? Why were they down here in Atlantic City?

'Officers Burke, Rodriquez, and myself are leaving Atlantic City.'

Parker stood quietly at the edge of the alleyway. He gazed up and down Indiana Avenue. The scene was strangely placid, especially when he considered the commotion just four blocks away.

Then something moved.

Something farther up the street caused Parker to pause at the mouth of the alleyway.

Somebody was moving on the sidewalk, almost directly across from where his car was parked. He wasn't sure what it was yet; his eyes strained to see in the dark. His throat was painfully dry.

Could be just neighborhood types, Parker thought. Maybe it was a street junkie or a wino? The odor in the alley was a fresh scent.

He quietly made his way back into the shadows of the

alleyway. Then he walked in a hurry another forty or fifty yards to Illinois, the street running parallel to Indiana. He wanted to come back onto Indiana, but behind the man loitering near his Audi.

Parker peered down another vacant alleyway. His chest felt uncomfortably tight.

He saw something move again. Shadows parted. Then the red ember of a cigarette traveled in a familiar arc.

The left side up ahead . . .

A distinct outline was poised at the end of the alleyway. A man was waiting near Parker's car. The man was only twenty to thirty yards away.

A run-down bar a block or so away provided dim lighting. The neon glow from the All-Star Lounge was enough for him to decipher a full silhouette.

Parker began to inch forward again. The waiting man was only ten yards away. He slid out his .22. Who the hell was standing there in the alleyway?

'Freeze! Don't move,' he finally called out.

The man dropped into a professional shooting crouch.

'It's Parker,' Isiah shouted, identifying himself.

The man paid no heed. He fired, and the round whistled past Parker.

Instinctively, Parker fired back. He fired a second time. Both hurried shots missed.

'Don't shoot, Isiah. Don't shoot, for Chrissakes!'

Parker recognized the voice, and he couldn't get his breath. Dread clutched him.

The man was Jimmy Burke. His own partner had purposely shot at him.

Burke suddenly darted from the alley. Parker could have fired. He didn't. There were too many questions. Maybe he couldn't have fired at Burke anyway.

Isiah Parker ran down the alleyway after Jimmy Burke. Spots appeared in front of his eyes, obscuring the scene.

All at once he stopped. A body was there; a dark shape was curled up beside a collection of rubbish.

There was enough light to make out features of the fallen man. A mop of curly black hair; a long beaked nose; two black holes in the forehead. Aurelio Rodriquez had been murdered.

Police sirens were screaming through the night again. Parker's brain was screaming. Finally, Parker began to run. He stumbled as he ran away from the police, from whoever was chasing him.

He disappeared into the darkness of Atlantic City . . . He passed New York Avenue . . . Then Baltic Avenue . . . The fear, the feeling of helplessness from just a few minutes before, were already being replaced by rage.

25

John Stefanovitch
Minersville, Pennsylvania

There had been a massacre, and he had been there. He had heard the horrible screams of death.

Relax, now. Don't overload, Stefanovitch told himself.

Let everything settle down first, then try to sort it out . . .

Stefanovitch's parents' house was visible down the winding road, beyond a dusty coal hauler they had been following the last few miles. The sky overhead was dark gray, stirred up but oddly beautiful over the sprawling Pennsylvania farmlands, which weren't all that far from Atlantic City.

'That's it on the right down there. The homestead.' Stefanovitch broke the silence of the past couple of minutes.

Rest, he thought again.

Get away from Atlantic City, from all of the death and chaos.

Tomorrow is soon enough to start again; to try to understand . . .

'So you really are a farm boy,' Sarah said in a soft whisper, her waking-up voice. It was just past two in the morning.

'Yes, ma'am. That's Stefanovitch A&M up ahead. Stands for Agriculture and Mining. My humble beginnings.'

Nobody was up at the nineteenth-century farmhouse; nobody except for Stink. Stink was a brown and white mongrel-collie, now officially retired from running the farm. Stink had a friendly, intelligent face, with the softest chestnut brown eyes. Stefanovitch called her to him, puckering and smooching his lips.

Stink began wagging her tail, working it into a blur. She was yipping and circling Stefanovitch and Sarah as if they were farm animals to be herded into a tighter pack.

'Get down, Stink. You been in that brook again, haven't you? That old creek in back.'

The dog was happy to see Stefanovitch, but also confused. It was the wheelchair – juxtaposed with the familiar face and voice. Stink had never gotten used to it.

'Let's go inside. Get some sleep if we can,' Stefanovitch finally said to Sarah. 'You can meet everybody tomorrow.'

Relax for now, he told himself again.

Forget about Midnight.

Sarah learned all about the Stefanovitch clan over Sunday breakfast. She heard tales of the famous Stefanovitch soup kitchen, which Isabelle and Charles Stefanovitch had maintained at the farm for twenty-five years; which they still kept open for anyone in the area needing a hot meal.

Stef's father told humorous stories about John and his brother, Nelson, growing up in the small town, both of them local sports deities; both boys also unusually sensitive toward the poor and unlucky, because of their soup kitchen duties.

Most revealing of all, Sarah witnessed a touching and special love between Stef's mother and father. She had never seen anything like it, especially among people their age. They were obviously best friends, intimate and loving.

'Do they ever fight?' Sarah asked as she and Stefanovitch drove around the countryside later that morning.

'One time when we were kids, she marched off to her sister's. She stayed for two weeks. Called it a long-overdue vacation. Most of the time, though, no. My parents are amazing people.'

'So what happened to you?' Sarah grinned as she asked the question. Her hair was piled up at the back of her head. Her clothes were early lumberjack. She looked like a local beauty.

'People always ask the same thing. I learned all of their bad habits, none of the good ones. I screwed up so bad, I became a cop in New York. A form of social work, in some opinions. What makes it worse, I have no major regrets.'

Sarah and Stef got back to work before noon on Sunday, finally beginning to talk about what had happened in Atlantic City. The investigation had to move along, to go forward somehow. At least they could think straight after a good night's sleep.

There had been a horrifying massacre. More than a dozen crime bosses had been murdered in cold blood.

By whom?

For what possible reason?

Strangely, by late Sunday, Stefanovitch was sinking into a black mood, a frame of mind he didn't understand, much less know what to do about.

He tried to work for a little longer, out on the screened-in back porch, with its view of the farm's silo and woodshed. He and Sarah kept returning to the same question about the investigation – who stood to gain from the shootings in Atlantic City?

That was the linchpin now, the huge unanswered question. Who would benefit because of the murders?

Stefanovitch's back ached, and his leg tingled unpleasantly. He hadn't had any exercise for days. He thought that he needed to go for a long walk; to *run* across these familiar fields the way he had for twenty-some years of his life. He needed to run full out now, until his lungs burst, until his legs collapsed underneath him.

'Hi there. Hey, are you all right?' Sarah finally picked up on his strange mood, his isolation over the past hour.

'I think I have to go. I have to leave,' Stefanovitch said, absolutely a shot out of the blue.

He couldn't run; he had to go. Everything was collapsing

in on him. The investigation. Coming home. Sarah.

It was too much to handle. He felt like he was finally cracking, a huge fissure starting at the base of his spine.

'Excuse me?' At first, Sarah didn't think she had heard him right. 'Stef?'

His face flushed, Stefanovitch began to push himself off the back porch. 'I have to go, Sarah.'

Everything was coming apart in his head. He thought he might be sick . . .

But mostly it was one thing, one impossible problem that he couldn't begin to deal with . . . He liked Sarah too much – and he understood in his heart that it could never work between them.

He couldn't stand that. Maybe people had to be stuck in a wheelchair to understand. Probably they did. But that was the way it was. He had to get out of there right away. The feeling had come over him like waves of claustrophobia in a crawl space. It was unbearable. Impossible to explain to Sarah or his parents.

Sarah might have stopped him, physically stopped him, but she didn't even try.

She let Stef take his things out to the van. She watched him say good-bye to his parents, apologizing for leaving so suddenly. It was all so weird, and so intense. Real life could be like that: the daily soap operas most families learned to live with.

She stayed on at the farmhouse for the night. She wanted to talk to Isabelle and Charles about their life out in Pennsylvania. She needed the background for the book, she told herself. Getting back to New York would be easy enough in the morning.

'I know John too well,' Isabelle Stefanovitch finally said to her in the brightly lit kitchen, where the two of them had talked for hours, sipping port wine. 'He would never hurt your feelings like this, not unless he couldn't help it. He would never purposely hurt your feelings, Sarah. He's very tense now.'

'I know that,' Sarah said. She thought that she understood what had happened. She could imagine his state of mind.

Her feelings were hurt, though. She couldn't help that either. That was reality, too.

Somewhere out on the Pennsylvania Turnpike, meanwhile, Stefanovitch drove with his foot pressed all the way down to the floor. The foot in his mind.

He was falling in love, and he couldn't bear it . . .

Stefanovitch forced himself to dwell on the Midnight Club the rest of the way back to Manhattan. The horrible screams he had heard in Atlantic City became background noise for the long ride home.

Who had ordered the massacre? What had happened to the Midnight Club?

Those were the questions he had to answer. That was the maddening puzzle he still seemed no closer to solving.

PART THREE

The Midnight Club

26

Everything that could change changed at six o'clock on the morning of July 11, a Monday.

All that had transpired since the first murders at Allure was suddenly redefined for everyone, especially the public, who would hear and greedily read about the new twists and turns the following morning at the latest.

The passenger tunnel inside the Air France terminal at Kennedy Airport was thickly carpeted, camouflaged in bright vermilion and blue. It was luxurious by most airport standards, reminiscent of the nouveau riche travelers it served. The long corridor was all serenity as it filled with well-dressed passengers exiting from the Concorde. The two-hour-and-fifty-minute flight from Paris had been a thing of perfection.

Among the final passengers to deboard the crowded jetliner was one who couldn't possibly be on the flight . . .

Alexandre St-Germain exited the plane.

The Grave Dancer was very much alive.

His dress was elegant, befitting his businessman image. A beige suit and salmon shirt were hand-tailored; his black half boots were soft Italian leather, as was the briefcase he carried. St-Germain's face was deeply sun-bronzed, his wavy blond hair meticulously combed back. Nor did his eyes betray any physical or emotional discomfort. They were dark, shiny stones that gave away nothing of what went on behind them.

A black Bell helicopter with gold racing stripes was waiting for him at the New York airport. He had to stoop low as he climbed into the close quarters of the cockpit. His eyes rapidly brushed over the repository of glass and shiny metal instruments inside the plane.

He encountered Jimmy Burke of the New York Police Department, who occupied the far left corner of the copter. St-Germain smiled knowingly, his head cocked slightly to the side.

'Hello, Jimmy B. I'm back safe and sound. Did you miss me?'

As the shimmering helicopter made its way out of the early morning airport maze, the two men talked for the first time in several days.

'I don't believe Atlantic City could have gone any better.' Burke was characteristically enthusiastic. He had developed a disarming smile and manner as a promising wise guy in the East New York section of Brooklyn. Like many of the local hoods, he had fulfilled his patriotic duty by joining the army in the late 1960s. He'd met Alexandre St-Germain in South Vietnam and immediately begun to smuggle and sell narcotics for the Grave Dancer.

St-Germain returned the easy, predatory smile. 'The old bosses, the ones who were never able to learn the new ways, are gone. The way is clear for necessary change. A new order has emerged. Not only in New York, but in Rome, Paris, London, Tokyo.'

Burke nodded. 'Everyone who matters is blaming the vigilante policemen, the so-called death wish squad. One reason is that the death squads actually existed in the New York Police Department long before this. I told you about the squads. Once that was leaked to the newspapers, everything else followed smoothly.'

'Yes, the media can be very accommodating. What about the others who were involved? The detectives. Rodriquez and Parker?'

Burke answered without revealing the trepidation he suddenly felt. He had prepared himself for the expected question, but not for the intensity in Alexandre St-Germain's eyes.

'One of them is dead. Aurelio Rodriquez was taken care of in Atlantic City. Parker is a little bit of a problem. Parker escaped.'

'What do you mean, he escaped?'

Alexandre St-Germain's eyes had become dark beads. His nose flared, so that momentarily the handsome face was almost hideous, a much older man's profile.

'Parker got out of Atlantic City. He's acting as if none of it happened. He hasn't even tried to contact me.'

'So the affair in Atlantic City *could* have gone better,' St-Germain said, his chin jutting menacingly. 'Well, I suppose it's not important. It's nothing we want to deal with at this time. For the moment at least, let it be. Let Mr Parker be.'

That afternoon, Alexandre St-Germain's yacht cut through a light chop about thirty miles off City Island. A comfortable breeze streamed across the deck, where St-Germain met with Cesar and Rafael Montoya, powerful drug underbosses from Colombia.

The music of U2 played somewhere on the yacht. Revolutionary claptrap. Bono grieving for Ireland and other lost causes.

Both of the Montoyas were impressed with the style and demeanor of the Grave Dancer. Neither of them would show it, however. They were the sons of one of the men killed in Atlantic City, but there was no problem there. They had agreed to set their own father up. The meeting this afternoon was to divide the spoils in South America, to move forward with the business of the new Club.

Alexandre St-Germain took Porsche sunglasses from his shirt pocket and slipped them on. 'So how is everything in Bogotá?' he asked the Montoyas.

'*Como siempre*,' said Rafael. 'I told you months ago, my father doesn't matter anymore. My father was nothing to anyone who matters.' Rafael Montoya had been educated at the University of Miami, but mostly he had learned in the jungles and mountains of his homeland. Rafael was twenty-six, one year older than his brother.

Something about the meeting caused St-Germain to smile. 'You know, the world is now run by men like us,' he said. 'Maybe it always was.'

'And what kind of men are we?' asked Rafael, who had been enrolled as a philosophy major at Miami.

'Psychopaths.' Alexandre St-Germain shrugged and his smile broadened. 'No one understands us. They can't put themselves in the minds of men who act without a conscience. They try to understand, but they can't.'

'I have a family.' Cesar Montoya spoke now. He had a pouty baby's face that reflected his soul. 'I have plenty of conscience. More than I need.'

St-Germain calmly took a shrimp from the platter set before them. 'You think so. Well, that's good, Cesar. Myself, I have no family, no attachments. I have only myself to be concerned about. You know, I even enjoy wet work. Wet contracts. I understand who I am. I am a monster. I was an assassin when I was twenty years old. Psychopath? Do you know that word? *Psicopata?*'

The brothers looked at one another, and then both bearded men laughed. This afternoon, each was wearing a white linen suit with leather sandals. The sandals alone cost more than the average yearly wage in their country.

'It is a time of great change,' Alexandre St-Germain went on. Although he was speaking to the brothers, he seemed to be staring through them. They might as well not have been there.

'For the past five years, we have been planning everything so carefully. There was very little bloodshed until Atlantic City. The other members, the bankers, the politicians, they don't like killing. They prefer the courts. In New York, in Rome, London, the Far East, in Bogotá, information was mysteriously made available to ambitious district attorneys and other prosecutors. The traditional ranks of the syndicates were thinned out in this efficient manner. Do you see what I'm saying? Then came Atlantic City. Years of work were consummated in a few moments. The old crime empire was eliminated. And now, a completely new breed exists. Here's to better business for us all.'

Rafael Montoya raised his glass of white wine. 'Congratulations on your victory.'

'Our victory,' said the host, still seeming to look through the skulls of the two Colombian drug lords.

The Montoyas smiled again, and seemed relieved by the last pronouncement. 'Our victory.' So, they were getting their father's territory after all. The Midnight Club had made its decision.

St-Germain gave the two brothers lunch, and they talked very serious business for the next hour or so. He was curious about their future plans, the future of the South American drug business. Suddenly, he seemed to want to know everything from them.

As he listened, he was thinking that Rafael and Cesar Montoya were the worst kind of sociopaths, the most dangerous of all. The brothers were bloodthirsty animals, yet they thought of themselves as family men. They had helped him plan the death of their own father; and ironically, their father had helped him plan this afternoon as well.

Wet work. Yes, he did enjoy it. Shattering the most sacred taboos was sport for him. His only true release. *Psicopata.*

The gun concealed in Alexandre St-Germain's waistband was small, less than ninety millimeters. It was over almost before it had begun. Two head shots fired on the deck of the luxury yacht. Both Montoyas dead. Perfect execution of the street law.

They were too uncontrollable to run South America, even Colombia. Their father had known that. Alexandre St-Germain knew it as well.

They were old-style gangsters, not businessmen. They had no place in the future of the Midnight Club, the new Club.

27

John Stefanovitch
One Police Plaza

John Stefanovitch had always tried to embrace life; to accept the good with the bad. Because of his philosophy, he often had the sense that he was racing, trying to cram enough life into too short a time span.

He had slept only two hours the previous night. At four in the morning, he woke rigid and sweating. He spent the better part of an hour crouched behind a darkened apartment window overlooking Second Avenue – thinking, plotting, getting more lost and confused than he had been in a couple of years.

He still didn't understand what had happened in Atlantic City. How could they have been so close to Trump's, and failed to stop the killings?

The Midnight Club? Who actually controlled it, if it wasn't the crime bosses themselves? Who had ordered the shootings at Trump's?

Then there was the matter of Sarah McGinniss. In some ways, Sarah was the most difficult and troubling problem. Why had he run away from her down in Pennsylvania? Because he was afraid she might be playing with him? No, that wasn't really true . . . Because deep inside he felt inadequate, unworthy of her? That was definitely closer to the mark. That was so close it hurt Stefanovitch to consider it.

It just couldn't work. *They* couldn't work. Stefanovitch was as sure of it as he was that the realization was one of the most painful of his life.

* * *

The sixth floor inside Police Plaza was choked with activity at nine in the morning. Like the seventh and eighth floors, the sixth was subdivided into departments. Outer offices were partitioned by enameled steel wall units to create compact but at least windowed offices. Each was large enough for a small sofa, work desk, and a chair or two. Stefanovitch wheeled past his own office, without bothering to look inside.

He was a few minutes late arriving at the commissioner's briefing. Captain Donald Moran was delivering a postmortem on Atlantic City. Two dozen high-ranking cops were huddled around, listening. They were mostly stone-faced, looking about as awful as Stefanovitch felt.

'Vincent Poppo died this morning. That's seventeen dead in Atlantic City. Santo Striga and Sammy Chum aren't expected to live. Despite the allegations in the newspapers, no one's been able to identify the hit men at Trump's. This police vigilante thing in the papers is total bullshit. We don't know why Aurelio Rodriquez was in Atlantic City. It's possible he was part of the team that hit Trump's, but not as a cop.'

Stefanovitch didn't want to, but he also got the opportunity to speak to the group about the investigation.

'I don't have a lot to tell,' he said. 'We're trying to cooperate with the FBI, and the Atlantic City police force. They're doing hotel-by-hotel checks up and down the boardwalk. There are special detective teams operating in Newark, Philadelphia, Miami, here in New York.'

Stefanovitch raised his hands palms up. He felt burned out, frustrated, and he knew it showed. What he wasn't telling the others was that the FBI and the local police had tied his hands in Atlantic City. They were playing jurisdictional games, which was why he'd left Atlantic City on Saturday night. The questions in his mind were: Why had the travesty down there been allowed to happen? Why was the NYPD being pulled back from the manhunt at this time? It was one more thing that didn't make sense.

Herbert Windfield, Stefanovitch's captain, got to speak next. 'We're pretty sure whoever hit Trump's knew we were right there at the Tropicana,' he began. 'One of the hitters closed the drapes before the shooting started. Coincidence, right? So we have no videotapes of the shooting. The recordings show that none of the hitters said anything once they were inside. Another coincidence? On the tapes, there's shouting from the mob bosses, gunfire. The hitters didn't say a word. Cold as ice. The whole thing was like a hit by a gang of fucking Darth Vaders.'

Following the round of Monday morning quarterbacking, Stefanovitch was one of the first out of the briefing room. He was surprised that the commissioner hadn't shown up. Why was that? Not enough teams had been assigned to do the follow-up work down in Atlantic City. Something had changed.

Back in his office on the Homicide floor, Stefanovitch flicked on the overhead lights. A familiar hum came with the lights. He hated the fucking buzz, hated everything mechanical in his life.

Suddenly he stopped. He stared at a man sitting in the wooden chair by his desk.

The man had a brown leather shoulder holster over a T-shirt that said 'PAL,' a police organization for helping kids around New York.

'Hello, Lieutenant Stefanovitch,' the man in the chair said. He didn't bother to get up.

Detective Isiah Parker had come to visit.

28

Isiah Parker
One Police Plaza

'I'm Isiah Parker. I work in Narcotics uptown. Nineteenth Precinct? We've met a couple times over the years. I don't know if you remember me or not?'

Stefanovitch shut the door behind him. He wasn't even sure why. 'Yeah, sure. How are you, Isiah? I saw your brother fight a couple of times. Terrific boxer.'

'He was a good fighter. Thank you.' Parker leaned forward until his elbows were on his knees. His legs and arms seemed too long for his body. There was a gracefulness in the way he moved, though. Stefanovitch thought he remembered that Parker had been a track star once upon a time.

Parker was serious and quiet as he lit up a cigarette. His eyes continued to make contact with Stefanovitch's. He seemed to be searching for some hint of recognition; something that would tell him who the Homicide lieutenant was, where he was coming from.

Finally, Parker folded his arms. He started to speak in a soft, calm voice, almost as if he were telling a story to a friend.

'Three police detectives hit Alexandre St-Germain, Lieutenant. I was one of those men. I also hit that scum Traficante. I was the one who got to Oliver Barnwell about a week later. Sorry to say, I don't think I have any regrets about it.' Parker took a long pull on his cigarette.

'I need to talk now. I need to talk about a lot of things that have happened lately, including what did and didn't happen in Atlantic City.'

The small office in Police Plaza seemed very still suddenly. Outside, there was the usual clamor of police business: phones ringing, typewriters and copier machines going at it.

Stefanovitch noticed a few things about Isiah Parker. Parker was a large man, even more physically impressive than his brother had been. He had workingman's hands and muscular arms, the physique of a construction worker, or maybe even a coal miner.

Stefanovitch knew about Isiah Parker by reputation. His brother's boxing career had drawn attention to him, but before that, Parker had been an item around the NYPD. Stefanovitch remembered that Parker had led Manhattan in arrests a couple of years back. He was known as a hard-ass. Supposedly he was an honest street cop, too. He was arrogant and bullheaded, but maybe with some good reasons.

In some ways, his career in the department matched up with Stefanovitch's. In other ways, they were worlds apart – about as far from one another as 125th Street in Harlem was from Main Street in Minersville, Pa.

'I think I need to back up a little, for you to understand some of this,' Parker said. His voice was still pleasant, as if the two of them were swapping department stories at a Blarney Stone.

Stefanovitch nodded. 'I was going to suggest something like that. I'll try not to get in the way too much. You go ahead and talk.'

'Let me try to go all the way through this one time. Then you can ask questions . . . I investigated my brother's murder against strict orders *not to* from upstairs. That's a serious problem I have. I don't obey orders real well, Lieutenant.'

'I can understand that. I've had similar problems a few times.' Stefanovitch broke into a smile. 'Maybe more than a few times.'

Whatever Isiah Parker might have done, Stefanovitch

172

liked him. Cop to cop, he was feeling a kinship. There was something down-to-earth about Parker. Maybe he was giving him points because of what had happened to his brother, but Stefanovitch didn't think so.

'My brother got his title shot by playing along with the New York mobs. It was the only way to go, he told me. Maybe he was right, I don't know. They wanted a lot of special favors in return.'

'What kind of favors?'

'They wanted to control Marcus. Own him. Say who he would fight. Where he would fight. After a while, he said no. Marcus didn't take other people's shit too well.'

'Your brother didn't seem like the type.'

'This went on for maybe a year. Most of the best fights in the fight game don't happen in the ring, Lieutenant. One day they brought him down to the Bowery. A place called the Edmonds Hotel. They murdered him there. The street law. In the newspapers, on TV, my brother supposedly died shooting up smack.

'Marcus had always been the people's hero. He was living their dreams, showing them the dreams were real. I don't know if you can understand? The people in Harlem dream a lot. They have to dream.'

'I understand some of it. I'm from out in the sticks originally. Lots of coal miners and farmers. Everybody out there lives on fantasies, too. Football and fast cars, mostly. Almost everybody wants to be someplace else, to be somebody else. Myself included.'

Parker nodded; then he went on. 'When I found out what happened, how Marcus really died, I went crazy inside . . . I went to see the police commissioner. I bothered Captain Nicolo in Narcotics a lot. I wanted to clear Marcus's name. I guess I needed to do it for myself as much as anything. People thought my brother was just another sports junkie. That hurt. It still hurts.'

Without hearing any more, Stefanovitch understood some of what Parker felt. There was something familiar about the detective's frustration. When he had tried to investigate the ambush at Long Beach, he'd gotten the same kind of runaround inside the department.

'I was obsessed with my brother's death. I stopped working on anything else. If I took another case, I'd only work it part-time. I couldn't sleep. Stayed on my own a lot. I wouldn't even talk to my partner about it.'

'Did anyone in the department try to help?'

'Nicolo did. In his own way, he did. He sent me to see one of the headshrinkers downtown. All I could think about was how Marcus had been murdered. How they kept increasing the junk load on him every day.'

'It's a trick they used in the war. Over in Vietnam,' Stefanovitch said.

'I talked to a couple of junkies from the neighborhood. They told me how it felt; how my brother suffered before he died. The Grave Dancer liked to torture his victims. As you know, Alexandre St-Germain was a butcher. A psycho.'

Isiah Parker tilted himself back on the spindly legs of the chair. He tapped out another cigarette, lighting up as he continued to speak to Stefanovitch.

'Back in February, I got called in by the chief of detectives. I was ready to talk about everything. I expected to be jived with. You know, a little tea and sympathy first. Then a reprimand that I shape up my act, or get out of the department. Fair enough. Chief of Detectives Schweitzer had been my rabbi once. Lieutenant –'

'I'm Stef. Or John, if you like.' Stefanovitch reached across his littered desk. He shook Parker's hand. 'What the hell, you know?'

'Well, it was nothing like what I expected, in Schweitzer's office. I'm coming to the good part now. This is what I came to talk to you about.'

'You've got my attention.'

'The chief told me he'd heard I was having trouble since my brother's death. He said not to worry about it. He said everything would work itself out. He's smart, you know.

174

He was very matter-of-fact about the whole thing. Caught me by surprise, because I was expecting something else.'

'You expected to get your ass chewed off, which you felt you partly deserved?'

'Right. Schweitzer is hard to read sometimes. At least he knows the rules of the street. Protect your ass; protect your partner's ass. We talked a long time in his office. He listened mostly. Schweitzer's a real good listener.'

'And you tell pretty good stories.'

'He asked me something I thought was a little strange. Schweitzer asked if I ever heard of death squads inside the department.'

Stefanovitch could feel his face flushing. 'Had you?'

'Yeah. I knew about a couple times somebody authorized certain detectives to go take somebody out. I knew about death squads.'

Stefanovitch continued to nod as he listened to Isiah Parker. This was getting heavy. Everything was tracking so far. He had a feeling that Parker was telling the truth. Stefanovitch also knew about police department death squads. They existed. Death squads in the New York Police Department were for real, although he'd only heard about them being used to go after cop killers.

'Maybe two weeks later, Schweitzer met me at a hotel bar. Trumpets in the Hyatt. He insisted it be a bar. Out of the office. He seemed like he was in a good mood that night. Loosey-goosey like. We had a couple of pops standing around the bar. Then he laid out what was on his mind.'

'This is the fun part, right?'

'Yeah. That's right. Schweitzer said he was planning to put together a squad. He had orders directly from Police Plaza. He said that a lot . . . He said we were in the middle of a guerrilla war with the street mobs. Nine cops had been killed in the last year. He asked me to think about that. Just to think it over. No pressure.'

'Yeah, no pressure except now you know somebody at

Police Plaza wants to shoot it out with organized crime. No pressure. Just go out and commit a few harmless homicides with some other vigilante cops.'

Parker smiled and seemed to enjoy Stefanovitch's sense of irony.

'The third time we met, it was up in Mamaroneck. This time it was at the house of Deputy Commissioner Mackey. Beautiful old house. Mackey was very intense and serious. He raised ethical considerations. But he showed us a lot of hard evidence. How many cops had been killed for breaking the street law. He said there was nothing the department could do legally. The mob was using guerrilla tactics, then hiding behind the court system with their expensive lawyers. There was no way the department could win. The mob kills a cop, maybe even a judge, a certain witness, anybody they want to kill. If we can make any kind of case, they hire the best lawyers and get themselves off.'

'Did it get any higher than Schweitzer and Mackey?'

'There was another meeting the next week. This meeting's up in Westchester, too. I get introduced to the rest of the team. Detective Jimmy Burke is former Vietnam and Manhattan South Vice. Detective Aurelio Rodriquez is from Queens Narcotics. His partner had been killed a few months before. I knew Aurelio. He wanted a little vengeance, just like me. The three of us were told that Commissioner Sugarman approved of the special unit himself. It almost sounded like it was Sugarman's plan.'

Stefanovitch could feel a cold spot forming in his stomach. 'This was a verbal approval from Commissioner Sugarman?'

'That's right. You got it. Mackey used a lot of the police commissioner's own words. He was trying to make us more comfortable. After that, we met only with Mackey. He'd give us the specific targets. Alexandre St-Germain. Traficante. Ollie Barnwell. Everything was very organized. We even kept a surveillance log before and after the hits. We recorded our time on undercover.'

'Do you still have the surveillance log?' Stefanovitch was

beginning to make a few written notes. 'You did keep the log, Isiah?'

Parker smiled. 'Sure I kept the surveillance log. It's in a safety deposit box. A girlfriend of mine has the key. Just in case I ever get into an accident, in case something unfortunate happens. I never completely trusted my partners, especially Burke.'

Stefanovitch rubbed his forehead, then his eyes. He believed what he was hearing – he just couldn't believe he was hearing it.

'I met with Mackey one more time. This was almost two weeks ago,' Parker said. 'He told me about Atlantic City.'

'Did you keep a surveillance log on the meeting? Do you have a record of the meeting?' Stefanovitch's heart was starting to beat faster. They were getting into what really mattered.

'The last meeting with Deputy Commissioner Mackey . . . I was wired. I wired myself. Like I said, I was very uncomfortable.'

'Jesus Christ. You wired yourself for a meet with Charlie Mackey?'

'The tape is in the safety deposit box I told you about. Safe and sound.'

'I'm beginning to see how you got all those narcotics arrests. Tell me more about Atlantic City. Everything there is to tell.'

There was silence as Parker lit up another cigarette. The detective seemed to be taking stock of what he had gone over, maybe what he hadn't gone over yet.

'We were supposed to check into separate hotels in Atlantic City. I was in Trump's. Burke stayed at Bally's, Aurelio Rodriquez was at Resorts.'

Parker told about the chaos and confusion after the shootings at Trump's. 'I saw you outside on the boardwalk. I also think I saw Deputy Commissioner Mackey in the crowd. Some coincidence, huh?

'Then Burke tried to kill me. Burke was waiting for me near my car . . .

'Rodriquez had already been murdered. The vigilante cops, right. Somebody pimped us. Somebody set us up, Lieutenant. I'm not even sure who. Mackey and Burke? The commissioner himself?'

'What are you doing now, Isiah?'

'I've been checking on my good buddy Burke over the past few days. Pulling some favors with a few friends. As it turns out, Burke met St-Germain in Southeast Asia. He worked for him there. One other thing you should know. It's the reason I came to see you, Lieutenant.'

Parker paused for a few seconds. John Stefanovitch waited for him to start again.

'I think that Jimmy Burke might be the one who killed your partner, Kupchek. I think some of the men who originally ambushed you at Long Beach were *New York City cops*.'

29

Sarah McGinniss
The Waldorf-Astoria Hotel

Madness was beginning to take over her world. Sarah couldn't stop thinking that way, because it happened to be the truth.

She was running, actually running, inside the formal and elegant Park Avenue entrance to the Waldorf-Astoria. Then she was rushing up the double-wide marble staircase. Finally Sarah entered the plush, floral-carpeted lobby, which extended a full city block to Lexington Avenue.

As her eyes focused on the scene, she selected sharply delineated objects and surfaces to concentrate on: a gilded sign for the Hilton Room; the entryway to the famous Empire Room, where café society had once danced to Frank Sinatra and Benny Goodman; a cocktail lounge called Peacock Alley. The hotel's interior was undeniably rich, but also harmonious. It blended various marbles, stones, friezes, matched woods, and marquetry panels.

Somehow, the Waldorf seemed almost perfect for what was about to happen. It was the hotel of kings and presidents, wasn't it? Maybe it ought to be the hotel for the highest intrigues as well.

She had to find Stefanovitch.

He'd called her at home, but she'd been out taking Sam to school. The message he'd left said there was going to be some kind of announcement about Alexandre St-Germain at the Waldorf. Stef didn't know any more than that yet. No one did. The message was so unexpected that as soon as she heard it, Sarah rushed to the midtown hotel. Now where was he?

She was feeling numb as she stood in the Waldorf, trying to catch her breath. Her face was flushed. Her neck tingled.

Finally she spotted him, down past Peacock Alley on the far right side of the lobby. He was spiffed up: wearing a car coat; a shirt and tie. He looked good, and was catching a lot of passing stares.

'I came as soon as I got your message,' she said as she hurried up to Stefanovitch. Even as she spoke, Sarah realized how hurt she'd been in Pennsylvania. She hadn't understood how much until that moment.

He sensed it. 'It's real hard for me to apologize,' he said. 'But I'm sorry. I should have tried to explain, but I'm not sure I understand what happened myself. I am sorry, Sarah.'

His hand brushed the sleeve of her dress. The slightest physical contact was made, but it seemed more than that to Sarah. Something about the strangeness of the relationship made all this incredibly intense to her.

Sarah looked into his eyes, but didn't say anything. She knew this wasn't the place or time.

'After this is over, we should talk. Sometime soon.' Her face quickly shifted away from Stefanovitch, those haunting brown eyes. 'Do you know where we're going? Where is all this supposed to happen?'

'The Duke of Windsor Room. It's up on the fourth floor. A lot of movers and shakers are already there. I did some scouting before you got here.'

'Well . . . let's go join everybody,' Sarah said. 'See what this is all about.'

More than a hundred reporters, all kinds, from television networks, from newspapers and magazines around the world, were already gathered in the formal room. Everyone who was anyone was there: the American networks, the BBC, CBC, Iron Curtain services; representatives from all over Latin America. There were gold moiré draperies everywhere. The walls were covered in gold damask. Several of the sofas and chairs were Chippendale.

Sarah recognized a few of the newspeople, colleagues and acquaintances. This was going to be a huge story. Possibly, it would be the biggest story yet. And it was breaking right here in the Waldorf's very civilized Duke of Windsor Room.

A cluster of microphones jutted from a stern podium set before rows of upholstered chairs. Alongside the podium, Sarah saw a man she knew, a high-powered New York lawyer named Morton James. She figured that James's law firm must be orchestrating everything. The idea angered her. Morton James belonged to a group described as 'New York's greediest.' He was definitely another class of criminal: pin-striped collar; blue blood; black heart.

The Midnight Club. The words played like a familiar tune inside her head. There was something uncomfortable about this juxtaposition: the ornate Waldorf-Astoria meeting room – and what was about to happen here. What *was* about to happen here? What did Morton James have to announce to the press?

In his inimitable way, Stefanovitch was clearing a path through the reporters, plowing down the right side aisle. He found two seats halfway to the podium.

It was almost eleven-thirty, the time scheduled for the press conference. Nothing had happened yet. Reporters continued to file into the hotel room.

A clique of lawyers from James's firm was congregated around a silver coffee urn, a very expensive-looking samovar. Sarah felt as if she were attending some kind of stockholders' corporate bash. It was a disturbing notion. Everything felt expertly orchestrated; everything was purposely expensive; so right, so respectable; so utterly reprehensible under the circumstances.

The lawyer Morton James was standing behind the podium and all the protruding microphones. What a pompous and self-satisfied creep. What a fine example of pond scum on the surface of life.

'Good morning,' he announced in a voice that was too silky-smooth and mellifluous, too pleasant by half. 'I would like to thank you all for coming to this press conference.'

Press conference? Is that what this is? Sarah thought to herself. She had to smile.

At that moment, Alexandre St-Germain appeared from behind thickset oak doors at the front of the formal meeting room.

Stefanovitch felt his stomach drop. His heart began to pound so loud he thought others around him could hear it. The killer he had been tracking for almost five years was walking toward the speaker's dais.

The Grave Dancer wore a conservative business suit, not unlike that of his Park Avenue attorney. His hair was slicked back, making his face more severe than ever. The Grave Dancer was back; and he looked as if he belonged inside the elegant Waldorf meeting room.

Alexandre St-Germain stepped behind the microphones. He seemed very comfortable and completely relaxed. Sarah suddenly felt as if she couldn't breathe.

Stefanovitch touched her arm. It was like electricity, live current being fed into an even stronger current. She wondered what this was like for him, being in the same room with St-Germain.

'I have prepared some remarks which should help to explain my sudden, much-publicized disappearance several weeks ago,' Alexandre St-Germain began in a strong, clear voice.

'On that evening, I received word that because of certain of my financial interests in Europe and the United States, an attempt would be made on my life. I was taken away from New York before a tragic shooting occurred here. A precaution, which turned out to be a necessity. My company's security team saved my life. I was transported to Kennedy Airport. It was felt that I would be safer at my home near Nice. We are all too aware of the assassination attempts against business leaders during the last few years.

'When I reached my destination in France, I learned about the tragic developments in New York. At the time, it was felt that I should remain in seclusion, until more was known about the attack.

'I discovered that two of the European corporations in which I own a substantial interest, Ferro and Maldo-Scotti Industries, had been infiltrated by members of a crime syndicate that has had dealings with leftist terrorists. Yesterday, the Sûreté arrested several men in connection with the attempt on my life. I am satisfied that my personal safety is assured, and so, I have returned to resume my business in New York.'

At that moment, Alexandre St-Germain discovered Stefanovitch in the audience. He glanced at Stef and the look was unbearably cold and detached. In an instant, he let Stefanovitch know how insignificant he was. *I have returned to resume my business in New York. You mean nothing.*

'Simultaneous with this announcement,' St-Germain went on, 'another meeting is being held in Europe, releasing all of the information there . . . my company's full security arrangements. Everything you need to know for your stories.

'Because of the notoriety the case has received, it was felt that such unusual steps were justified, and in fact necessary . . . I would gladly answer any of your questions now.'

At the conclusion of his prepared statement, Alexandre St-Germain smoothly handled questions without any assistance from his lawyers. He gained confidence as he spoke, becoming almost glib on the podium.

He could easily have been mistaken for a high-level executive from a major corporation. He had been expertly coached and prepared for the morning's meeting. Sarah sensed that he was actually winning the group over. They were starting to laugh at his clever jokes, appreciating his style, which was sophisticated and urbane.

Alexandre St-Germain seemed so terribly *respectable*. He didn't act like the Grave Dancer; he didn't even look like the Grave Dancer, the underworld figure she had once photographed on Fifth Avenue. He had never been more dangerous.

Stefanovitch turned to her. He was clearly disturbed. His body was tense, almost numb. 'Let's go,' he finally whispered. 'I've heard as much as I need to. As much as I can stomach for today.'

The Grave Dancer was alive. It was starting all over again.

30

Alexandre St-Germain
The Seventy-ninth Street Boat Basin

A completely new order would exist now, a sixth estate rising out of the impossible chaos of the old mob structure. It would be in effect everywhere that mattered: in the United States, in Italy, West Germany, in England, France, Holland, Spain, all through Japan, Hong Kong, the rest of the Orient. In all the major cities and countries of the world, *respectability* and *anonymity* would be the foundations for the future of organized crime.

The Midnight Club would operate like any multinational corporation, almost like a government. There was no room for gangsters, for unpredictable dons and bosses, when hundreds of billions of dollars were at stake. What was necessary was strong local representation, and even stronger central control.

Tonight there would be celebrations, respectable parties, the kind that any successful business might throw after a victory over the competition.

Tomorrow, the orderly investment of profits would begin. Two dozen legitimate takeover targets had been identified on stock exchanges around the world; real estate opportunities had been found in every major city.

Alexandre St-Germain's luxury yacht was named *The Storm Rider*. It was docked in its accustomed port at the boat basin at Seventy-ninth Street.

The guests had begun to arrive around nine-thirty. They were congregated on the aft deck, where every kind of drink, assorted shellfish and caviar, red meat, and exotic bird was being served by William Poll's gourmet catering staff.

Live music played: European disco, Brazilian sambas, slightly dated punk rock. The guests of Alexandre St-Germain included New York artists, their stodgy patrons, old eastern stockbrokers, executives from multinational corporations, Broadway actors and actresses, musicians, the usual hangers-on for each of these groups. Enormous wealth was everywhere. The confident aura of power and prestige was unmistakable.

Alexandre St-Germain was completely at ease among the wealthy party-goers. He had selected a light gray suit that was subtle and elegant. He understood his role tonight: helping to seed the new order; securely establishing his own place in it. Long ago, he had discovered that facades and surfaces were everything in any society. It was as true on this yacht as it had been in the underworld of Marseilles. The difference between the two worlds was that one operated on deception, the other on self-deception.

The distinguished guests, with their ingrained oh-so-serious looks, found him witty, charming, even better-looking than had been rumored. They were easily convinced that the stories about Alexandre St-Germain were apocryphal; media-inspired exaggerations. There was no way this European gentleman could be the things he was said to be.

Respectability, he remembered all through the night. It was a mask he wore easily; one of his more subtle disguises.

Late in the evening, he stood alongside Jimmy Burke on the yacht's deck. For several years, Burke had been carefully preparing the way for St-Germain's emergence in New York. Now, the two men watched the glittering, super-rich party from shadows falling across the second deck of *The Storm Rider*.

'The crème de la crème of New York society,' Alexandre St-Germain said. 'A peculiar thing, the conversation of most American men – there is rarely any content, no depth of

186

thinking or knowledge. It's a consistent trait, I find. All that they know about is making money, and not so much about that as they think.'

St-Germain pointed toward the main deck. He indicated a tall, striking blond who was dancing there. He felt the need to do something that wasn't so respectable. Something for himself tonight.

'You see the one I like? The blond in blue. Quite stunning. Do you happen to know her?'

'I can find out for you.'

'Yes, find out for me. Bring her around. She's the most beautiful creature here tonight. Tell her that. Tell her I would like to meet her very much.'

When the last of the guests left in the early morning, the young blond woman, Susan Paladino, remained on board the yacht. She couldn't have possibly left the main state-room by herself.

She was feeling uncomfortably warm inside the elegant and luxurious room. She was having trouble getting her dress up over her head and off. Underneath the cumber-some blue Azzedine, she wore nothing. She had planned to meet someone important and interesting at the party tonight. She just hadn't been sure who.

Susan Paladino was feeling sleepy, but also sexy, and wonderfully important in the stateroom, which she knew belonged to Alexandre St-Germain. She had the intoxicating thought that she had come a long way from Buffalo. She was somebody now; she really was.

The exotic shipboard room seemed to be moving around her. The walls and ceiling occasionally blurred, coming in and out of focus.

Finally, she had to lie down on the huge double bed. It was a good place to wait for him to come back. Alexandre St-Germain. Handsome. Blond. Very, very rich . . . Susan Paladino. Very, very naked.

She tried to sit up, but it was no good. She wanted

to speak, but couldn't get control of her voice.

How could she be so drunk? She never let herself get like this. She felt completely separated from the scene, from her own body.

She suddenly noticed Alexandre St-Germain there in the stateroom, along with a few other men, but he didn't say anything to her. How strange. Hello? Hello there? Was she saying that out loud?

She tried to smile.

But he didn't smile back at her.

How different he was. How interesting and provocative. How stunning with his long blond curls.

Why don't you smile, Goldilocks? she wanted to say. Don't take everything so seriously or you'll ruin tonight for both of us. Why don't you say something?

He sat in a chair across the room. His long legs were draped across the chair's arm. He never said a word to the girl. He watched the other men use Susan Paladino. The Grave Dancer merely watched. Later, he watched as they injected her with cocaine, almost 90 percent pure.

There was nothing that compared with this forbidden thrill: watching someone die, especially a frightened, beautiful woman. It was one of the last taboos in a world that claimed to have none. It was an experience he had known Club members pay fortunes to witness . . .

The drug threw her body into convulsions. The convulsions went on for several minutes. Technically, she suffered a stroke. She seemed to be coming as she died. Who was the poet who had enjoyed that image? Lord Byron, wasn't it? Watching her die, Alexandre St-Germain was as excited as he ever became.

The men in the stateroom discarded the young woman's body somewhere around Sandy Hook. Susan Paladino sank quietly into the dark waves of the sea. She was weighted around the waist and ankles, and wouldn't be found until spring, if ever . . .

Just another dance for the Grave Dancer.

31

Sarah McGinniss and John Stefanovitch
East Hampton

Sarah composed an opening for a very pivotal chapter in *The Club*, maybe the turning point of the book.

She was sitting at an old schoolroom desk, framed in a dormer window of her beach house. She eyed the main road rather than the ocean, watching as the cars steadily arrived. She wrote to distract herself as much as anything:

> Everyone we could trust, possibly even trust with our lives, had been asked to come. Seven men and two women were invited out to the house in East Hampton, a list whittled down from twenty. A harrowing task in itself.
>
> They began to arrive as early as six forty-five in the morning. The first was David Wilkes, who'd traveled from Washington. Stefanovitch and I had prepared everything as well as we could under the circumstances. Neither of us entirely believed what we had decided to do, only that something had to be done.
>
> For Stefanovitch, there was no issue: he had to go after Alexandre St-Germain again. There was no choice for him. No choice at all.

Stefanovitch busied himself stoking a modest fire in the living room. He tried not to think about what was going on here; about the fact that St-Germain was alive.

He used oak and pine shavings Sarah had brought from Vermont during the spring. After twenty minutes, the house began to smell sweet and good, like New England on a crisp fall morning. The atmosphere was deceptively pleasant, as homey and traditional as any countryside inn.

Stefanovitch saw that it was still spitting rain outside. The sky was gloomy cardboard gray, pressed down and hugging the ocean. Sam raced along the top of the dune in a bright yellow slicker. He was an irrepressible spirit, an irresistible little boy. Sam seemed oblivious to all of what was happening, the possible dangers.

As he shuffled a final log onto the fire, Stefanovitch noticed his hands were unsteady. A very troubling question remained for him: had they chosen these people wisely enough? Could every member of the group be trusted?

The night before, he and Sarah had made the necessary phone calls. A meeting was decided on. The house in East Hampton seemed like a good place, as secure as any.

Sarah finally appeared downstairs. She stood beside one of the dripping bay windows, talking with Isiah Parker. Stefanovitch had told her everything about Parker. He had shown her the detective's personnel file, which he'd been able to copy at Police Plaza. Parker had been a superior policeman for his twelve years with the department, but Parker was also an enigma.

'I guess we should start,' Stefanovitch said at last. 'We're all here now.'

They began to settle around an old oak serving table in the dining room. The room was filled with antique furniture, also humorous knickknacks Sarah had picked up both in the East and around California. They helped to lighten the mood of the room, but not enough.

Three lawyers, one man and two women, were there from the district attorney's office. They all sat together at the table. Stefanovitch had known each of them for years. Stuart Fischer had been the right hand for the district attorney over the past several years.

David Wilkes had flown up the previous night. He'd accepted the invitation immediately; he seemed well aware of problems with the ongoing investigation in Atlantic City, the mysterious lessening of police resources.

Stanley Kahn from the *New York Times* had been asked to come by Sarah. The reporter accepted without too many of his difficult questions being answered beforehand.

David Hale and Terry Marshall from New York's Organized Crime Task Force were already seated at the dining table. So was John Keresty from US Customs. So far, none of them knew why they had been invited, except that it had to do with the reappearance of Alexandre St-Germain.

Sarah remained standing as the others quietly seated themselves. Small details seemed charged, and terribly important that morning. The shore house felt as if it were holding more of the morning's chill than usual.

'I might as well start with a few things that are on my mind,' she said from her place.

'For reasons that should become clear as I go on, we decided against Police Plaza for this meeting. We also decided against the district attorney's office. Or even the *Times* offices, on Forty-third Street, Stanley.'

She bowed in the direction of the *Times* reporter, who looked slightly bemused.

'If you think you hear a little paranoia in what I'm saying, I'm afraid you do. We don't know exactly whom we can trust in police departments,' Sarah said. She paused to let the implication of her words sink in. 'Or in the district attorney's office. Or at the *Times*. Or in the Treasury, or FBI. Did I leave anybody out? I assume I have everybody's attention now?'

'Rapt,' Stanley Kahn said from behind tented hands.

Sarah watched the tightening circle of faces. None of the men and women seemed overjoyed to be among the trusted few. That was understandable. The notion that so many others weren't trusted was overwhelming to consider.

A chair scraped against the wooden plank floor. A body hunched forward. Mostly there was silence.

'Where to start is part of my dilemma,' Sarah continued. 'Maybe if I go back closer to the beginning . . .'

Stefanovitch was getting an uncomfortable sense of déjà vu. He had been here before and he'd been burned badly. He had trailed St-Germain into a trap. His wife had been murdered. Stefanovitch finally spoke up from his place at the table.

'What we're here to discuss is the possibility of playing by their *law*. Not just the *street law*. It's not that simple. We're talking about the unwritten *laws* of supranational corporate executives around the world. And the *laws* practiced by governments and military juntas. The *laws* of the super-rich, people who think they're above ordinary laws.

'We want to talk about a crime syndicate, an entirely *new* kind of syndicate. It's called the Midnight Club. It represents what's become of organized crime.'

Late that afternoon, after all the others had left, Sarah and Stefanovitch sat up on the deck overlooking the water. The rainstorm had finally passed. A pale wafer of sun was trying to break through the cloud cover.

For the first twenty minutes or so, they talked about the important meeting that had just finished. Had they sounded too paranoid? They didn't think so. Not based on the reactions; especially the questions asked toward the end of the session. The *new* Midnight Club had the full attention of everyone invited to the meeting.

'Maybe we should talk about something else for a while,' Stefanovitch finally suggested. 'Sarah, I really am sorry about what happened in Pennsylvania,' he went right on – while his nerve was up.

'It's over now.' Sarah shrugged. 'I'm not sure if I understand exactly what happened, though,' she couldn't help adding.

'I think I understand it okay,' Stefanovitch said. 'I'm not so sure I can put it into the right words, and then get the words out.'

Sarah didn't say anything. She had a sense that Stef had to do this his own way, or not at all.

She looked into his eyes. He had deep brown eyes, but too often, they seemed on the edge of sadness.

Sarah realized that part of her wanted to make the sadness go away. She didn't know if that was possible; if it was a wise thing to want to try to do; if it was healthy for either of them. She *did* know that they needed a break from both the Midnight Club and Alexandre St-Germain.

'I've tried to be with somebody a few times since the accident,' Stefanovitch said. As he spoke, he watched children playing in the surf. 'One time it was the woman I mentioned meeting in Gramercy Square Park, a nurse named Pat Beccaccio. I wanted to get close to her. There was this ache inside me. I was afraid, Sarah. The more I needed somebody, the more afraid I got.

'I'd go over to Gramercy Park, hoping she'd be there after work. I'd think about her a lot during the day. If I saw some tall woman with dark hair in the neighborhood, my heart would start to slam around, thinking it might be her. If she wasn't at the park, I'd be incredibly disappointed and hurt . . .

'I'd imagine that she didn't come because she didn't want to see me, didn't want to stop and have to talk to some cripple. I decided she was avoiding the park, so she wouldn't have to see me.'

Sarah felt she was getting closer to whoever John Stefanovitch really was. For better or worse, Stef had this old-fashioned code of honor. It was stuck like a broken record in his thick skull. He would probably have it for the rest of his life.

There are features I like besides his eyes, she was thinking as she listened to him talk. Like a scar that ran like the serrated edge of a knife over one of his eyelids. It made the eye sag a little, which gave his face more character. He'd been *bitten* in a high school basketball game, he'd told her. She could understand how someone might want to bite him sometimes.

'I don't know if you can understand any of what I'm saying, Sarah? I couldn't bring myself to call Pat Beccaccio and make a date. Sometimes, I'd be in my apartment at night, with my hand right on the phone receiver. *I couldn't make myself call.* I don't want you to feel sorry for me. I don't feel sorry for myself. I just want you to know what's been building up inside me for a long time.'

'I understand a little,' Sarah finally said. She wanted to reach out for him suddenly, to hold him and be held, but she didn't. She listened. She let him talk.

'This may not sound like a cop talking, but I was afraid. Afraid of you. I was scared you might reject me, right when I was starting to feel something.'

'Maybe that's okay. Maybe you're getting back in touch with something important?'

Finally, Sarah came closer. He could smell her perfume, which was light and flowery. The whole thing had an extraordinary this-isn't-happening aura. It fit with a lot of other experiences lately.

It was Sarah's turn to be confused, though; time for her head to be whirling. She wasn't sure exactly who started it . . .

They began to kiss. The kiss was sweet, more tender, gentler, than she would have expected it could be. That was the thing. Stefanovitch was always full of surprises.

She wasn't sure whether this was the right thing, or absolutely the wrong thing for them. Sarah wasn't sure how she felt about anything right now. Her mind was reeling a little. No, her mind was reeling a lot. She knew just one thing for certain: she wanted to kiss Stefanovitch. She needed to be held by him, and to hold him back. Beyond that, she wasn't sure of anything.

Suddenly, Sarah kissed him hard, their teeth hitting. She sucked at his mouth and squeezed his body as tightly as she could.

'I guess this breaks the ice a little more.' He finally was able to speak again.

'Now you know how I feel, at least. No more guessing games. I like you so much, Stef.' Sarah smiled. 'I have from that first day at Police Plaza.'

32

The Midnight Club
New York City

At a few minutes before eight, Alexandre St-Germain arrived inside Tower Two of the World Trade Center. Some of the most powerful men and women in the world had journeyed to New York to meet with him that morning. They were congregated upstairs, in a plush suite of business offices on the eighty-sixth floor.

The crime syndicate was about to begin operations. Except that it really wasn't a crime syndicate anymore; it was a federation of business, government, and political figures.

. . . With the power of influence.

With respectability.

With invisibility.

There were twenty-seven members now. All of them were up on the eighty-sixth floor of the Trade Center . . .

The Old Guard of organized crime was no longer operating. All that had changed in Atlantic City. There was too much money, too much political influence involved to trust it to crime chiefs. Sixty-five billion dollars was put on the table every year; that was the profit from organized crime around the world – enough to pay off the banking debts of entire countries.

Sixty-five billion dollars. In profits.

The evolution of leadership had actually been taking place for a decade. First it had happened in Western Europe; then in the Far East; finally in the United States, where the mob had been strongest, and also had government ties going as far back as the OSS.

The original Club had included nothing but the Old Guard of crime – the powerful and erratic dons and bosses. Then, Alexandre St-Germain had begun to shape a new direction. The Club had taken on 'advisers' from Wall Street and all over Europe. Only St-Germain operated in both the old world and the new.

Now the advisers, plus Alexandre St-Germain, were the Club.

The words of a speech flowed through St-Germain's head as the elevator rose through the Trade Center. This will be my second formal speech in two days, he considered. The price of respectability.

Look around you, he planned to say to the august group gathered in a suite overlooking New York Harbor. *Think about the differences between the old order and the new. We make billions of dollars by giving speeches, by holding business meetings, by attending political caucuses and dinners. How different that is from the syndicates of the past. How important to the recharging of the world's money supply, the world's cash flow.*

For twenty days I was dead. Just as the old ways are dead. From today on, there will be a more organized way for us to do business. The world's governments are limited by their own internal politics; by absurd, almost Neanderthal policies for dealing with one another. We have no such restraints. We are the most efficient, the wealthiest, and most powerful governing body in the world.

Our policy will be to maintain tight control of the world's economic markets. New York. London. Los Angeles. Paris. São Paulo. Frankfurt, Rome, Amsterdam, Tokyo. Hong Kong. The cities from which you come. We will move on to control the Third World at some time in the future.

Look around you and think about this. There is no one who can stop us from taking whatever we want.

At eight o'clock, Alexandre St-Germain swung open the glass doors leading into a sun-drenched conference room. Inside the well-appointed room, they were quietly waiting for him.

The club members had taken their places on either side of an oval, polished glass conference table. Most of the men were outfitted in dark expensive suits, the women in conservative dresses. The group had the look and feel of money; of real money; of power without any limits.

To the surprise of Alexandre St-Germain, the twenty-seven members rose as he entered the room. They stood, and they applauded. The newly constituted Midnight Club had finally been called to order.

That night, a dark blue Cadillac eased to a stop in front of 10 East Seventy-fourth Street, two doors from the wilds of Central Park. A stretch limo parked in front of the federal-style town house wasn't an unusual sight. Number 10 seemed to get more than its share of expensive cars, even in a neighborhood of prestigious foundations, embassies, and consulates.

The wrought-iron front door of the town house finally swung open. Four strikingly beautiful, very young girls came outside. The girls were talking and laughing as they hurried to the waiting car.

The Cadillac limousine quietly slid north on Park Avenue, then picked up speed onto the FDR. The girls were asked to put on black satin sleeping masks during the ride up into Westchester.

Alexandre St-Germain
Bedford Hills

Inside the dark paneled library of an estate house in West-chester, Alexandre St-Germain played with a Cuban cigar, which happened to coordinate with the mahogany walls. The layout brought to mind the clubs of London: Boodles, Brooke's, the Savile, but especially the Hurlingham out in Fulham.

Old money.

Quiet excess.

Respectability.

The polished wood library was the gathering place for an Eastern Establishment group that effectively controlled much of the American banking system, but also the all-important communications industry, and, as much as any clique of Americans could, the major activity on Wall Street. The four regular members were also part of the Midnight Club.

The subject of the meeting that night was an important one – oil prices and the heating of the West, without undue panic or economic collapse, for the coming winter. All those in the room agreed on one thing: it was a decision far too complex and delicate to entrust to the politicians and bureaucrats in Washington, or elsewhere around the world.

As the men stiffly filed out of the library around twelve, Alexandre St-Germain was aware of an arm firmly sliding around his shoulders. A Wall Street power broker named Wilson Seifer spoke confidentially to him.

'There's a party planned. Private affair. Why don't you come with us.'

Seifer led the way down a corridor with resplendent tapestries and medieval heraldry on every wall. Baccarat chandeliers swung overhead, like priceless necklaces and pendants.

The room that the men entered was lit by gold and rouge flames coming from a fieldstone fireplace. Overall, it had the appearance of a mead hall.

The girls inside the room stood in an orderly school row. They were grouped in front of the crackling, blazing fire. Their bare skin and long hair gleamed beautifully in the burnishing firelight. The oldest girl looked sixteen, the youngest might have been twelve.

They were naked. All were shaven between their legs. Each girl wore a black satin sleeping mask.

Old money, Alexandre St-Germain thought, and had to stifle a smile.

Respectability, indeed.

The best things about the Club never really changed.

33

John Stefanovitch
East Forty-third Street

Stefanovitch was nervous as he waited on the corner of East Forty-third Street.

He listened to a cacophony of noise just starting up at six-thirty in the morning – the usual cries and moans of early Manhattan traffic. He was sipping juice from a cardboard box when Beth Kelley finally showed up.

'Long time no see, Stef,' his physical therapist said when she saw him. 'What's it been, nine days?'

'Yeah, but who's counting.' Stefanovitch shrugged. His face and neck had begun to turn red.

'Nine days, no word. Not even a postcard.' When it finally came, the therapist's smile was brittle. She was hurt and disappointed. She had invested a lot in Stef's rehabilitation; more than a year of her time and expertise.

'You didn't get the card yet? Man, those local mails.'

A slight smile came from Beth Kelley, a real one.

'How do your legs feel? They're real strong, I'll bet,' she said. 'Upper thighs, calves especially.'

His legs felt terrible, as a matter of fact. He couldn't believe how much strength he'd lost already, how his legs had atrophied in such a short period without exercise.

'I'm on a case. It's a huge, complicated mess.'

Beth Kelley said nothing to that. 'You coming inside? Or is this just to say good-bye?'

'No, I'm coming inside. I'm here for a workout. If you'll promise to be nice.'

Kelley said nothing to that either. She turned and walked into the gym ahead of Stefanovitch.

Ten minutes later, he was straining under weights that seemed impossible for him to have ever lifted. Sweat was rolling off his body. His upper thighs were burning. He needed to work out for emotional as much as physical reasons, he knew. He needed a release from the tension.

I'm going to walk, he finally began to repeat over and over to himself. I'm going to walk.

It was like the way he used to issue chants as a boy back in Pennsylvania, as if by force of will he could do whatever he wanted to, or had to.

I'm going to walk.

'Goddamn it, I'm going to walk!'

Stefanovitch yelled the words inside the loudly echoing gymnasium. All the workouts at the Sports Center suddenly stopped.

Heavy Universal weights were suspended perilously in mid-air. Other weights dropped with loud, clanging noises. The aerobics people – the heavy-weight freaks – the blue-clad, holier-than-thou instructors – were all staring at him, all attention on the man in the wheelchair.

Then they began to clap. What Stefanovitch had said, what he'd shouted above the noise in the gym, had gotten to the usually schizoid and narcissistic exercise group.

'Fucking-A right you are, Stefanovitch!' Howie Cohen, the muscle-bound manager of the center, hollered from his usual sedentary perch, high up on the running track.

Laughter erupted at Cohen's words. Even the ax-faced DI's grinned. Then the regular grunts and groans of torture resumed in the gym. It was business as usual.

I not only intend to walk again, Stefanovitch was thinking as he strained and lifted and groaned. I even intend to live through the week.

John Stefanovitch and Isiah Parker
Central Park West

At half past eight, Stefanovitch sat with Isiah Parker in the front of a light green police-issue sedan. The two of them sipped lukewarm coffee, and ate bialys off waxed paper and the outside of brown paper bags. That morning, the plan conceived at Sarah's beach house was going into effect. They were trying not to think too much about what the consequences would be.

'It doesn't get much better than this,' Isiah Parker said, mocking a TV beer ad. He was as cynical as Stefanovitch, almost as bad as Bear Kupchek had been.

Stefanovitch watched the action at a newspaper vending machine across Central Park West. It was being stocked with morning editions of the *New York Times*. A big, sky blue *Times* truck was parked like a moving van in the middle of the street.

Some New York crazy had spray-painted 'LIES! TRASH! PROPAGANDA!' in red and black on the sides of the newspaper machine. Stefanovitch was thinking that he wasn't too enthused about graffiti artists. He kept waiting for the graffiti artists to start up on private cars. He imagined some poor New Yorker crossing the Painted Desert, with 'Pepe 122' or 'Louis 119' scrawled all over the hood.

That morning, though, he was feeling a little closer to whoever had painted 'LIES!' and 'TRASH!' Some national papers had already reported LIES and TRASH about whatever had really happened at Trump Plaza in Atlantic City. LIES and TRASH were a sign of the times.

As the morning sun rose over Central Park, Stefanovitch and Parker talked. It was real cop-to-cop chitchat. Laid-back and offhanded and easy. They covered their early days in the police department. Then general fear and loathing on the streets of New York. Both of them were still feeling each other out, slowly and carefully searching for soft spots and also points of connection.

'I went through the Police Academy in 'seventy-six. Everybody had some version of the same story back then,' Stefanovitch said as he slurped coffee.

'Which story was that?' Parker was wearing a rumpled crimson and white T-shirt that said 'Viva Mandela,' plus a black leather vest. He managed to look relaxed, very easygoing, at all times.

'They were all planning to put in their twenty. Get the regulation pension. Then buy a money-maker bar or restaurant somewhere in Florida, out on the Island. But everybody kind of wanted to make the city a little better place to live along the way.'

Isiah Parker laughed. It had been pretty much the same bullshit when he had gone through the academy two years earlier. His eyes narrowed. 'They always said you were going to be the PC someday. You were supposed to be connected. Rabbi at Police Plaza? That true?'

Stefanovitch shook his head. Now it was his turn to laugh.

'You know how it is, cops like to collect their little stories. I can tell you my own version in about a sentence. I like it on the streets. Right here. Like right now. I keep telling them that down at Police Plaza. They can't completely envision a wheelchair cop on the street, though.'

'The street gets into your blood, all right.' Parker had to agree. 'Outsiders, anybody you talk to, they don't understand that too much. Only cops understand. Only another cop can listen to a cop and not think he's crazy.'

Another fifteen minutes slowly passed on the surveillance watch. Then half an hour . . . Suddenly Stefanovitch pointed through the sedan's grimy windshield.

'Here we go loop de li. I hope. That's the car arriving now.'

A long blue limousine was easing into the no-parking

zone in front of the canopy at 85 Central Park West. A broad-shouldered chauffeur, in a tight black suit, started to climb out of the limo.

'Marco Gualdi,' Stefanovitch said. 'An associate of Mr St-Germain's from Sicily. I think they played on the same bocci team or something.'

The heavyset driver stood in front of the Central Park West luxury building, smoking cigarettes and schmoozing with the captain-doorman. Stefanovitch noticed that both of them laughed in the side-of-the-mouth, conspiratorial way high lackies seemed to favor around New York.

His powers of observation were coming back a little. Yes, he did like police work and the streets. Maybe it was an extension of the do-gooder soup kitchen his parents ran? Some kind of quixotic urge to try and do the right thing? He didn't really know why, but he liked it, maybe he loved the life of a street cop.

'This might even be some fun,' he finally smiled and said to Parker. 'Mind if I cover this one myself? Start things off right?'

Isiah Parker pushed his long legs up against the bottom of the steering column and the front dash. He peered over dark sunglasses at Stefanovitch.

'Be my guest. You holler, I'll come running pretty damn fast.'

Stefanovitch was smiling as he swung open the passenger side door, then the back door of the sedan.

In the same fluid motion, he pulled his lightweight racing chair out of the car, and set it on the sidewalk. Using the racer on the job was something new and different; it was even vaguely exciting.

There was something that got into your blood about police work, about the streets of New York. He was thinking that as he assembled the Chair. Maybe the act of wearing a gun did it? Maybe it was having so much raw power in your hands? So much life-and-death responsibility? . . . Whatever it was, he needed it right now, and he was getting a good dose.

Stefanovitch slowly made his way down Central Park West toward the parked limousine.

He was about to cross West Seventy-seventh Street, another half block to the Grave Dancer's limo, when Alexandre St-Germain emerged from the elegant apartment building, Number 85.

Horns were tooting up and down Central Park West. A manhole cover clattered, then was still again.

Alexandre St-Germain was there on the sidewalk. The Grave Dancer was walking crisply, looking good in a tailored charcoal gray suit. He motioned for his driver to get back inside the car. Two more bodyguards fell in on either side of St-Germain as he came out from under the apartment building's canopy.

A faded red gasoline truck turned down Seventy-seventh Street. It was blocking Stefanovitch's view of the limousine and Alexandre St-Germain.

'Son of a bitch. Hey. Get the hell out of the way,' he said out loud, to no one in particular.

His heart had really begun to kick in. His forehead felt hot, beaded with sweat already. He was still thirty yards from the limousine and Alexandre St-Germain.

Suddenly, he realized he wasn't going to get there in time. There was no way.

'Son of a bitch.' Stefanovitch squared his mouth and cursed.

A matronly woman waiting on the sidewalk glanced over at him. She saw the wheelchair, and tempered her initial reaction. They always did, and it drove him crazy.

Stefanovitch's hands bored into the hard, black rubber wheel guards of the wheelchair.

The chair was dropping off the curb, moving into the street against the red light, against the traffic making a right turn on Seventy-seventh.

'Hey!' he shouted up the sidewalk, completely ignoring the traffic. He was moving as fast as a wheelchair could move. 'Hey! Hey!'

The racing chair's wheels were lifting off the ground at each crack. It was dangerous, because the chair was so light it could go over.

'Hey, you! . . . Hey! Hey! . . . *Grave Dancer!*'

The two bodyguards had stopped moving. They didn't seem to believe what they were watching up ahead. They were definitely looking his way, though. Stefanovitch had their undivided attention.

They both touched under their jackets, feeling for handguns. What the hell was this coming down the street?

Alexandre St-Germain slowly turned as he was getting into the backseat of the limousine. The blond hair, the smoothly handsome face, came back into view. The Grave Dancer was only a few yards away from Stefanovitch.

St-Germain straightened to his full height. He stared up the sidewalk, at the man coming in the wheelchair, coming pretty fast, too.

Stefanovitch could feel the Grave Dancer's eyes burning into his skull. He was slightly out of control, wired to his limit. He'd been waiting so long for this moment. It seemed bizarre and unreal now that it was here.

'Yeah, you. I'm talking to *you*,' he called out again.

He couldn't help himself anymore. He was exploding forward on a burst of adrenaline and emotion.

None of his instincts, no common sense was working for him. It was a dangerous time. Christ, St-Germain was blond and handsome. He looked like the good guy.

Stefanovitch's thoughts were silent screams. They echoed around the caverns in his head . . . *Revenge* . . . Some kind of justice was what he had in mind. Like smashing the fucker's face for starters.

When the wheelchair got close, Alexandre St-Germain finally spoke. He talked in a low, even voice, like someone addressing an excitable child.

'Are you yelling at me for some reason?' he asked.

'Yeah, I am. I'm John Stefanovitch with the New York police. I'm yelling at you.'

'Yes? Can I help you?'

'We met a few years ago. We sort of met on the back streets of Long Beach. You gave me this wheelchair to remember you by.'

Stefanovitch's hands were clamped down hard on the arms of his chair. He was out of line, and he knew it. He just couldn't stop himself. There was no way he could stop this thing from being played out.

'I never got to thank you in person, to see you like this, man to man. Actually, there are a couple of reasons I wanted to meet you one day.'

The Grave Dancer interrupted. 'Well, you've had your long-awaited pleasure. I'm afraid that I have some business meetings to attend this morning. You're very welcome for your present, the one given to you at Long Beach. It seems that maybe you'll deserve another present soon.'

Alexandre St-Germain started to slide into the shiny black limousine.

A hand grabbed onto his shoulder. The hand crushed the soft padding of his expensive suit jacket. Then Stefanovitch suddenly yanked St-Germain backward.

Both of his bodyguards moved forward, but St-Germain waved them off. His throat and cheeks were bright red, swollen with blood. His blond hair had been mussed in the scuffle, little twists standing on end.

'Take your hand off my arm,' he said to Stefanovitch. 'You knew the rules. You decided to break them. You wanted to play in the big game, the big leagues.'

'Those were *your* fucking rules,' Stefanovitch shouted. 'Now you're going to hear my rules.'

Stefanovitch held on to the Grave Dancer as tightly as he could. This was a street fight; there couldn't be any backing down from here on.

'No matter what else happens, we're going to shut you down, motherfucker. I'm going to shut down your Midnight Club. I'm going to get *you*.'

Stefanovitch let go of Alexandre St-Germain. He jerked

the wheelchair around, a move he'd seen kids pull on skateboards.

His back was to Alexandre St-Germain and the body-guards. The wheelchair was squeaking – *skee-skee-skee-skee*. The sound was absurd. It was as if the chair were mocking him, mocking everything he was attempting to do, but especially his trying to be a cop again.

Back at the car, Isiah Parker was sitting in the front seat, his legs still propped up. He looked as if he hadn't moved since Stefanovitch had left.

When Stefanovitch got close, he saw that Parker was slowly clapping his hands. Parker was also grinning. It was the first real smile Stefanovitch had seen from the black detective, a great goddamn smile.

'That was real fine. You're off to a flying-A start with the man. I like the way you serve notice, serve papers. Now he has to kill you, too.'

Stefanovitch's heart was beating so hard he could hear it over Isiah Parker's voice. He was thinking that he still didn't care enough about what happened to himself.

He felt like he was flying, though, and that was good enough. He felt as if he had been released from some max-security prison where he had been slowly rotting, wasting away, dying of old age at thirty-five.

It was all beginning again.

Maybe it could be revenge against St-Germain and the Club.

Maybe retribution, some kind of justice finally.

Or maybe it would be something Stefanovitch couldn't bring himself to imagine – a world where justice no longer had a place.

34

Sarah McGinniss
One Hogan Square

Sarah had to get *The Club* right. She was obsessed with the book, focusing all her energy on it. The issue was proper documentation; the hard part was getting people to believe truths too horrifying to believe.

Stuart Fischer had suggested she come to One Hogan Square for a briefing with some of his people. The meeting was actually held in what amounted to the attic of the district attorney's office.

Sarah had talked Fischer into letting her bring a tape recorder. She was planning to take written notes as well. Documentation was so important.

'Why doesn't everybody grab a seat in this comfortable little nest of ours.' Stuart Fischer addressed the small group that was filing into the makeshift office. The tenth-floor loft had originally been furnished, however sparsely, when the DA's office was secretly investigating the New York Police Department in 1986. It wasn't much to look at, but it was out of harm's way.

'I have some news for you, unexpectedly good news. We're going after Alexandre St-Germain again.'

The office was nearly silent as they huddled closer around Fischer. The young lawyers were clearly in shock.

Sarah watched a young assistant perched on a peeling windowsill. A *brrrrr* sound emerged through his lips and an overgrown, bushy mustache.

A few of the others seemed to avert their eyes. There was a definite similarity to the meeting at Sarah's

210

house in East Hampton. A sudden chill was in the air.

'When we prepared our case against St-Germain last year, we were accused, maybe justifiably, of being too conservative. I don't know if that's true. I don't particularly care about the sins of the past. I promise you, though, conservatism won't be the problem this time.'

Fischer glanced at Sarah, who was the only one who understood exactly what he meant.

'I want to be particularly clear on that,' Fischer continued. 'I want all of you to understand exactly what I'm saying. If this sounds like a personal vendetta against Alexandre St-Germain, then I'm communicating pretty well so far. Because that's what we're going to try to conduct here. Anybody? Questions?'

There were none. Not yet. Just complete surprise that they were going after Alexandre St-Germain again.

'All right. We're going to be contacting other key agency heads this morning. The FBI, the French and Italian police, Customs, a few bosses in Treasury. I've already spoken to the IRS. They're in. They understand that we can get St-Germain this time.'

One of the assistants finally spoke, a striking blond woman who couldn't have been more than twenty-seven or twenty-eight. 'We're going all the way with the IRS? I should say, they're going all the way with us? Power to seize and confiscate? St-Germain's bank accounts? The companies he supposedly owns? That kind of all the way?'

Fischer nodded at the young lawyer. He smiled at her. '*That* kind of all the way, Louise.'

Sarah made a note about the tenor, the feel of the meeting. There was very little of the usual self-deprecating humor. The assistants understood exactly what was involved in mounting a case against a mob head like St-Germain; how painstaking and thorough it had to be.

'Absolutely all the way.' Fischer amplified his answer to the assistant's question. 'Actually, we're going to proceed down two avenues this time. We'll go after St-Germain with the Continuing Criminal Enterprise Law ... and with RICO.'

The lawyer sitting on the windowsill whistled appreciatively. Two or three of the others finally allowed themselves to smile, to glance at one another for quick reassurance. They were getting the general idea. This *was* a vendetta.

'I've asked the six of you here to be briefed privately. We're going to be acting as a highly confidential unit. We'll be contacting other agencies and departments, but none will have the whole picture the way we do.

'We already have a lot of evidence on St-Germain, some of which dates back at least ten years. That ought to constitute a continuing criminal enterprise in somebody's mind.'

Fischer laughed, and Sarah could see that his high spirits were becoming contagious. He had purposely shocked them. Now he was bringing them back up, slowly, rather masterfully. When they left the office in Hogan Square, they would all be flying high. Stuart Fischer was a very good lawyer, an even better motivator, and Sarah was feeling terrific that she and Stefanovitch had decided to call him on this instead of the DA. She had serious questions about the district attorney himself.

It was all documented in her notes; it would all appear in *The Club*.

'St-Germain will use James, Henley and Friends,' Fischer continued. 'As usual, their people will outnumber us about five hundred to one. That's why I want two separate charges operating. It's perfectly legal harassment.

'It's the way a good small law office would handle this. We'll hit them with the first piece as early as tomorrow afternoon. I don't care which charge it is. Something juicy and controversial. While James's staff is still reeling, we'll move in with our RICO motions. Get them coming and going. Everybody with me so far?'

'I love it.' The young mustache spoke from his perch on the windowsill. 'Hey, listen, though . . . did the mob ever knock off an entire DA's office before?'

The room broke into raucous laughter. For a change, they were being asked to do what they all had become lawyers for in the first place, to prosecute with the full force and intent of the law.

Sarah's eyes roamed around the attic room, studying the faces of the young attorneys. She wanted to remember everything, every look.

Fischer had begun to speak again. He wasn't smiling. 'In answer to your question, they knocked off a DA's office in Bogotá, Colombia. Seventeen men and women. So yes, counselor, there's precedent for that.'

The laughter inside the office stopped. Sarah froze that incredible tableau in her mind, too. Just that look on all of the young lawyers' faces.

She was trying to help in any way she could – whether it was something major, or taking care of details she was afraid no one else would remember.

Sarah spent the rest of the morning of July 17, and most of the afternoon, on the phone with Customs.

Then she was on the phone with an official from Scotland Yard.

Finally, she spent an hour with one of the best researchers at CBS Network News. She thought of it as 'tightening the noose.' She wasn't sure whose necks the noose was around, though. The look on the faces of those young lawyers kept flashing back to her.

The key to everything was patience. Harassment would work, but it took time. There was no other way to go after Alexandre St-Germain and the Club.

John Stefanovitch and Isiah Parker
One Police Plaza

Stefanovitch and Isiah Parker were dragging badly when they left Police Plaza one night later that week. As he pushed his wheelchair across the pedestrian mall, Stefanovitch looked up at ragged clouds whipping across the sky. That was the way he felt; torn apart by hidden forces.

'All things considered, it's going better than we ought to expect,' he finally said to Parker. 'What's St-Germain up to, though? Why is he sitting back and taking it so calmly?'

'He's deciding how he wants to handle our little disturbance. He's been harassed before. He's waiting for something. Some mistake he thinks we'll make.'

'It's almost like he knows what mistake we're going to make.'

'Maybe he does. He's been here before.'

'I also think he's trying to keep his nose clean. He's playing the maligned and completely misunderstood businessman.'

'That could be. It would explain a few things.'

Both Stefanovitch and Parker knew that the New York police practiced more illegal harassment than had ever been reported anywhere by the media. There were major and minor tactics. Stefanovitch had seen senior detectives putting sugar in the gas tank of a mobster's Cadillac. He'd watched oil rags being stuffed up the exhaust pipe of a pimp's Caddie Seville parked in Times Square. Cops knew that most wise guys would tear up a parking or moving violation ticket, but the computers kept extensive records. With a well-placed phone call, any detective could get a scofflaw drug dealer's car towed to the city garage. The result was incredible bureaucratic red tape, and frustration, and occasionally a hotheaded mistake.

In the area of more serious harassment, the city's environmental agencies always cooperated with Police Plaza. They could shut down a mob-owned factory for violations, or a favorite restaurant in Little Italy because of flies, rodent droppings in the kitchen, faulty ventilation, even improper signage in the bathrooms. Then there was every policeman's best friend, the Racketeer-Influenced and Corrupt Organizations Act. The special conspiracy law was aimed directly at organized crime. The RICO Act permitted officers legally to seize a suspect's bank accounts, automobiles, speedboats, even a house or place of business, which was precisely what they were doing to St-Germain.

At the parking lot entrance, Stefanovitch and Parker stopped and shook hands. They renewed the emotional pact made a few days earlier in Stefanovitch's office. Both of them were used to long surveillance stints. This looked like it might be a beaut.

Stefanovitch avoided saying what was going through his mind: Watch your ass going home.

'Good night, Isiah,' he said. 'Tomorrow's going to be our day.'

Parker's face was well defined in the moonlight. There was something reassuring about his physical presence. 'I like working with you, Stefanovitch. I'll never forget you grabbing that motherfucker out of his limousine.'

Stefanovitch liked working with Parker so far, too. Isiah understood that this was about getting Alexandre St-Germain, snaring the Grave Dancer, no matter what happened to either of them.

The two policemen finally separated. They made their way into private compartments of darkness and mystery.

35

Sarah McGinniss and John Stefanovitch
East Sixty-sixth Street

Sarah and Sam were like an old married couple sometimes, a late-1980s version of the Odd Couple.

For a good fifteen minutes that night, the two of them discussed the alternatives for dinner. They finally decided on Ray's Famous Pizza, a bottle of apple cider, homemade tollhouse cookies, and a Spielberg movie called *Goonies*.

They didn't watch much of the movie, because they started gabbing about the trip upstate with Roger. Sam asked Sarah whether she and his dad were ever going to get together again. As gently as she could, she told Sam probably not. He seemed to accept that.

Sarah had to keep biting her tongue as she listened to Sam's stories about his two weeks with his father. Roger had given in to every whim Sam had, refusing to set any limits. He had been perfectly awful.

'He's sure a great guy,' Sarah said as she tucked Sam in around ten. She was really biting her tongue now. 'He loves you a lot, Sam.' Which was probably true. Who wouldn't love Sam?

He was so vulnerable. Sam's eyes looked so sad.

'What's the problem, Sam?'

'Dad loves me,' Sam finally began to answer. 'I love him, too. But Mom –'

'I'm right here.' Sarah leaned forward. She kissed Sam's cheek, nuzzled him affectionately.

'I love you. I missed you every single day on our trip. Promise you won't leave me, okay?'

He raised his small, fragile arms toward her, and Sarah

had to stop herself from crying. Suddenly she wished that the problems between herself and Roger could have been worked out. Sam deserved to have a father.

After Sam was finally tucked into bed, Sarah went around the apartment straightening up. If it hadn't been for her housekeeper, Annie Leigh, the apartment wouldn't have been much different from a crash pad shared by a couple of bachelors.

More often than she liked to admit, Sarah slept collapsed on the down comforter on her bed, in her clothes. She also played a lot of Spite and Malice with Sam, and occasionally solitaire, with the TV turned on. Late at night, she practiced an old Fender guitar in her room, playing Ry Cooder and Muddy Waters songs at two in the morning. She'd learned the blues in Washington Square in Stockton.

Sarah liked Stefanovitch a lot, and that was something she wouldn't have thought possible a few weeks before.

She had questions, lots of questions, but she was intrigued. So much so that when he'd called from Police Plaza and asked if he could come over for a while, she said yes, even though she was exhausted. Now she couldn't wait for him to arrive.

Sarah couldn't make up her mind about Stefanovitch, but she knew one thing: she liked being with him more than she'd enjoyed being with anybody for a long time. He kept surprising her, revealing new layers of himself.

Stefanovitch knew about things that were fresh and interesting to her. He talked about his police job sometimes, but also about her job; about politics in the world; even unlikely subjects like his cooking theories, child psychology, modern art. He read more than she did; he enjoyed classical music, jazz, and rock. He was familiar with fashion designers, even the names of the top New York and Paris models. He told her that a lot of cops were pretty well read, and had varied interests. They just happened to be cops.

Most important, John Stefanovitch thought that she was beautiful, inside and out – and she needed to be told that very much right now. Sarah needed to believe it about herself again.

When they had kissed at her beach house, Sarah had actually experienced some light-headedness. She hadn't felt that way in years; and she found that she'd missed it a lot, more than she had known.

The elevator eased to a stop and the polished oak door slid open noisily. Sarah smiled when she saw Stefanovitch. This was like a date. How many people their age were dating nowadays? A lot, she suddenly realized.

He had obviously spiffed up after work. His thick brown hair was combed; his faded blue work shirt looked pressed. He would always seem a little Pennsylvania-barnyard, but there was also a subtle polish to him, something that went beyond Minersville, a dash of Manhattan cynicism. And he definitely was handsome, even in the Chair.

'Hello there, Stef.' She suddenly felt shy, the way she did whenever she overthought a social situation. 'How'd it go?'

'Well, it was a long day, but a pretty good start.' He immediately retreated into talk about work.

So did she. 'How was Isiah Parker? How was he to be with?' she asked. It was partly a nervous question, but she did want to know.

'A lot better than you and I on our first day.' Stefanovitch smiled. 'I like him. He wants St-Germain. His brother was a lot of his life. There's something else, though, something Parker's not willing to tell me yet.'

It had suddenly occurred to Sarah that they were holding this conversation in the hallway, where they were easy prey to eavesdroppers.

'Should we go inside?'

'It's a nice hallway and all, but I guess we should move inside. Sam Snead, winner of three Masters and three PGAs. Is he still up and around?'

'He went off about an hour ago. Will you have a drink with me? I have some wine.'

He liked the way she looked in jeans, bare feet, and a faded Western print shirt. 'If I have that drink, I think I'll turn into a vegetable.'

'That's okay. I'll feed you something if you like.'

Sarah made cheese and herb omelets, and she opened a bottle of Château Margaux. It was quiet in the kitchen, where they sat; nicely peaceful after the long, frantic day.

While the eggs were cooking, Stefanovitch finished the last of the tollhouse cookies.

'I've gone past the point where sleep is possible. You know that feeling?' he said after he'd polished off his omelet and half the bottle of wine.

'I know the feeling right now. Another omelet? More wine? Cookies?'

'Please.'

'Really?' Sarah's eyes widened. The light from the lamp overhead played through her hair.

He nodded and grinned. He was feeling almost human again. There was something so luxurious about the cheese omelet and wine at midnight. He hadn't eaten like this for a long, long time. Part of his life was getting so good, so much better, that it frightened him.

After the second helping, he sat at the table with a satisfied smile spread across his face.

'Beautiful, talented, and she can cook like a whiz. What's the catch? What's wrong with her?'

Sarah sighed, her brow puzzling slightly. 'She's divorced. Has a small child who needs lots of love and attention.'

'What else? Nobody would ever object to Sam. Nobody worth too much, anyway.'

'She can be a workaholic sometimes, which might make her seem too self-centered to some people.'

'There's more than that, isn't there?'

'Probably. I think so. Oh, I don't know. Stefanovitch, do you want to go to bed with her tonight?' Sarah said, and suddenly she could barely breathe. It was out now. No turning back.

A look of concern drifted over his face, a definite mood shift.

'Do you think that's a good idea right now?'

'I have no idea. It's what I'd like to do, though.'

As if in a dream, the two of them left the kitchen and proceeded to the bedroom. The world seemed a little fuzzed at the edges. Moonlight was streaming through the picture windows. They began to undress, both of them feeling a little strange, suddenly quiet and private.

As her fingers clumsily unbuttoned and loosened clasps, she kept thinking, I want to make love to him. A warm and pleasant sensation was spreading through her now, almost a glow. She wanted him very much. She had for a long time.

Sarah came to him. They kissed, and it was as sweet as the kiss at the beach. Yes, there is definitely something here, Sarah thought.

'Is this going to be all right for you?' she said against his cheek. She didn't know how to ask certain awkward questions. She didn't want to rush or pressure Stef in any way. She wanted this to be right for both of them.

'Yes, it's good for me. After I got hurt, I thought there might not be any feeling. There is, though. I mean, you know what I mean. I can do something about what I'm feeling.'

Sarah understood better after the first few minutes in bed. For one thing, he had the gentlest touch she could imagine. Using his fingertips, he stroked her back and shoulders, then her face and neck, then lower on her body.

She wondered if he had always been so tender. He wasn't what she had expected at all.

He was completely aware of her body; very sensitive and warm.

As they became comfortable, the inhibitions began to go away, layer upon layer, like taking off bulky winter clothes.

Sarah straddled Stefanovitch. Admiringly, she noticed that he had the body of a twenty-five-year-old: firm and hard, especially his stomach, but also his arms and shoulders. He was powerful, but so careful in the way he touched her.

Sarah kissed his chest, loving his smell, which was fresh and clean.

His fingers lightly kneaded her back and neck. He was relaxing her, inch by inch, her body starting to melt.

'Where did you learn to be so nice in bed? So sweet?' she whispered.

'Backseats of old cars out in Minersville. The Middleview Drive-In Theater. South Junior High parking lot.'

'No, Stef. Uh-uh.' She kissed him again.

'I was in love once. Remember?'

She placed a finger over his lips. 'I love the way you feel. The way you touch me,' she whispered in the darkness.

'Everything is going to be fine. We don't have anything to be afraid of,' he said.

'I was petrified on the way to the bedroom.'

'So was I, Sarah.' Stefanovitch smiled. He also blushed in the darkness, and was glad that she couldn't see.

'I'm not anymore. I'm not afraid.'

'I'm not either. Oh, maybe a little bit.'

'Make love to me, Stef. I love the way you touch me. I really do love it.'

36

John Stefanovitch
New York Harbor

The harassment continued the following morning.

It was the only way to get to St-Germain.

A forty-foot launch transported nearly a dozen officers from US Customs and the Drug Enforcement Agency, as well as Stefanovitch, out to a freighter called the *Osprey*. The Turkish ship was anchored just inside New York Harbor, near the Ambrose Light.

Captain Mohammed Rowzi silently cursed the fates as he examined a five-page document stamped with the official seal of the Customs Service, Department of the Treasury. A filterless cigarette that was half ash hung from his bloated, white-scabbed lips. Gulls circled and shrieked overhead.

Captain Rowzi's command of the English language was poor, but he recognized enough words to understand that he and his ship were in serious trouble with the New York City police.

In particular, Captain Mohammed Rowzi knew that he was in big trouble with the unsmiling police lieutenant seated in the wheelchair before him on his ship's deck.

'What is meaning this paper?' Captain Rowzi folded both arms across his broad chest, the papers flapping against the wind. He was trying to appear completely mystified as he talked to the police officials.

'This is just your basic court order,' Stefanovitch said in an innocent voice. 'It means the Customs Service has received information deemed reliable, passed on by the police department or another law enforcement agency. Your ship is suspected of carrying contraband, specifically narcotics. Drug Enforcement and Customs now have the power to search the ship. They also have the legal power to seize any narcotics and other contraband they find.

'They have the power to destroy your ship's cargo on the spot, actually. This is Inspector McManus. The search is at his discretion now. His call. Maybe he can tell you more.'

Stefanovitch glanced over at a US Customs officer, Barry McManus, with whom he'd worked several times before. The most amazing thing about this charade was that it was perfectly legal, even commendable.

Captain Rowzi glared into Stefanovitch's eyes. 'Paper means nothing!' he said, and started to turn away.

'Glad you think so.' Stefanovitch shrugged. 'I just hope the people who own all the cargo on board feel the same way. Inspector McManus, you can search the boat now.'

A half-dozen New York Customs inspectors immediately, and rather joyfully, went to work. They began their search by ripping apart several wooden crates filled with Turkish cigarettes, pottery, and phony Oriental rugs.

Next, the inspectors carefully went through the ship's books, checking the bill of lading line by line against the ship's actual contents. The inspectors found the usual discrepancies, but they made much of them. The search was as noisy as a New Year's Eve party in Peking.

Five hours later, John Stefanovitch, Inspector Barry McManus, and a very unhappy-looking Captain Rowzi were back together again in the captain's small, untidy quarters.

Outside the open door, a uniformed policeman stood with a riot shotgun poised across his chest. The freighter captain was already under arrest. Several million dollars' worth of uncut heroin was being guarded on one of the police launches off the bow.

'I know nothing of drugs. Someone puts drugs on my ship,' Captain Rowzi solemnly, but nervously and unconvincingly, protested. 'I am ship captain seventeen years.'

Barry McManus shook his head. He revealed a trace of sympathetic regret, but mostly bureaucratic indifference. His stiff stare was enough to bring strong men to tears. It had done just that more than once in McManus's career.

'We want to talk to the owners of the cargo on board.' Stefanovitch repeated his bargaining appeal to the freighter captain. 'I think I've been consistent on that point.'

The Turkish captain wearily shook his head. His khaki shirt was black with sweat stains that ran nearly to his belt. The cramped bunk room smelled like a horse stable.

'I told you name. Star of Panama Company,' he said again, emphasizing syllables with spit. 'Star of Panama Company.'

'Yeah. The Star of Panama Company owns the ship. But not the cargo. Not the heroin, Captain Rowzi. We already went through all this crap. It's on the bill of lading.'

'Captain Rowzi,' Inspector McManus broke in. 'Captain, we legally searched your vessel, and we found uncut heroin. We also found perfectly legal pottery, cigarettes, machine-made rugs, specie. All that cargo is in jeopardy now. All of it. Do you understand what I'm saying?'

The round, bullish shoulders of the ship's captain sagged further. His neck had almost disappeared.

'Know nothing of drugs,' he repeated.

Stefanovitch looked at the Customs inspector first, then at Captain Rowzi again. 'Tell him, Inspector. I think he deserves to know. The owners ought to know, too. The owners of the cargo.'

'In accordance with provisions of the RICO Act,' McManus said to the freighter captain, 'I've ordered my officers to destroy your vessel's shipment of goods. Everything on board. All of the cargo. Everything you've brought to New York.'

Captain Rowzi couldn't believe what he had just heard. Were these policemen insane? Entire ship cargoes were never destroyed. His eyes nearly fell out of his face. Such dangerous, unbelievable English words were being spoken: heroin . . . destroy . . . cargo.

'No! What I tell owners?'

Stefanovitch leaned forward in his chair. The stench of garlic and sweat coming from Rowzi was overwhelming in such close quarters.

'You can tell Mr St-Germain and his friends that under federal law there will be no restitution for any of their losses. Tell them that this is all legal. It's the fucking law . . . Our law. And this is just a *start*.'

Stefanovitch started to leave the captain's quarters, but he paused and turned back.

'And tell him that Lieutenant Stefanovitch said hello. We're old friends. Old, old friends, Mr St-Germain and myself.'

At eight-thirty that night, Stefanovitch pushed himself between crowded dining tables inside the Lotos Club on East Sixty-sixth. The Lotos Club had originally been opened as a gathering place for people in the literary arts. Nowadays it was a favored locale for business meetings, lectures, and lavish parties for executives.

That evening, the main-floor dining room was filled with men and women gathered for one of the hundreds of honorariums that plague New York every night of the year.

Up on the dark wood podium, Alexandre St-Germain was addressing the room. He saluted the honoree, but also multinational business in general, a subject he was well versed in.

Stefanovitch temporarily parked his wheelchair beside one of the tables. He listened to the Grave Dancer talk.

He also watched – both St-Germain and the other so-called business leaders. He wondered how many of them were legitimate in their multinational business dealings. Were any of them in the Midnight Club? They all looked so above it all; so beyond reproach; so perfect in every way.

Finally, Stefanovitch began to push himself forward again. He tried to clear his mind, refusing to second-guess himself about what he was doing here tonight.

He was flashing painful scenes from Long Beach on the night of the ambush. He was remembering things about Anna; how she had died that night in March.

When he got close to the speaker's rostrum, Stefanovitch raised his voice above the din in the room.

'*St-Germain!*' he called. 'I have a warrant for you to appear before the grand jury. It's in connection with violations of the Continuing Criminal Enterprise Law. I'm serving you here, with all these very reliable witnesses present.'

Conversation around the room ceased immediately. The waiters stopped serving dinner. Silverware froze halfway to open mouths. St-Germain's face was a dark red mask of embarrassment.

Stefanovitch stared at the drug dealer and murderer for a long moment. No one in the dining room looked as if they could possibly belong to the Midnight Club. But nothing was as it seemed anymore.

Stefanovitch finally pushed himself out of the Lotos Club dining room. He was getting to Alexandre St-Germain. He was sure of it.

Stefanovitch went home after the Lotos Club. He felt better than he had at any other time during the St-Germain investigation. All his instincts told him that they were doing this right. Just right so far.

He took a hot shower, dried off, and popped open a bottle of beer. He called Sarah, and told her about the scene at the Lotos Club. He wanted to talk about everything with her, but he knew enough not to try. He was too worn, absolutely fried, unfit for anybody's company tonight.

Finally, Stefanovitch dropped off to sleep on his couch, half watching a movie. The late-night feature was *Chinatown*,

Jack Nicholson at his most brilliant and mesmerizing as J. J. Gittes.

Sometime later the phone rang – a jangling up somewhere near the head of the sofa. Stef woke in a disoriented blur.

The room was a cubist puzzle. The picture window was on the wrong side of the bed. All the lights were still on, throwing glaring reflections from the windows back into the room. He finally realized that he was on the couch in the living room, not in his bedroom.

He reached for the phone, nearly pulling it off the stand in the process. He knew it could only be Sarah.

'Hello, this is Stef.' He imitated a phone-answering machine. 'When you hear the beep, tell me last night wasn't a dream. What time is it? Oh yeah, hi.'

There was a strange silence on the other end of the line.

It felt like the physical reality of being somewhere in pitch-blackness. Like falling into a deep tunnel, or drifting into the unfathomable mysteries of death.

A voice finally filtered through the receiver's tiny black holes. Stefanovitch's pulse quickened as he listened.

'I wanted you to know one thing, Stefanovitch. I shot her myself. I took the job personally.

'I stood in the hallway of your pathetic little apartment building in Brooklyn Heights. When the front door opened, I fired the shotgun. You can imagine the rest, I'm sure. You get the picture. Good night for now.'

37

John Stefanovitch and Isiah Parker
Central Park West

I wanted you to know one thing . . .
  I shot her myself . . .
  You can imagine the rest . . .

The unnerving explosions inside Stefanovitch's head hadn't stopped since the phone call.

At six-thirty in the morning, he was on East Forty-third Street waiting for the Sports Center to open. He'd been up since four.

For once, Beth Kelley was sympathetic during the workout. She pushed him, but didn't try to break him. Something about the wounded look on Stef's face had quieted her down.

By eight o'clock, Stefanovitch and Isiah Parker were back on Central Park West, waiting for Alexandre St-Germain to come out to his limousine again, for the chase to resume, the real chase. Maybe the final one.

The Grave Dancer had gotten to Stefanovitch with the phone call.

He hadn't been able to sleep after the call. He lay awake remembering the months of pain, the suffering after Anna's murder and the shooting at Long Beach.

I wanted you to know one thing . . . I shot her myself.

He had waited more than two years; now he needed justice, some form of revenge for everything that had happened.

When he had been growing up, there was a lesson a priest in Minersville had taught. It mirrored his current frustration. In order to explain the concept of infinity to children, the priest would ask his classes to think back to the very beginning of infinity. The process always created a tremendous ache in Stefanovitch's head. Obviously there could be no beginning. No matter how far he went back, billions and billions of years, he could never reach the starting point of infinity.

Stefanovitch felt that same overpowering frustration now. Alexandre St-Germain's freedom and arrogance mocked him. The Grave Dancer had placed himself above the law, outside of every moral and ethical system.

When the front door opened, I fired the shotgun.

You can imagine the rest, I'm sure.

'He's kind of late getting going this morning. Must be having his Cocoa Puffs.' Isiah Parker finally spoke up inside the surveillance car.

Stefanovitch had told him about the phone call from St-Germain, and Isiah knew it had shaken him. Lately, he, too, had had nothing but sleepless nights. Two, three hours at the most. He was completely committed to the case they were building against Alexandre St-Germain. He thought of it as his own personal survival kit.

'Why do you think he called me?' Stefanovitch asked. 'Why now? What the hell is going on?'

'Maybe the pressure's getting to him. You embarrassed the shit out of him yesterday. Before that, you treated him like some cheap punk in front of his apartment. He's arrogant. I could see that the first time I looked into his eyes.'

'No, there's something else. Something about that phone call.'

'I don't think so. Only that he's still in control.'

'Maybe he's taking control again,' Stefanovitch said. His eyes were trained thirty yards down the street. On the Grave Dancer's car.

The blue limousine continued to wait in front of the apartment building. The motor running, smoke curling lazily from the exhaust. Taxis, other private cars arriving for pickups had to park in front of or behind the almighty limousine.

Eight-thirty became nine on Stefanovitch's watch, a gift from his father when he'd left Minersville. The old Bulova still kept time. It also kept his fashion image right about where he wanted it on this particular morning – early racetrack.

Something was happening right now. His cop's instincts told him that as he and Parker sat watching Alexandre St-Germain's building, another complex universe was operating, completely separate from theirs. St-Germain's sordid universe; the Midnight Club's universe.

'This is getting a little too familiar,' he finally said. 'The stakeout routine. Maybe that's what's bothering me. I've got ten past nine. He's never this late. The limousine's just sitting there. What do you want to do?'

Isiah Parker pushed open the car door and stepped out onto Central Park West. Traffic noise rushed inside the car. 'I'll go this time. Bet I get that asshole chauffeur to roll down the window in the limousine.'

'I'll bet you do, too.'

Isiah Parker walked up Central Park West toward the waiting stretch limousine. His long stride ate up the sidewalk distance quickly. His dark glasses seemed to ward off glances from the other people on the street.

When he reached the limo, he knocked hard on the driver's door. The window was mirrored. Parker could see himself, and the cars sliding past on the street. Finally, the glass eased down.

Isiah Parker smiled as he leaned in toward the driver. It was a typical New-York-cop-versus-New-Jersey-wise-guy confrontation, the kind that happened every day on the street. The driver wore a shiny black monkey suit. His smile was typically smug, behind dark Ray-Ban sunglasses.

'Where's the Grave Dancer, my good man? Your boss is going to be late for work today,' Parker said.

The driver shrugged and he issued a coarse grunt. The

gesture signified a what's-it-to-you kind of attitude that Isiah Parker just loved.

'Mr St-Germain's already gone to work. He left a message for you, though. He says for you two traffic cops to go ahead, give me the morning's traffic ticket. He told me to tear it up in your faces. He says you have your laws, he has his. He said to tell you, and your buddy the cripple, that the game's just beginning. It's just the beginning, Dick Tracy.'

Moments later, an emergency call came over the police radio in Parker and Stefanovitch's car. Something had happened. The Grave Dancer had gone to work all right.

38

Alexandre St-Germain
New York

Alexandre St-Germain rode through the city in grave silence that morning. He was pondering recent actions he had undertaken: a temporary end to respectability; a clear defiance of the Club's new rules and its stated desire for invisibility.

Stefanovitch had been tracking him for too long. Somehow the detective had escaped death once; he'd wound up in a wheelchair. The stubborn policeman kept coming anyway.

He had publicly insulted and goaded St-Germain. He was responsible for a freighterload of heroin's being confiscated; for the intolerable RICO harassments; for other serious embarrassments during the past weeks.

St-Germain had encountered diligent policemen before. Sometimes they were driven by some mysterious need for revenge; sometimes by the strictest morality. But in Stefanovitch's case, it seemed even more than that.

St-Germain had asked Jimmy Burke to investigate the Homicide lieutenant. Burke had copied records from Police Plaza. The files mechanically reported on Stefanovitch's past and present. He had been a navy officer, decorated twice in the Middle East. He had entered the NYPD in 'seventy-six, and quickly established himself as a fast-track performer. He was tireless; he appeared to be honest; he was liked and respected by the powers at the top. Even confined to a wheelchair, he was viewed as a key performer in the police department. Stefanovitch was still a rising star.

Two things were clear from the file: Stefanovitch was bright for a policeman; and Stefanovitch was relentless in his duty. In a way, he was a very old-fashioned police officer, almost an anachronism. He seemed to have an obsessive preoccupation with right and wrong; he had a moral code and work ethic left over from another era.

There was really no choice for St-Germain.

The street law had to resume.

39

Sarah and Sam McGinniss
East Sixty-sixth Street

There was still a small island of serenity for Sarah; a thread of sanity remaining in her life.

Sam stood underneath the formal forest green canopy of their apartment building, talking to his best friend, Austin, another seven-year-old from the neighborhood. Sarah was posted off to one side. They were early for school, which was just around the corner on Park Avenue.

It was a nice way to spend a few extra minutes – Sam yakking about baseball and transformers to Austin; Sarah renewing some casual, New-York-apartment-style relationships with the other tenants. Watching Sam, Sarah felt as if the life she'd been leading lately was completely unreal.

'I think we'd better scoot,' she finally called over to Sam.

He said good-bye to his friend, suggesting they have a hard ball catch out in the back alley after school. The superintendent usually let them play there – unless he was working on the water pipes, which he seemed to paint or scrape down every other week.

Sarah and Sam headed east on Sixty-sixth Street, toward Park. She watched Sam out of the corner of her eye.

He was like a curious little bird sometimes, idly pecking around the home nest. He knew nearly every square inch of the block, in fact. He would comment on the appearance of a new neighborhood face, or somebody's pet, even on the blossoms of the dogwood trees fenced along the sidewalk.

This morning, he was a little quiet, and Sarah thought she knew why. She was spending too much time on the investigation and on her book. Sam wouldn't come out and say it, but he was feeling neglected.

'Are you okay? Tell your old mom the truth,' she finally said about midway down the block.

'I'm okay. I'm fine.'

Sarah draped her arm over Sam's shoulder.

'Hey, guess what? I don't believe you. You lie, small white man.'

Sam began to laugh. She could usually make him smile.

Sarah figured that maybe if she joked a little with him, Sam might come out of his funk.

'Hey. Have I told you how happy I am that you're back? I can't remember. Did I tell you that, Sam?'

Sam laughed again. 'Only about a hundred times, Mom.'

'How many out of the hundred did you believe me? About one?'

Sam continued to smile at her joke. That was one of their things together: they could laugh about almost anything.

'How about if we go out to the beach on Saturday? I promise not to work. I'll make Belgian waffles with fresh strawberries. Then some swimming. Wiffle ball, of course. Chinese fighter kite flying. Couple of our favorite movies on the VCR. And that's just the morning.'

Sam took Sarah's hand as they walked.

'What about Stef? Will he come with us to the beach?'

Sarah hadn't expected the question, though she wasn't completely surprised. 'Do you want Stef to come?' she asked.

'Yeah, he's funny. We're friends.'

'Well, that's good. I'd like him to come, too.'

Still holding hands, Sarah and Sam turned the corner onto Park Avenue. Traffic on Park was the usual bumper-to-bumper variety, for the morning rush to glory.

The sidewalk was hopelessly crowded and seemed almost frantic. Men in light-color summer suits; determined-looking women in expensive business suits and dresses, half of them wearing running shoes.

One man in a lightweight tan suit looked particularly lost and perplexed at the corner of Sixty-sixth. New York could be a Twilight Zone horror story for its visitors. He turned to Sarah as she and Sam passed.

'Third Avenue? . . . Excuse me, do you know which way that is? I got turned around, I guess.'

Sarah began to point east across Park Avenue when she was struck by the flat of the man's hand.

The unexpected blow against her chest was paralyzing. She was knocked to the ground, flat on her back.

Sarah suddenly had no air in her lungs. She couldn't get her breath, couldn't call out for help. A terrible pain shot up her spine.

The man in the tan suit lifted Sam off the sidewalk . . . *It was as if he were hugging Sam.*

The boy didn't know what to do to get away from the stranger. He tried to fight, but he didn't have the strength to break the man's grip.

'Upsy-daisy now.'

The man said it loudly enough to be heard by the other pedestrians.

'Here we go, big fella, in the car with your dad. Off we go. We're off to the races.'

The man was laughing. He was playfully tickling Sam . . . *so that Sam couldn't cry out.* The man had a German accent. Who was he? What was happening?

Sarah still couldn't get her breath. She couldn't scream for help. Oh God, no more . . .

It *looked* as if Sam were squirming because he was being tickled by the man . . . the man who was *playing* at being his father.

Sarah gasped out loud. She still couldn't scream, couldn't get her voice back.

She had never felt so powerless, except in dreams, terrifying nightmares about losing Sam.

Sam was being lifted into a waiting black sedan. That was all she could distinguish from her view on the ground. Maybe it was a BMW? An Audi? She couldn't tell . . . The German voice? The accent?

The car slowly pulled away, disappearing into a cortege of heavy eastbound traffic.

Still terribly dazed, Sarah tried to push herself up from the sidewalk.

People gathered around her, trying to help, not understanding what had just happened.

Her vision was badly blurred. The close-up faces all merged into one.

Finally, Sarah screamed out loud on Park Avenue. Unbelievable words came from her mouth in the middle of all the people heading for work.

'Please help me! Somebody please help! They took my little boy!'

John Stefanovitch
East Sixty-sixth Street

Sarah waited in her apartment for the police, but she was waiting mostly for Stefanovitch. She couldn't stop herself from sobbing.

For the hundredth time, she went to the picture windows in the living room and gazed in futility onto Sixty-sixth Street. She was numb, and numbness was the only thing that saved her.

She was trying to imagine that there had been some terrible mistake with Sam and the man on Park Avenue, but she knew better.

The doorbell rang. The police had arrived.

There was still no patrol car out on Sixty-sixth Street. The detective and patrolman had walked over from the local precinct house. The detective held a black leather pad and a pen in hand. He looked as if he were ready to give out a traffic ticket. It wasn't the most compassionate way to greet someone after a kidnapping.

'Your little boy is missing from school?' asked the detective. 'I'm Detective Cirelli,' he added.

'He isn't missing from school. He was kidnapped off the street. I was there. We always walk to his school together.' The words suddenly poured out from Sarah. 'A man in a beige suit took Sam in a black car. I think it was a BMW. He knocked me down.' She was crying again. She couldn't help it.

The detective stiffened. He was overweight, with a florid face. He almost looked angry at her for being in tears.

'Could it be that you let your boy walk to school by himself this morning? That's what often happens.'

Sarah was thrown even further into shock. She was used to working with intelligent policemen: she'd forgotten about the other kind. She overcame the urge to hit this man, to scream at him, to break down completely.

'No, of course not. Detective Cirelli, this is unbelievably hard for me. Why are you making it harder? I was with Sam. I was with my son when it happened.'

'All right, Mrs McGinniss. Try to relax, please. Could we have a description of your boy? It is a boy, you said?'

'Yes, he's seven years old. He weighs a little under fifty pounds. I'm not sure how tall Sam is right now. He has brown hair, not very long. His father just had his hair cut.'

'Is the boy's father here?' Detective Cirelli asked.

'No. We're divorced.'

'Could the father be responsible for taking the boy? What I mean is, were there any custody problems recently?'

The front doorbell rang again. This time it was Stef. He came inside and Sarah hugged him fiercely. Stefanovitch didn't need to hear about what had happened. He knew already. He understood completely . . . The street law.

After the detective and patrolman from the Nineteenth

Precinct left, Stefanovitch and Sarah held one another in the living room.

Finally, he swallowed hard and said, 'Everything that we can do right now is being done. That's the truth, Sarah.'

'Stef, what if we turned it all off?' She spoke the words softly, very tentatively. He sensed that she already knew the answer.

'We could try, but I don't think it would make any difference to St-Germain and his people. We broke the street law. We have to think of some other way to get Sam back. And we will, Sarah. We'll find Sam. We'll do whatever we have to do.'

Alexandre St-Germain
The Hunts Point Market

At the intersection of Randall Avenue and Halleck Street, in the Bronx, the road dead-ends at a vast two-story shed that is the New York City Terminal Market at Hunts Point.

The buildings themselves are in the shape of a fork, with four separate tines; each has approximately sixty stores. Inside are truck docks, loading platforms, display areas, and private offices for the owners. Produce and meat trucks enter the building complex at a toll plaza in the late evening, usually between eleven and one A.M. The peak of activity is between three and five A.M., with buyers driving through the market, parking and shopping at their preferred stores. As a rudimentary security system, ID is required by the city's Department of Ports and Terminals, but the ID is available to anyone.

On July 24, Alexandre St-Germain's dark blue Mercedes limousine silently moved down the tightly packed corridor of storefronts and loading docks that marked the beginning of the market. Inside the car, the Grave Dancer was as emotional as he allowed himself to become.

It was three fifty-five in the morning. The stores had already been open for hours.

The glistening limousine didn't seem out of place among the dilapidated storefronts and tractor trailers. Several wealthy store owners, and obsessive Manhattan restaurateurs, came to the marketplace in their expensive cars.

Alexandre St-Germain saw the dark brown sedan before his limousine reached the meeting place. He knew that it contained part of the hit team from Atlantic City, the European mercenaries.

As the limousine approached, the sedan's front and back doors swung open.

A few seconds later, the first of three men climbed inside the limousine. The men wore open-necked shirts but also sports jackets, and in one case, in spite of the summer heat, a light brown leather car coat.

'Hello, *signore*. *Piacere di vederla*. How are you this fine morning in New York?'

The first man spoke to Alexandre St-Germain in confident but also respectful tones. The man was Sicilian. He had a strong jutting jaw that seemed to restrict his ability to smile. His skin had a greenish brown hue. His name was Salvatore Crisci, but he was known throughout Europe as *Cacciatore*, the Hunter.

Cacciatore was a killer whom Alexandre St-Germain had used several times in Europe. He had never been inside the United States before the affair in Atlantic City. Cacciatore had no use for Americans, though he had nothing against American money.

The second man who entered the limousine was a German; his name was Franz Engelhardt. He had planned and executed more than twenty assassination-bombings throughout Europe. Years before, his preferred killing tool had been a handmade stiletto, with a nine-inch blade. In Rome he had gotten the nickname *Arrotino*, the Knife Grinder. It was Engelhardt who had abducted Sam McGinniss on Park Avenue.

The third member of the group was Jimmy Burke, the New York police detective who had met St-Germain in Vietnam.

The two Europeans and Burke were powerful-looking men. Although their faces were hardened, it was obvious that they feared Alexandre St-Germain. They avoided unnecessary contact with the unforgiving eyes. They were here to report, but also to listen.

'We've followed Stefanovitch and Parker for the past few days,' Cacciatore said in a surprisingly high-pitched voice. He appeared to be a homosexual, with a flair for the extravagant. His hair was orange-red, piled in a high pompadour. His pants were extremely tight, and he wore makeup. The conscious effort toward extremes helped to create this false impression. The impersonation served as a useful distraction in the underworld.

Cacciatore used both hands when he spoke. 'I bought a pack of cigarettes. I was standing right next to Stefanovitch in a small store on Eighty-fourth Street. I could have taken him then. You told us to wait. Parker is staying with a girlfriend. A model on the East Side.'

Alexandre St-Germain looked away, into the bustling, early morning marketplace. His anger was more in control. Actually, he felt comfortable in the workingman's environment. The smell of fruits and cheeses reminded him of his youth, of early mornings on the streets of Marseilles.

He considered the fate of Stefanovitch. Others in the Club wanted him to ignore the policeman. To be patient . . . But he couldn't wait and be patient any longer. Stefanovitch had to be dealt with. The policeman was determined, and he was resourceful. One day he might get lucky.

'Do it now. I don't care what the rest of the Midnight Club says about this. I don't care about their Harvard Club rules. *Do it now!*'

John Stefanovitch and Sarah McGinniss
East Sixty-sixth Street

Sarah and Stefanovitch had been awake during the longest and worst night of Sarah's life. She had never been more aware of the sounds in her apartment. Sarah glanced at her wristwatch and saw it was twenty past four. She would have guessed five or five-thirty. The passage of time was leaden.

A detective from the local precinct was stationed in the apartment for the night. He waited by the upstairs telephone.

The last call had been before midnight. It had been Roger, finally reaching her from California. She'd tried a dozen times to get through to him. His call was highly emotional and concerned, but it was also filled with recriminations regarding Sarah's move to New York, where 'things like this happen.'

At seven-thirty in the morning, Annie Leigh, the house-keeper, arrived. Annie was a generally helpful and loving woman from St Martin. She had been with Sarah and Sam since they'd moved to New York, almost two years ago. Annie Leigh loved Sam as if he were her own little boy. She needed to be comforted and consoled by Sarah, and Sarah almost broke down under the additional burden.

Later in the morning, Stefanovitch tried to eat something. He sat at the kitchen table, listlessly picking at bakery rolls and sipping black coffee. The telephone still hadn't rung. The kitchen, the whole apartment, felt unnaturally quiet, almost as if he had never been there before.

'It's so unreal, Stef. So bad. I can't believe this has happened. Why wasn't I more careful? I should have known this could happen.' Sarah couldn't eat.

'Stop. You couldn't have known.' Stefanovitch reached across the table and held her hand. He wanted to help her, but there didn't seem to be any way. Everything possible was being done. He had already seen to that.

'Soon we'll hear from the police about the canvassing they did in the neighborhood yesterday. There might be something to help us. Somewhere to start us at least.'

Stefanovitch had requested that the precinct canvass reports be delivered to Sarah's apartment as soon as they were tabbed. At ten o'clock, the copies finally arrived via Detective Cirelli. Included was a crime-scene sketch drawn from what Sarah remembered, plus the few details other witnesses had supplied. Detective Cirelli was his usual obliging self.

There was also a sketch of the perpetrator, as he had been described: a white male, in his middle to late thirties. Cleancut, in a beige summer business suit.

He looked like any of a thousand businessmen who walked down Park Avenue every morning. Sarah had thought that he could be German, so they were working with Immigration to check recent visitors from that country.

To pass time, Sarah and Stefanovitch read all the verbatims from pedestrians who'd been on either Park Avenue or Sixty-sixth Street at the time of the abduction. Several had noticed the man carrying 'his little boy,' and 'playing with him,' 'taking him over to their car.'

Not one of the witnesses had understood that he or she was actually watching a kidnapping. At the end of every statement were the capitalized letters NR, meaning 'negative results.'

That was all they'd gotten for the past twenty days. *Negative results* on the initial investigation of the shooting at Allure; *negative results* on the massacre at Trump Plaza in Atlantic City. Now this. Alexandre St-Germain always seemed to have the upper hand. Somehow, he was always in control.

Throughout the rest of the morning and early afternoon, the horror grew for Sarah . . .

At noon, Sam would have come home from school ... By twelve-fifteen, he and Sarah would be eating a lunch she prepared when she broke from her writing, but today there was no Sam. The silence, the emptiness in the apartment were palpable and unbearable.

Sarah finally wandered back to Sam's bedroom. Stefanovitch went with her. She understood it was the worst thing to do. She began to sob once again, folding her arms over her eyes. She'd never been so completely out of control, or felt so empty.

Goose bumps swelled over her arms and legs. Sam's belongings, his ball glove, a taped hockey stick, his neatly folded clothes, were all around the cheery room. A favorite childhood book, *Harold and the Purple Crayon*, was propped on the windowsill. His things seemed to be accusing her. She had never thought of herself as the hysterical type, but she'd never lost her son before either.

'We'll get Sam back,' Stefanovitch whispered. But he wasn't sure anymore.

He was finally beginning to completely understand Alexandre St-Germain. He understood that as intelligent as he'd thought St-Germain was, he had seriously underestimated him. St-Germain was thorough. He would do anything to win – commit any crime, order any murder, any unthinkable act. That was the pattern, in fact: unthinkable acts. Obscenity on obscenity. The Grave Dancer was a psychopathic killer. He had no concept of right or wrong; no conscience; no morals; and there was no legal way to stop him.

Alexandre St-Germain had beaten them again and again.

The Grave Dancer had won everything that was worth winning. Men like him completely controlled the world now. The crumb-bums.

40

Isiah Parker
East Seventy-fourth Street

Isiah Parker had the sense that he'd been followed for the past few days. He hadn't actually seen any of the trackers, but he'd felt their presence several times.

Late that night, he wandered around his old neighborhood in Harlem. Starting at 119th Street, he headed west across Morningside Park, which was alive with crack and other secretive drug deals. Teenage dealers were now using electronic pagers to signal one another. A dozen crack houses lined a single block.

He continued down Broadway toward Ninety-sixth, into the so-called gentrified neighborhoods, what the young whites were beginning to call Sohar, which stood for 'southern Harlem.'

Occasionally, people waved to Parker as he passed. He was known to be a cop, but he and his brother, Marcus, had been part of the neighborhood for so long, even that didn't matter.

Isiah Parker smiled at some of the familiar neighborhood faces. For others, he was cool and expressionless. He knew how to play the hometown crowds. He and Marcus had always known how to play the Harlem street audience.

He had a flat, cold feeling inside, brought on by the realization that he couldn't hide like this for much longer. A numbness edged into his body. He would have welcomed the rage that had driven him for the last several months but the knifing anger wouldn't come. He had to get it back – one more time at least.

All the best plans – the constant surveillance cars, the

other forms of harassment – were just more police games to Alexandre St-Germain. St-Germain had seen the eye of combat before. He had survived gang wars in Rome, Paris, Amsterdam, and Macao. He was always protected; a step, several steps ahead of everyone else, including the police.

Isiah Parker ducked inside a neighborhood coffee shop on 106th Street, across a wide stretch of Broadway from the Olympia Theatre. He sat at the counter with a brimming cup of bitter black coffee, and a stale sugar doughnut. He watched the street, but saw nothing to alarm him.

The coffee shops are all going to the Orientals lately, he thought. New York considered the Chinese and Koreans 'good little workers,' but they made shit coffee. There wasn't much left for black people.

Neither of the two young Korean counter boys said boo to him. They probably looked down on black people, too. Parker left them a tip anyway, and he went back out on the street.

Something was bound to happen soon. Something was definitely going down. It had begun with the kidnapping of Sarah McGinniss's son. Also, the late-night phone call to Stefanovitch. Thinking about the incidents, he had an image of somebody walking up and shooting him in the back. It almost seemed inevitable now.

He didn't want to take any chances that someone might be following. He played subway games from 103rd Street down to West Seventy-second and Broadway.

He was the last one on a crowded, buzzing subway car. Then he would suddenly jump off at a stop. He'd get back on just before the electric doors closed.

He was finally pretty sure he wasn't being followed. At the corner of Seventy-second Street and Broadway, he took a Checker cab crosstown, to the East Side.

He made the cab stop inside Central Park. He got out and walked the rest of the way.

Nobody was following. Or they were so brilliant, so good at this, that it didn't much matter.

At eleven-thirty, he rang a tarnished gold doorbell inside the dreary, semidarkened foyer of an East Side brownstone. Parker rang the bell a second time. There was no working intercom in the grim foyer, just the rusted shell of one.

By midnight, Parker was in bed with a model named Tanya Richardson.

Tanya was a girl he'd been seeing on and off for the past few months. He felt safe in the East Side apartment. Almost no one knew about him and Tanya. The few who did, Parker knew he could trust . . .

At one-thirty in the morning, Parker lay awake in bed thinking about everything that still had to be done to get at St-Germain. He was feeling paranoid and jumpy in spite of the late hour. Finally, he decided to take a walk. One last check around. Then maybe he could sleep.

As quietly as he could, he rose from the bed. It was a Byzantine, frilly affair with pipes and sideboards painted white and gold. Springs creaked, but Tanya didn't stir. He kissed her long neck, her flowing brown hair. Then he left.

Outside the apartment, harsh streetlights were glinting off all kinds of surfaces, shining up brightly into his eyes. The glare temporarily blinded him.

He started to walk down Second Avenue, the old favorite singles scene, the great White Way, still crowded this late at night.

Parker rounded the corner onto Seventy-fourth Street. He continued only a few steps.

Crouching slightly, he stared through the windows of cars parked up and down the side street. His eyes were still adjusting to the lights.

Finally, he saw what he had been looking for, but hoping not to find. Noisy alarms sounded through his body.

Two men were sitting in Goodfellow's, a popular restaurant and bar on Second Avenue. Parker watched them for at least sixty seconds, just to make sure.

He was sure. He'd noticed the one with red hair earlier that day. They were following him.

They hadn't seen him approach on Second Avenue. They were too busy watching the brownstone where he and his girlfriend were supposed to be sleeping. They were clearly watching the brownstone. The Grave Dancer had his trackers, too.

Isiah Parker crossed Seventy-fourth Street. He walked among a few couples, out for a night of grazing in the neighborhood bars and restaurants. Except he was moving faster than the others.

He ducked inside Goodfellow's, his gold detective's shield out and ready.

He said, 'I'm a police officer. You stay right here, all right? Don't let anybody else in. *Capisce?*' He spoke quietly but firmly to the blond Irish bouncer-maître d' stationed at the front door.

'Yeah, yeah. All right, man. Sure.'

He could make out the heads and shoulders of the two hit men. They were positioned at the rear of the tinted Plexiglas bubble attached to one side of the bar, nearest to Tanya's apartment. The trackers.

Both men wore dark, European-style sports jackets. Parker was sure they carried concealed weapons underneath.

The heavyset bouncer at the door hadn't moved. He was obviously smarter than he looked. Patrons of the East Side restaurant were crouched over their greasy burgers, their shell steaks, and wilting house salads. An air conditioner dribbled water onto the red tile floor.

As he peered around a white stucco pillar, Parker bent down suddenly. He took a .22 revolver out of a holster strapped tightly to his right leg.

Right then, the killer called the Hunter saw him.

The gunman's right hand disappeared into his jacket. He was fast and smooth for such a large man. The very affected orange-red pompadour made most policemen underestimate his fighting skills.

The other hit man seemed to work in slow motion by comparison. He was moving, though, going for the kill out of synch with his partner.

Isiah Parker fired at Cacciatore first.

Cacciatore was hit and he crashed back through the restaurant window. His expensive black boots were suddenly up on the dining table. His body hung out through shattered glass onto Seventy-fourth Street. He was like a diver frozen in midair.

Parker's gun flashed again.

The second assassin suddenly dropped his weapon, which clattered loudly. Then he fell awkwardly to the tile floor.

Parker had been grazed by the gunman's first shot. His left cheek was burning. Customers in the restaurant were screaming, trying to get out onto Second Avenue, away from the sudden explosions of gunfire.

'I'm a police officer,' Parker said to anyone within hearing distance. 'It's all over! Everything's all right. Everything's all right now.'

It wasn't all right, though, Isiah Parker knew.

Alexandre St-Germain was coming after them. For some reason, he had waited – but now he was coming hard.

41

John Stefanovitch and Sarah McGinniss
East Sixty-sixth Street

'Good evening, Mrs McGinniss. Evening to you, sir.'

'Hello, Mr Sullivan,' Sarah said to the doorman posted inside the foyer of her building. Mr Sullivan had once told Sarah he'd worked at the building for more than fifty-five years. He considered the tenants to be his immediate family, though some were more family than others.

'Excuse me for asking, but is there word? Might there be anything about Sam that you can tell us?'

The obvious concern in the elderly doorman's voice brought back so many painful images for Sarah. How many times had she and Sam stopped to talk with Mr Sullivan before heading up to their apartment on evenings just like this?

Partly because Sam's father didn't live in the building, and partly because Sam was so outgoing and friendly, the doormen had adopted him as their own. They had adopted Sarah as well. It was a prototypical New York family situation.

'No, there's nothing yet,' Sarah said. 'As soon as there's anything, I'll tell you first thing, Mr Sullivan.'

The ancient doorman revealed the most gloriously white set of teeth, complementing his full head of white hair. 'Well, you folks try to have a peaceful evening, under the circumstances. I'll say a prayer tonight.'

'Nice old man,' Stefanovitch found himself whispering as they continued through the marble front hall toward the elevator bank. He wanted to keep Sarah's mind off Sam, if he possibly could. She needed sleep, or soon she wouldn't be any good to anyone. For the first time since he had known her, she looked terrible. All the pain and exhaustion showed on her face.

'My neighborhood up in Yorkville is filled with doormen who work in midtown,' he said. 'Families pass these jobs down from generation to generation. Manhattan doorman jobs have been known to appear in wills.'

Sarah finally had to smile. 'You love any kind of street gossip, don't you? You're a closet sociologist, you know.'

'Park Avenue is a street, too,' Stefanovitch said and winked at her. 'I'm getting into this Park Avenue life-style a little. I'd love to hear the real dirt from this street.'

Up on Sarah's floor, they stopped to kiss in the deserted hallway. Sarah tenderly held his face in both her hands. Maybe she was fooling herself, but some of the sadness seemed to have left his eyes.

There was something about those brown eyes, windows to the real John Stefanovitch . . .

It struck her, suddenly, how sad it would be if they never got to find out any more about one another. If their story had to end right at its beginning.

That was a possibility, wasn't it? They had broken the street law. They had gone after Alexandre St-Germain and the Midnight Club.

Stefanovitch sensed that he was blushing as they held one another in the hallway. He felt vulnerable lately, completely at Sarah's mercy.

Finally, they pulled apart. Sarah clumsily tried to find the house key, groping inside her purse.

'You're the writer. Say something clever to break the silence,' Stefanovitch said.

'I can't find my damn key.'

The two of them laughed as they entered her apartment. The laughter was a relief, because it came so infrequently lately. The heavy wooden door slammed shut behind them.

Locks clicked tightly into place.

* * *

The digital clock radio inside Sarah's bedroom went out at three-seventeen in the morning.

The almost imperceptible electric hum inside the apartment suddenly stopped. The buzz from the refrigerator and the illuminated face of an old 'Pepsi Cola Hits the Spot' wall clock in the kitchen disappeared.

Sarah stirred slightly. She rolled toward Stefanovitch, but she didn't wake up.

The building's electricity had gone off.

Downstairs in the lobby, the night doormen cursed the building's prehistoric wiring. Their usual night of card games, paperback book reading, and paid catnaps was going to be ruined.

The fire exit stairway leading to all floors, the roof, and the basement was illuminated in a widening arc from a powerful flash lamp. The fifth-floor hallway eventually appeared in the jouncing lamp's bright light. Then the imposing dark wood door to Sarah McGinniss's apartment was revealed in the narrowing cone of light.

Low rumbling voices could be heard in the hallway. Three dark figures stood huddled together behind the search lamp.

More words were spoken softly. A ring holding several skeleton keys was produced. One after the other, the keys were inserted and tested in the Medeco lock.

One of the passkeys began to turn slowly in the lock . . .

Sarah was certain she had heard something outside the bedroom door. The noise was different from the usual nighttime sounds inside her apartment. She was surprised the tiny sound had awakened her at all.

Something was *different.*

Her eyes were wide open, revealing a field of total blackness stretching out around her. For a brief moment, it gave her the illusion that she might still be dreaming.

A few seconds of concentration were necessary to accustom her eyes to the dark. Finally, she could discern the outlines of both large picture windows inside the bedroom. The sounds of car horns and pneumatic bus brakes drifted up from the street, but no noise came from *inside* the apartment.

Sarah began to look for her clock.

Where was it? She couldn't find it anywhere on the night table.

She thought she heard a floorboard creak. Did it come from the hallway?

Maybe a board under the living room carpeting? Someone was in the apartment.

Her breathing was already coming in short, rapid bursts. She couldn't get enough air into her lungs.

Sarah concentrated on listening . . . listening . . . just listening to whomever . . . whatever . . .

She was sure that she heard another distinct sound, and she desperately wanted to cry out, to call out and question whoever was there. This wasn't just night frights. Not some ordinary New York apartment scare . . . Somebody was actually inside her apartment.

Oh God. She was a fighter, but not against something like this.

Who was it? Alexandre St-Germain? The Grave Dancer? That horrifying, truly bizarre night and early morning in Atlantic City came flashing back at her . . . The murders. Out of nowhere, it had seemed. How had they gotten in so easily?

'Stef?' she whispered as softly as she could. She moved over to touch his shoulder.

He wasn't there.

'Stef? . . .'

'I hear them.' A voice came from a few feet away, off to the left.

He had gotten himself into his wheelchair. He had moved across the bedroom, away from Sarah. His revolver was cradled in his lap.

'Go lock yourself in the bathroom.' There was no mistaking

the policeman's command in his voice. 'If anybody so much as touches the bathroom door, start screaming like hell. Once you start screaming, don't stop for anything.'

'Stef? . . . Who do you think it is?'

'I don't know. Get into the other room, please. There's going to be shooting here.'

John Stefanovitch heard the creaking bedsprings, then Sarah's light footsteps padding across the bedroom carpet.

She understood what was happening . . . the imminent possibility of gunfire in the bedroom. There was no arguing or discussing with him this time.

Stefanovitch tried to maneuver the wheelchair, and to catch his breath at the same time. He wondered how good he would be in this kind of situation . . .

He never could have imagined how unnerved he would be by the presence of an intruder inside Sarah's apartment. Rage surged in the corridors of his brain, balancing some of the fear.

How many of them were there? Would they come into the bedroom firing? Maybe they would creep up to the bed and fire at close range.

How would Alexandre St-Germain want it done? The street law had to be observed. That was it, wasn't it? Another important object lesson to be taught to the world.

I wanted you to know one thing . . . I shot her myself.

I stood in the hallway of your pathetic little apartment building. . . .

Suddenly, Stefanovitch imagined exactly how it had been that night. For a terrifying, sickening instant he saw everything, the unbelievable horror of the killer coming right into his home. How Anna must have felt at the end.

The awful silence made him feel he was trapped in a jar.

As Sarah stood inside the bathroom, a hundred conflicting thoughts rushed through her mind. Her body felt heavy and almost useless. This isn't happening to us, she thought over and over. It was impossible to accept that they had actually come into the apartment.

Her mind kept grabbing on to one thought. *Alexandre St-Germain is inside my apartment. The Grave Dancer is here.*

Sarah couldn't control her breathing. She could hear the amplified pounding inside her chest. She had a sudden urge to double over and throw up.

She almost began to scream for help. For a second, she was absolutely going to scream, but Stef had told her to wait, to stay quiet until they actually tried to come into the bathroom.

Sarah stood very still. She waited. A wave of exhaustion rolled over her. It was instantly followed by another wave.

Outside in the apartment hallway, the unidentified noises had stopped. There were only honking car horns, and the acceleration of buses out on Madison Avenue.

Stefanovitch was certain that one or more hit men were outside the bedroom door, listening before they crashed inside – before the insanity began.

How many of them would there be? Was there anything he could do to stop this from happening? He knew there wasn't. That was the worst part.

Had Alexandre St-Germain come himself? That was the question he needed answered.

Stefanovitch wished it weren't pitch-black inside the bedroom. He thought about pulling the window drapes back, but it was too late for that. He didn't dare make a noise and lose his advantage: that they didn't know he was up, waiting for them.

Another floorboard creaked.

His heart boomed against his chest; it felt as if it were physically exploding.

There was a loud click.

The bedroom door opened.

They were coming in.

Stefanovitch raised his revolver until it extended straight out in front of his face.

Fleetingly, he thought that he hadn't fired a gun at

255

anybody in nearly two years. He had never gotten used to shooting at another person.

Both his arms were rigidly straight. These could be the same men who hit Trump Plaza with submachine-gun pistols, he was thinking. There was no hope, no way out if they had machine guns. There was no hope for either him or Sarah.

Alexandre St-Germain had started out working the streets himself, Stefanovitch was thinking. He had done much of the early killing in Marseilles, in Paris, in a place called Long Beach. He seemed to enjoy it, to thrive on wet work. Would St-Germain have come himself? . . . Would he take that risk? What drove the bastard to do anything that he did?

A single light flared – a powerful search lamp was shining into the room.

Stefanovitch tried desperately to grab hold of his mind. Concentrate, he urged himself. Focus.

Instinctively, he wanted to jerk back, to move farther away from the probing light, but there was nowhere to go.

He heard the distinctive snick of a pistol action working across the bedroom. Definitely a pistol.

How many of them are there? he wondered again. Unanswered questions. The most important ones of his life. Of Sarah's life, too.

Were they all inside the bedroom now? They were as quiet as rats working in the darkness. Spasms of fear twisted through his body.

A second flashlight blinked on. Its beam revealed an empty bed. No one sleeping there. Now they knew . . .

Suddenly, John Stefanovitch fired at the lead flashlight. He aimed half a foot above the source of its piercing ray.

A man screamed, wounded and shocked by the unexpected ambush. A body hit the floor with a hollow, sickening thud.

The second flashlight blinked out instantly.

There was the sound of muffled voices, of men speaking in a foreign language.

Stefanovitch couldn't be sure of anything that was happening in the pitch-darkness.

He thought they were moving farther into the bedroom, though – not back into the hallway. Rats rushing into a dark hole at night. He and Sarah trapped in the hole.

He could hear their shoes, vague shuffling sounds on the carpet, their clothes brushing against furniture.

Then the eerie silence took over the room again. As if no one were there.

The bedroom was near-total darkness, but his eyes were finally adjusting to the scene.

He thought he could make out vague, subtle shapes. That shape over there was – Sarah's vanity table? Or was it that he knew where the vanity table was? Was he seeing, or remembering? The distinction was so important.

He could see the shadowy outline of the bedroom door leading out into the hallway. Could he see the mirror hanging on the bathroom door?

He saw moving shadows then, like something liquid being spilled against the bedroom walls.

The air was gone from his lungs. He needed to stand up, to get his breath.

Could they see him?

He kept wondering whether their eyes had become used to darkness. The question was screaming inside his head.

The mirror on the bathroom door caught an image.

He saw a shape crossing past. It moved very quickly – running, darting to the left.

He had to do two things, almost at exactly the same time: fire and move away. Fire just to the left of the mirror door; move away in his wheelchair. At the same time . . .

The revolver flared in his hands. An instant later, his left arm reached back and pushed hard off the bedroom wall. All his arm strength went into the motion.

The second gunman crashed loudly against the hollow-sounding wall, then stumbled to the floor.

The flashlight! His thoughts were so loud it seemed as if he were talking to himself, babbling in desperation. There was at least one more of them. Maybe two.

Maybe one gunman was without a flashlight. A very smart one? The grand cocksucker himself?

Frightened tenants in the building were beginning to cry out from the relative safety of their apartments. A woman screamed close by, probably on the same floor of the luxury building.

Finally, Sarah began to yell for help. Her back was up against the closed bathroom door; both bare feet were wedged against the cold porcelain of the tub.

'Call the police! Somebody call the police! Please call the police!' Sarah screamed at the top of her voice.

A handgun roared like a small cannon inside the bedroom.

A terrible shock of pain poleaxed through John Stefanovitch's body. He reeled violently to his left; he almost went over in the wheelchair.

One of the hit men was behind him.

The third man?

The fourth one?

He felt the same searing heat he'd experienced at Long Beach. The sheer force of the gunshot had almost thrown him from the wheelchair, ripped him from his seat.

A fire burned down the right side of his spine, searing into his flesh. He moaned softly, against his will, but he couldn't control the sound.

The gun muzzle bloomed again. *Behind him.*

The pain that pierced his brain was excruciating. His eyes started to blur. He could see a bright tunnel of light. It was Long Beach all over again.

At that instant, the bathroom door flew open. Sarah was

out in the clear. Her silhouette was cast against the wall. Then she disappeared back inside.

What was she doing?

'Sarah, no!' Stefanovitch shouted at the top of his voice.

Suddenly, a glass object crashed against the bedroom wall, near the closet. Another glass shattered. She was hurling things out of the bathroom. Distractions! Trying to help any way she could.

'Sarah!'

The gunman fired again, this time point-blank into the bathroom.

'Sarah? Sarah? . . . *Sarah!*'

Stefanovitch steadied his arm where the bright flash of gunfire had been. His hands were shaking. He aimed behind the last of the ghosting gun flashes. He squeezed the revolver tightly in both hands. Rage had taken over.

Both shots missed.

Chaos followed. Seconds later, all the appliances and lights in the apartment building came back on. The effect was startling temporarily, the shock jarring.

He saw the third gunman slip out the bedroom door. There had only been three of them . . . Had the last one been Alexandre St-Germain? He couldn't tell.

'Stef?' he heard Sarah cry out. Then he saw her coming through the widening crack in the bathroom door. 'Are you all right? Are you hurt?'

'I'm okay,' he said, not wanting Sarah to know he'd been shot. He was having trouble breathing.

Someone was pounding loudly on the upstairs door of the apartment. Muffled shouts came ringing through the walls. 'Are you all right in there? Mrs McGinniss? Mrs McGinniss?'

With a tremendous physical effort, Stefanovitch stubbornly started the Chair forward. Inside his head, there was no other choice. He propelled himself out of the bedroom, then down the hall to the upstairs doorway and, finally, out of the apartment itself.

Once he was moving, it was much better – so long as he didn't lean too far to the left. If he did that, the sudden pain knifing into his back became unbearable.

The elevator on the fifth floor was sitting there. He and Sarah had probably been the last ones to use it that night . . . The final gunman must have gone down the fire exit stairway, the way they had entered. Stefanovitch took the elevator.

Downstairs, the lobby was rapidly filling with tenants. A wall of blank, terrified faces greeted him.

Stefanovitch pushed his way through the milling, frightened crowd. He was oblivious to everything around him, to the frenzy and commotion. All Stefanovitch cared about was the third gunman.

'Open the front door,' he called ahead to the doorman. I'm not useless in the street, he thought. It was some consolation.

Then Stefanovitch was outside in the hot and humid night air. Finding the gunman suddenly seemed hopeless. He didn't have to think that way for long.

A running figure dashed from the alleyway, about half the building's length away. The man didn't pause to look back; he just sprinted toward Madison Avenue.

Stefanovitch immediately began to follow him up East Sixty-sixth Street. Was it the Grave Dancer?

As he reached the corner of Madison, Stefanovitch could see that the other man was limping. He was wounded, too.

Stefanovitch turned onto Madison, heading south after the gunman, steadily picking up speed. The wheelchair jumped a low curb at the corner.

Then he was out in the street, right out on Madison Avenue.

The street was flat and its surface was a lot faster for the wheelchair. He would be able to sprint – truly to race.

He hadn't counted on a flurry of traffic at a little past three A.M. The New York bar scene began to close down at three. Traffic had obviously picked up since then. A burst of yellow cabs and other vehicles was barreling up Madison, coming almost directly at him.

The drivers of the automobiles saw a man in a wheelchair riding the wrong way against traffic – a crazy-looking man in a wheelchair, wearing a bathrobe. A hospital escape? Even in New York, the sight was completely unexpected.

It instantly got worse.

Stefanovitch pulled the .22 revolver from the folds of his bathrobe. He began firing down Madison.

Stroke the chair, he remembered, not knowing if he had any real hope of closing the distance between himself and the hit man.

Traffic began to swerve wildly in order to avoid him. Taxis and other cars angled sharply out of the inside lane, their angry, blaring horns underscoring the danger he was causing.

Was it Alexandre St-Germain up ahead? There was no way Stefanovitch could tell. He had to close the gap. He tried to remember everything he'd learned about racing in the Chair.

Stefanovitch found that he was gaining ground as his head rose for another quick look at the running man. His chest was on fire, but he was gaining. Inches, but something. His body was tingling all over. He could feel wetness underneath him, and he knew it was his own blood, pumping out with each heartbeat.

Stroke! he repeated to himself.

Stroke!

Watch nothing except the lead racer.

Nothing else exists.

The gunman had stopped. He was turning back, standing less than thirty yards away. The gunman was leveling his gun at Stefanovitch – who was wildly caroming into better range.

Stefanovitch recognized his potential murderer. He knew the man . . . Chaos . . . madness filled his head.

John Stefanovitch swung up his revolver, losing control of the wheelchair as he did. The lesser of two evils, he thought in a flash. *Maybe.*

He fired before the other man. He didn't see anything after that, because he was heading directly into the side door of a swerving yellow cab. The taxi was only inches from his face.

He caromed hard off the cab door, and was instantly hit by a speeding, low-slung red sports car.

Horns were screaming everywhere on Madison. A startled, angry swarm was all around him – brushing him, almost touching, desperately trying to not run him down.

The wheelchair had begun to fly. It was something he'd wanted to do for so long, one of his recurring fantasies. Just to fly away.

Only it was sheer terror to be flying, actually flying.

He knew he couldn't possibly make the chair land on its wheels. The angle to the ground, to the blurry street pavement, was almost sideways. He was going to hit on the bad side, too, where he had already been shot.

There was nothing Stefanovitch could do to control his fate. All he could manage was to go along for the ride.

He struck the ground, and lost consciousness for an instant – not sure if he went out before or after he hit the street. He touched down partially with his left shoulder, partially with the side of his face; then the rest of his body followed. Wildly rolling over and over again. Over and over and over.

'It's not St-Germain!' was the next thing he heard. 'It's Burke. He's dead, Stef. You got Burke.'

Stefanovitch nodded. The words vaguely registered somewhere in his mind.

He'd seen Jimmy Burke with one fast glimpse from the rampaging wheelchair. Burke from Long Beach, and now Sarah's apartment. Of course, Alexandre St-Germain hadn't come himself. He had never given it a thought, had he?

Sarah was with him in the middle of Madison Avenue. So were an awful lot of policemen, and EMS ambulance people.

Some character in a white dress shirt and tuxedo trousers peered down at him through owl-rim glasses. A doctor? Stefanovitch hoped he was.

Sarah held his hand tightly in both of hers. The look on her face was so frightened that it scared him, too.

'I'm glad you're all right,' he whispered behind a crooked smile. He was amazed at how weak he felt – helpless, yet strangely peaceful, sprawled there in the street.

His face felt out of kilter somehow. It matched his body, which was twisted and bent, lying like a broken doll in the bus lane of Madison Avenue.

Finally, he winked up at Sarah, and then both his eyes closed. His eyes felt so heavy. His head lolled gently to the right, settling on the thick white traffic line.

Fifteen yards farther down Madison Avenue, the sad wreck of Stefanovitch's wheelchair lay flipped over on its side.

42

Sarah McGinnis
Milton, New York

It wouldn't stop . . .

The terror wouldn't stop coming at her.

For days, Sarah wondered if she might be losing her mind. The relentless pressure of the past weeks had been overwhelming. Now it was even worse. At the same time, she felt that her wits were somehow sharpening again, as if a kind of clarity came with walking through fire.

Whenever she drifted off to sleep, she would bolt awake, terrified by the indescribable images in her head. Her brain would throb with a dull pain; her body was sore all over. She had lost more than ten pounds.

She looked gaunt and felt depressed. There were so many disturbing moments that she couldn't erase from her mind; so many obsessive thoughts that wouldn't stop flashing.

Sarah visited New York Hospital a dozen times. No one could, or would, tell her how Stefanovitch was really doing. There were vague, hopeful, and polite niceties – but no one told her the truth. No one would even tell her if he was going to live.

There was no news on Sam either. She wouldn't allow herself to speculate on the reasons. She closed off certain regions of her mind, like rooms in an overly large house during the dead of winter.

Alexandre St-Germain seemed to have disappeared from New York again; perhaps he'd fled the country. The police hadn't been able to reach him for questioning.

The daily newspapers overflowed with stories about the terrible shooting at her apartment. She and Stefanovitch were emblazoned across all the front pages. The scenario had the staccato, slightly unreal feel of Hitchcock melodramas. Or was it more the feeling of an actual nightmare?

The phone call finally came early on Wednesday morning, three days after the vicious attack at her apartment. It was a brief call, not long enough for a police tracer of any kind.

Sarah picked up the phone downstairs, in the hallway off the living room. She heard a disturbing silence first; then an almost distinguished voice over the telephone.

'We want you to know that your little boy is fine . . . He's safe as he can be. Not a hair on his head has been harmed,' she heard.

Then the telephone wire went dead.

Sarah leaned up against the wall. She couldn't take any more of this. Her heart physically ached. She was suddenly trembling all over, her hands, her entire body.

Who had that been on the telephone? Why were they calling her now, then hanging up? What did it mean – *your little boy is fine*?

There was nothing else they could take from her. So why had they called to say that? Sam wasn't fine at all. How could he be fine?

Who was the call from? St-Germain? The Club? She didn't understand the kidnapping, and now this call. But why should she suddenly understand the inner workings of the Club?

Sarah stayed within steps of her telephone for the remainder of the interminable day. During the early afternoon, she noticed her reflection in the mirror in the foyer. It startled her. She had never looked so drawn, so completely exhausted. Sagging black and purplish bags hung beneath both eyes. Her hair looked as if she'd used it to dust the apartment. . . .Where were they keeping Sam? What could they want from her now? *What could they possibly want?*

There was no follow-up phone call the next day. Twenty-four hours passed, with nothing but the torture of her inner thoughts to occupy her.

Keeping her in this nightmarish state was clearly part of the plan. Why, though? For what purpose?

She couldn't go outside her apartment without meeting reporters camped like an aging neighborhood gang on Sixty-sixth Street. They wouldn't leave her alone, and suddenly Sarah understood what it was like for victims besieged by newspeople after a tragedy.

She felt as if she had visible open wounds, and the newspapers and TV reporters were shamelessly picking at them. She had never been brutal at these kinds of news scenes herself, but she had certainly been a part of them. Only now did she understand what it felt like on the other side; to be besieged for news the public 'deserved to know.'

One morning, when Sarah was short-tempered with the reporters, they sharply reminded her that she, of all people, ought to know better. She did know better, she told them. And so should they.

She visited New York Hospital again that same afternoon. Stefanovitch had just undergone a major operation.

The only blessing was that his doctor was excellent, a tireless healer named Michael Petito. Dr Petito wasn't one to dispense false hope or a misleading prognosis, however. He told Sarah that he didn't know if Lieutenant Stefanovitch was going to come out of it.

Finally, someone had at least told her the truth.

'We want you to do something for us, Sarah . . . If you do it, we'll bring your little boy home to you.'

The second phone call came as suddenly and unexpectedly as the first.

Both times, Sarah could picture the man who had taken Sam on Park Avenue. That moment was still so vivid in her memory.

266

'Yes . . . What do you want? *Please*,' she whispered hoarsely into the receiver. She knew she was hoping against hope: she was truly desperate now . . .

The telephone had woken Sarah from a rare sleep on Friday morning. She tried to concentrate on each word she heard. She needed to understand and remember every nuance.

The voice on the phone told her what to do next and what the consequences would be if she didn't. It was all put very clearly.

At the end of the conversation, the caller even offered a measure of reassurance.

'There is no need for you to worry about your little boy. We want you to get your son back. It's up to you. If you cooperate on this one thing, he's as good as home. . . .We don't want any more attention drawn to us.'

It was all up to Sarah. The explanation had been that simple. She had her instructions to follow. Whether she trusted the caller or not, she had no choice but to go.

As she drove north toward the upstate New York village of Milton, Sarah finally began to understand. There had been a simple and very direct logic to it all, right from the beginning. She knew all the rules; she just had to follow them as directed.

We don't want any more attention drawn to us.

Their rules.

Always.

Although a few people still seemed to reside there, the small village at the end of her journey was like an eastern version of a ghost town. Paint was peeling off most of the dilapidated houses. Foundations were collapsing. Front porches were caving in everywhere in Milton.

Nearly every backyard seemed to overflow with mechanical relics: rusting refrigerators, the shells of automobiles and pickup trucks, bent and twisted machine parts that couldn't possibly have a function.

267

As she drove down closer to the Hudson River, the scenery changed for the better. There were larger houses, many of which appeared to be country estates. Birds sang in the trees, which were mostly maples and elms and graceful old evergreens.

Occasionally, the river peeked through drooping leaves, looking blindingly blue, oblivious to anything but its own monolithic beauty.

Following instructions, Sarah finally parked the Land Rover at an overgrown driveway bearing a wrought-iron signpost indicating that the house belonged to a certain J. Kamerer. She could see a large estate house from the road.

The house was off-white, graying in spots, with its paint peeling and chipped, but not beyond the ministrations of a handyman. An acre plot of lawn was overgrown, yet had obviously been shorn once or twice during the summer.

Why had she been asked to come to this place? Is Sam being kept here? she wondered. She climbed out of the Land Rover.

'Hello,' Sarah called. 'Hello. Hello there?' she called again, her voice cutting sharply through the screen of summer's insect buzz, the persistent bird chirping in the woods.

She had been calm on the drive upstate. Her state of distraction had served as a tranquilizer. Now she was aware of how vulnerable she was, standing here and looking around. Where are they holding Sam? her brain screamed.

'Hello? . . . Hello? . . . Is anyone there?' Sarah called out again. Still no answer came back.

She wondered if anyone was watching her. She had the disturbing intuition that someone probably was.

Intermittently, a solitary car or pickup truck drove by on the winding country road that had led her to the house. J. Kamerer? She didn't know anyone by that name. Not that she could remember, anyway.

Finally, Sarah decided to do what she had been told. She slowly walked back to the Land Rover, to fetch her package. What they wanted from her. This was the hardest part yet, harder than she'd imagined when she received the instructions.

When she reached the vehicle, Sarah put her hands down into the front seat. She paused for a moment, trying to calm herself, trying to breathe.

Her writing and research for *The Club* were there, sitting on the car seat. All other copies had already been destroyed.

She gathered the bundle of papers up in her arms and began to carry it across the front lawn, almost like a small, injured animal.

Sarah understood that she was a loose end for them, no more than that. They didn't want her book published. It would be embarrassing. That was what this was about. Saving the Midnight Club from discomfort and embarrassment. Preserving their respectability; their invisibility.

Their goddamn rules.

She was almost certain someone was watching. Where were they keeping Sam? Oh, Sam, where are you, baby?

Could he be right here, in this woodsy neighborhood, with all of its somber nooks and dark crannies? Could he be in that house?

Sarah realized she was feeling light-headed and feverish in the summer heat. Blue jays continued to sing from the trees. Crickets and other insects buzzed, almost like an electric current in the air.

Sarah listened for another kind of sound. A human sound? A small, innocent boy's voice calling her name?

She shuffled unsteadily from the Land Rover, toward the oversized, ramshackle house. Tiny insects seemed to swarm around her. A woodpecker issued its *tat-a-tat-tat* from the trees. There were no human sounds.

Is this the end of it, then? she wondered, almost speaking out loud. Was this going to be the finish of everything?

Had they won every point, Alexandre St-Germain and the Midnight Club? They *had* won, hadn't they. They always seemed to win. Sarah wanted to scream.

She left two years' worth of research and writing for them. She did as she had been instructed.

Their warning had been clear and coldly logical. If there were copies, if the notes were ever reconstructed in any way, she knew the consequences.

As she drove back to New York, she thought she had never felt so drained, so completely used up and unreal. Maybe it was going to stop now. Maybe it could just end.

43

Sarah McGinniss
East Sixty-sixth Street

Forty-eight hours after the trip upstate, Sarah was walking in a slow, aimless, and drifting way. She shuffled west on Sixty-sixth Street, moving in the direction of Park Avenue.

After she'd left Milton that afternoon, she'd been filled with hope, even with a kind of strange joy. Since then, Sarah had become almost disconsolate. She'd done exactly as they had asked; she had played by their rules.

What more did they want from her? Where was Sam right now? Was he still alive?

There was something satisfying about not having anything to work on, at least. There was no book, no investigation. Walking around her neighborhood, Sarah had been noticing odd, unimportant things for the first time in months. Slants of sunlight bouncing off the hard city surfaces; colorful flowers growing up out of the sidewalk; a new northern Italian restaurant, a hopeful menu in the window.

The trouble was, there was no one to share it with anymore. She shook her head, to brush away the thought.

She saw the dark gray Mercedes moving along the street toward her, almost as if someone were searching in vain for a parking space.

She felt herself go cold, for maybe the hundredth time in the past few weeks.

Her eyes never left the slow-moving car. Two men were in the front seat. Hulking men in dark suits.

For an instant, Sarah thought about running up the stone

stairs, hiding inside the brownstone she had just passed. Were they coming after her now?

The scene seemed to happen in slow motion.

Sarah had a horrible feeling about this car. She had no logical reason, just a gut reaction. They were after her. But why? She'd given them all her writing; the truth as she understood it; her research. It would take her more than a year just to reassemble *The Club*, and it would never be as strong a book.

The gray sedan stopped alongside Sarah, less than a foot away. She froze. The electric door locks sprung open. The rear door swung toward her.

A tall, gray-haired man stepped out of the Mercedes. It was no one she knew. He stared directly at her, a slightly quizzical look about his eyes. Obviously, he didn't care whether she could identify him. He operated with no fear. He knew he was in control.

He seemed so *respectable*. Just a man in a business suit.

'Mrs McGinniss?' he asked, and she nodded without saying a word. She really couldn't speak, didn't want to speak. 'None of this happened,' the man said. 'Please understand that. We don't want to read about any of this in any newspaper. We really wouldn't appreciate that.'

Then Sarah's mind seemed to disconnect from the rest of her body, from the entire scene on Sixty-sixth Street.

She saw Sam being helped out of the car, but she couldn't quite make sense of what was happening. It was like looking at a photograph that had come to life. She had never been so completely detached; not at any moment in her life.

'Mommy, Mommy,' Sam cried. She was suddenly afraid that they were going to let her see him, then take him away again, whisk him back inside the car.

Instead, they let Sam go, and he ran straight into her outstretched arms. The gray sedan continued up the narrow street canyons and finally disappeared, as if, indeed, none of this had happened.

But then why would she and Sam be crying in the middle of their street?

44

The Midnight Club
Beverly Hills, California

Discreetly hidden among the hills and canyons north of Sunset Boulevard, the suburb of Bel Air is almost exclusively residential, accessible for the most part through steel gates occasionally guarded by private police.

Nestled among the lush, low hills is the Hotel Bel Air: classic, palatial, secluded; unique for its understated and tasteful landscaping, its petal-strewn walkways, its swans.

Almost everything about the California hotel is beautiful, and best of all, respectable.

During the first week in November of that year – gloriously sunny days, consistently in the high seventies – there were no rooms or suites available to any of the business travelers, the movie studio executives, the movie stars, who frequent the Hotel Bel Air.

Instead, the eleven-acre, ninety-room retreat was reserved for an unusual meeting. Twenty-seven business executives, government leaders, and high-ranking military men were in attendance. They met each morning, over breakfast served in the Pavilion and Garden Room, more typically used for expensive weddings and lavish bar mitzvahs. Every night, the participants dined as a group in the hotel restaurant, which had also been booked for the five days.

The talk of the Bel Air was the usual sort from the twenty-seven members of the Club, although it could hardly be considered shop talk . . .

– There was the important subject of narcotics, now a $23-billion-a-year business, with a profit margin over 65 percent.

– There was borrowing and lending, once known as loan-sharking. This banking function now accounted for $14 billion, $10 billion of that profit.

– There was prostitution, computed at less than $1.5 billion. Still, 40 percent in the black.

– And gambling – about $12 billion net, half of it positive earnings.

One evening at dinner, there was a disinterested discussion about how the Cubans were getting into the numbers racket in New York, Baltimore, and Philadelphia.

The Nigerians and the Pakistanis were involved in heroin dealing lately, and also the seemingly unrelated false credit card business. Why did ethnic groups always seem to have their specialties? None of the members really cared.

This was big business, with profits in the area of $59 billion to $60 billion a year.

During the week in Southern California, refinements were made in distribution channels; changes were agreed on in the pyramid-style management system that would affect business in every major country around the world – elemental changes in the way things had run for perhaps a thousand years. At the top of the new infrastructure was a chief executive; then came a chief operating officer; a general counsel; and finally the other major executives.

What the twenty-seven members had finally done was to control crime.

They had succeeded in making organized crime one of the most powerful and wealthiest business entities in the world. They were now eleven times more profitable than IBM, with no competition in the mid-range of their product line.

Only one important Club member was missing for the high-level meeting in California.

Alexandre St-Germain was not among the group sequestered in the hills of Bel Air. He purposely had not been invited. However, he was the subject of important conversations at the hotel.

The discussion was one of business practices, of the new way versus the old, of *respectability* and *anonymity*. The Grave Dancer had fallen back into his violent ways. There was the style in which he had attempted to enforce his will recently in New York. Shootings. An unfortunate kidnapping, in which the Club had finally intervened. There was the matter of a missing young woman named Susan Paladino.

Alexandre St-Germain had been necessary in the original plan to eliminate the Old Guard of crime. He had a shrewd understanding for business and politics, the instincts of a Machiavelli; he had personally charmed several of the twenty-seven current members. He had originally brought them into the venture, in fact. But now: what to do with the Grave Dancer?

In the early morning of November 16, David Wilkes led FBI agents and members of the LAPD onto the private grounds of the Hotel Bel Air. Three dozen officers and agents in business suits and duty uniforms trotted briskly across the strikingly beautiful landscape.

Riot shotguns and a variety of handguns caught the glint of the morning sun. Bolt actions slid into readiness, waking the swans, causing the hired Vietnamese and Mexican help to duck into laundry closets and a few unoccupied rooms.

One of the Club members was arrested during his morning swim. Another member was stopped while jogging down nearby Bellagio Road. The majority of the members were roused from sleep.

The raid was led by Wilkes of the FBI, but the team also included Stuart Fischer, from the New York district attorney's office. Sarah McGinniss was there in spirit. So was Stefanovitch.

The raid was the culmination of four months of strategic planning and unusual cooperation, not only among US agencies but also governments around the world. Known

Club members had been under surveillance for weeks before the California meeting. The documentation necessary for prosecution filled several large rooms in Wilkes's offices in Washington. Duplicate material was stored in warehouses in New Jersey and, for safety, at Interpol headquarters in Europe.

The RICO Act was cited over and over again to the twenty-seven businesspeople, then to their expensive teams of attorneys.

So much for respectability; for the Club's being civilized and blending in; for euphemism of any kind. The police were finally learning the rules of the game. There were no rules at all. Except to shoot to kill.

45

Alexandre St-Germain
The World Trade Center

Seven-fifty a.m., and he was alone. He was more alone than he had ever been in his life. Am I suicidal? he wondered. He had no definite answer for himself.

He hurried across the sterile expanse of marble and stone inside the World Trade Center lobby. He took one last deep breath at the elevator banks, to steady himself, to get himself ready.

He pulled out an Ingram machine-gun pistol. The compact weapon came from underneath a loose-fitting black sports jacket.

It happened so quickly that no one could have reacted any differently. A man pushing an Au Bon Pain bakery cart distracted the bodyguards at the last moment.

'No one moves. That means you and you especially. No point trying to be heroes here. No need to die for this piece of shit.'

Alexandre St-Germain recognized Parker an instant before he saw the submachine gun. Parker had reached the elevator doors simultaneously with St-Germain and his entourage.

The plan was skillful in its execution, almost effortless. To work, it had to be.

Parker immediately pushed St-Germain inside the elevator. He pressed the black muzzle of the Ingram hard up against the man's throat.

'Don't sweat it,' he said to the Grave Dancer. 'Everything is cool. We've already thought of everything. No body doubles this time.'

Both of Alexandre St-Germain's hands were thrust out,

palms forward. He was holding back his own people. 'I will take care of this,' he said. 'I'll handle this.'

The doors slid shut without a sound. Parker and St-Germain were alone inside the elevator, facing one another across the empty passenger car.

'I'm sure we can work something out. Come to an agreement.' St-Germain spoke very softly.

'Just shut up, Pusherman.'

Parker jabbed the button marked '108,' the tower's top floor. Up there was the famed observation deck, where ordinary folks could pay to peer out over New York, New Jersey, Connecticut, the whole metropolitan area.

The passing floor numbers registered on the indicator lights. The elevator-car cables whined like ropes of steel scraping together.

As the numbers reached thirty-seven, thirty-eight, thirty-nine, Isiah Parker watched closely; then he jammed the emergency button. The elevator bucked slightly, then slowly scraped to a stop. The alarm bell inside went off, a loud wailing that was painful to the ears.

'You thought you had it all figured out,' Parker said. He held the machine-gun pistol so it touched Alexandre St-Germain's chest. He wasn't feeling much of anything yet, as if he were drifting away, finally cut loose from the world.

'Apparently not.' The Grave Dancer's tone was supercilious.

'You killed off the competition. That was like firing the old executive team. What was supposed to come next?'

Alexandre St-Germain's face remained difficult to read. He had the cold, distant eyes of a wolf. He was completely self-absorbed. 'I've met policemen like you before. Many times before,' he finally said. 'You understand very little about life, but you think you know it all. Self-delusion can be extremely dangerous.'

Isiah Parker smiled at St-Germain. 'Something else I was told. You fed my brother junk for ten days. Got him addicted. You played with my brother, poisoned him slowly . . . You hurt him, to teach another of your lessons.'

St-Germain shook his head back and forth.

'A few missing details in your story . . . Your brother was an addict before we ever got to him. Whenever he needed it, we were there, of course. He was crazy, depressed, and very dangerous at the end. You should have seen that. Except that you were using cocaine yourself. A great deal of cocaine, as I understand it.'

Isiah Parker leaned back hard against the elevator wall. He smiled, a little sadly this time. So. He had shown the first weakness. Alexandre St-Germain was still winning.

The emergency phone inside the elevator began to ring. The familiar jangling sound came with its own echo.

Parker reached back behind his head. He plucked the phone away from its rack. 'Yeah? Elevator man.'

'Who is this? Who's up there?' he heard over the line. 'Who the hell's in that elevator?'

'It's Alexandre St-Germain. And a friend of his. We're in conference right now.'

Isiah Parker hung up the telephone. He realized that he was feeling strangely giddy. He wouldn't allow himself to lose concentration, though. He took the phone receiver off the hook again.

'No more calls,' he said to St-Germain. 'We'll hold all your important calls for a while.'

Parker waved his gun to the left of where St-Germain stood. 'Have a seat. Slide down nice and easy against the wall. Where do you get your suits, man? Barney's Boystown? You're the best-dressed killer in town.'

Parker could hear the steady wail of police cruisers arriving outside. It made him understand how spectacular and bizarre the moment was.

'Who knows, maybe they can rescue you,' he said in a quiet voice. 'Maybe they can figure out something. So sit back and relax. Let's try to imagine how it's going to turn out. Make a guess. You're supposed to be smart.'

Time in the elevator car passed slowly. A half hour. An hour. Almost two hours. All according to plan. Parker had been on the other side of police emergency situations before. He knew how they were reacting out there. He'd planned on that, too.

Both he and St-Germain were soaking in their own sweat. Somebody had shut off the elevator's fresh air supply. The first smart move by the NYPD.

Everything had become a slow, floating dream in Parker's mind. He'd been thinking about Marcus, remembering moments between them. They'd been neighborhood heroes. It was a hard feeling to explain. He thought back to when his brother had been champion. Being at the top of the world like that made you soar, made you feel you were somebody special. Everybody looked up to Marcus, and they knew they could get out of Harlem, too. Escape was possible. Then the dream had been destroyed – because of this man on the elevator floor.

Policemen, several of them, were stationed at the elevator bank below, and on the fortieth floor above. Every so often, they hollered up or down to the stalled car. They cajoled; they threatened. Parker never said a word back to them.

His eyes were starting to burn. Rivulets of sweat seeped out from his hairline. He felt as if his body were soaking in a warm pool.

St-Germain's linen suit had turned a lifeless cardboard gray. His wavy blond hair was plastered over his forehead. He wasn't the invincible Grave Dancer anymore. He was a monster, though, and Parker could feel his skin crawl.

'I'm going to tell you how it goes from here on,' Parker said. His voice stayed low, but kept an edge. 'Then we'll be even, you and me sitting here in this hot box. You'll know as much as I do.'

'You're in control now, my friend.'

'Yeah, that's right.'

Isiah Parker raised the black, snub-nosed submachine

gun. The Frenchman's dark eyes registered the slightest confusion. Alarms seemed to go off in his head.

St-Germain had decided that Parker wasn't suicidal: he was too much in control of the situation to let himself die here. The police detective obviously wasn't going to shoot him inside the elevator. What was he going to do? What was he planning now?

'You don't have *anything* figured out,' Parker whispered across the elevator.

'You seem certain about that.'

'Yeah, I am. You still think you're going to get away. That's your fucking arrogance. You think I've put myself in a box here. No way out. No escape for me.'

St-Germain said nothing. A smug expression remained on his face. He always won. Somehow, he won.

'You're wrong. I just wanted you to suffer, like my brother, Marcus. Like you did to him in the Edmonds Hotel.'

Isiah Parker raised the Ingram machine gun and smiled. With his free hand, he took out a sealed Plasticine bag filled with fine white powder.

St-Germain's eyes widened. Finally, he understood something.

'I wish we had more time for this,' Parker said. 'Never enough time these days.'

He took out a lighter, an ordinary Bic.

He took out a small silver spoon.

A hypodermic needle and a plunger appeared next.

He raised the Ingram to the level of St-Germain's eyes. 'Take off that coat. Get comfortable.'

'What if I won't?'

'Then everything goes real quick. Less time for any rescue attempts. Roll up your sleeve. Either arm's okay.'

The Grave Dancer reluctantly took off his suit jacket. After removing his gold cuff links, he rolled up his shirt sleeve.

'Now fix your own cocktail.'

'I don't use the stuff. I never use narcotics.'

Parker gestured over with the gun. 'Now you do.'

He watched in eerie silence as Alexandre St-Germain cooked up a speedball with the shooting paraphernalia. A familiar acrid odor took over the closed space. When the hypodermic was loaded, Parker spoke again. His voice was low, but in command.

'Good stuff. Very popular up where I live. Take a taste, Grave Dancer. *Do it now.*'

St-Germain raised the hypodermic, its plunger extended.

'Just a little taste now,' Parker said. 'Then we talk some more. Nothing to be afraid of yet. Twelve-, thirteen-year-old kids do it every day in my neighborhood.'

St-Germain slowly and carefully inserted the silver needle into his vein. The arrogant smile had finally started to fade.

Seconds later, his head lolled back, then forward again. It was a junkie's patented nod-out routine. His eyeballs rolled up sharply into his skull. Suddenly he started to dry-heave.

He knew he'd been given an overdose. Fear was in his eyes. He was going into cardiac arrest on the elevator floor.

Isiah Parker's eyes never left St-Germain's face. What he saw was his brother. The Edmonds Hotel. Maybe a touch of justice, finally.

Alexandre St-Germain went into severe convulsions. He couldn't get his breath, but he could hear Parker's voice. 'How do you like it, Pusherman?'

St-Germain had a stroke sitting against the elevator wall. He had a second agonizing stroke forty-five seconds later.

Parker stared at the pathetic, slumped figure, the head now twisted at an impossible angle. Alexandre St-Germain was dead, dead like a pitiful street junkie on the floor of the elevator.

There was no remorse inside him; no attacks of conscience

for Parker. He had done what had to be done. He'd done what the police ought to be permitted to do.

Then one thought dominated Parker's mind: to escape and survive. That would be something, wouldn't it.

He pulled the emergency-stop button back out. The elevator rumbled and shook to life. The amber indicator lights over the door blinked on and off again.

The elevator car began to soar upward, resuming its ride as if nothing had happened. A few seconds later, Parker stabbed the stop button again. The elevator halted at the forty-sixth floor.

Isiah Parker jumped out of the car and dropped the Ingram. He ran to an emergency doorway marked 'Fire Exit.'

He buttoned his sport coat as he continued to race downstairs. He shook perspiration off his face. He dried his head with his jacket sleeve. He went down past forty-five, forty-four, past forty-three. Don't panic. Just hurry, he reminded himself.

Finally, he emerged from the fire exit stairway, onto the fortieth floor. He saw policemen waiting with drawn riot shotguns and squawking walkie-talkies. Silence followed in the hallway. Parker told himself, *Now be very cool . . . You're a cop, too.*

'Isiah Parker, Nineteenth Precinct,' he said to the patrolman closest to the fire exit door. Somehow, he managed a blank poker face. 'What the hell is going on?' Parker asked.

The patrolman stared at him. Doubt glistened in his sober blue eyes. His bulky riot shotgun was held at chest level, pointed right at Parker's stomach.

Isiah Parker carefully shook out his portfolio wallet, showing his detective's shield. He forced a smile, then loosely shrugged his shoulders. 'Hey, relax, huh? What the hell's happening? We heard the elevator take off. What happened?'

A black detective in the hallway spoke up. 'Hey, I know him. That's my man Parker. Hey, Isiah.'

The patrolman with the shotgun finally shook his head. He slowly lowered the Remington. 'That's what we were wondering, too. Where's the elevator? Where's St-Germain?'

More patrolmen and detectives began to swarm out of the fire exit stairway. Isiah moved among them, joining in with the general confusion, contributing his part. They all had the same question – What was going on? Where had the hijacked elevator gone?

After a few minutes on the fortieth floor, Parker started down the fire exit stairway again. This time, he walked in the company of two other detectives. The deserted elevator had been discovered on forty-six. The Grave Dancer was dead inside.

Once he was in the lobby of the Trade Center, Parker continued toward the bright daylight of the street. Outside the soaring twin building, everything was chaos, even worse than up on the forty-sixth floor.

Police blockades had been set up everywhere. EMS ambulances, police cruisers with their turrets blazing red, were parked up on the sidewalk. Several thousand people were assembled behind rows of blue police barricades and street cops in pith helmets.

Escape and survive, Parker thought. Just like after Allure, and Cin-Cin, in Soho.

He continued north on Chambers Street, which was also blockaded with bright blue police sawhorses. He kept walking past the blockades, once or twice showing his detective's shield along the way.

As he walked north through the city, Isiah Parker wished that the world was still simple. All he had ever wanted was to get Marcus's murderer. Whether he did that through the police department, or not, didn't matter. All he had wanted was a little justice.

Parker wound up in the Bowery, somewhere around Grand and Canal streets, with their legions of panhandlers. The trembling stewbums, always looking like they had just wet their pants. The sad and desolate Edmonds Hotel. He stood on the street, thinking about his brother, Marcus, their past, all of the promise and hope destroyed by an insane drug pusher.

Isiah Parker didn't feel like an assassin anymore. There was no guilt attached to what he had done. He had blasted the Grave Dancer straight back to hell.

He continued to walk north, toward his home. He was a crime-busting detective after all. The best in Harlem. He still liked the idea of that.

One Last Dance

46

Sarah McGinniss
New York

On an afternoon near the end of April, Sarah found herself skirting along a familiar blue tape line, which led her around the Byzantine corridors on the ground floor at New York Hospital.

She had been coming regularly to the hospital every day for almost nine months. She knew the place by heart. That included most of the porters, a lot of the nurses and doctors, Linda and Laurie and Robin in the gift shop. Just about everybody knew Sarah, too.

The seventeenth floor, where she was headed, had an eighty-by-forty gray-stone terrace, which looked out over the East River; that big old Pepsi sign; the boroughs of Brooklyn and Queens. As hospitals went, it was the most impressive and beautiful one she'd ever been inside.

On that afternoon in the spring, Sarah went directly to Stefanovitch's room, actually his seventh room so far. Each room had been on a different floor inside the sprawling medical center.

Stef was up and waiting, as she'd expected. His mother and father, Nelson, Nelson's wife, Hallie, were all crowded into the room.

'Well, this is quite a happy Fizzies party, isn't it?' he said when Sarah arrived. He had his best smile turned up full. He brought to mind soldiers recovering in army hospitals.

He was peering across the sun-spattered hospital room. He seemed to be carefully studying his visitors. There was a wonderful twinkle in his eyes. Sarah didn't know how he managed it – especially today.

Finally, Sarah's eyes found Michael Petito, the tall, balding neurologist who had been to see Stef every day for the past nine months. It was nine months now since three killers had broken into her apartment, and tried to murder both of them. They had succeeded in inflicting two horrifying gunshot wounds, one in Stef's side, the other in the small of his back.

Dr Petito had made the decision to operate two days after the shooting. At the time, Stefanovitch had been listed in very critical condition. A half-dozen family members had driven up to New York from Pennsylvania. He hadn't been expected to live.

Stefanovitch had been in intensive care when his mother and father, Sarah, and Dr Petito had come to visit. 'You don't look so bad,' Petito had told him. 'I've seen worse after pro football games.'

Stef had liked the irreverent doctor immediately, maybe because Michael Petito had come up from the streets of New York, and acted a little like it. Or maybe because Petito was the team doctor for the New York Giants, a specialist on back and leg injuries.

He told Stefanovitch that he wanted to operate on his back again, that the new bullets had to come out of there anyway.

'What are the chances?' Stef had asked, struggling with every word.

'About sixty–forty, your way. Let's say fifty-five–forty-five, that you don't end up a full quadriplegic.'

'The other doctor said eighty–twenty, the other way. The last time I got shot up like this.'

Petito shrugged. 'Overly conservative, in my opinion. Your other doctor was protecting himself, in case he screwed up. I won't screw up, but those are the real odds. And they're not great. Especially the prospect of being a quadriplegic.'

Stefanovitch had agreed to sign the necessary releases. He had gone in for the operation, one that could leave him paralyzed from the neck down. As Dr Petito had said, though, the new bullets had to come out anyway.

Nine months later, he was still in New York Hospital.

The pain following the operation had been unbearable; it seemed to be endless. Petito hadn't told him about that, the excruciating pain after a second major back operation.

Day after day, Stefanovitch was rolled upstairs to physical therapy, where they thought it was an occasion for champagne if he touched his index fingers together once out of every couple of times, or wiggled his big toe. Every day, as he was wheeled back to his room from therapy, he was soaked to the skin, his entire body screaming from pain.

If he had been forced to do it again, he didn't think he could. Sarah had been there every day, for nine months straight. Sarah and Sam. Bringing him presents, and dinners from Rusty and Abe's Steak House, and most of all, hope.

'Sixty–forty my way? Those are the odds?' John Stefanovitch asked now.

His voice suddenly sounded hollow and distant. His family and Dr Petito were silhouetted against one of the sunny hospital windows.

'I thought I told you fifty-five–forty-five.' Petito's gaze was steady, his opinion firm.

'Yeah, you did. You know, I was feeling okay this morning, up in physical therapy,' Stefanovitch said. 'Now, I'm kind of spacey. Rubbery legs. My adrenaline is mainlining.

'Listen, Sarah.' He smiled, only his brown eyes were mostly glazed and vacant. 'I think I need something to motivate me. Would you, uh . . . why don't you stand over there. Would you stand right there by the door?'

'Don't be so bossy. Just because you've been laid up doesn't mean you're allowed to be cranky,' Isabelle Stefanovitch said. Sarah had watched her operate over the last few months. She could make Stef toe the line; at the same time she was communicating the most touching affection for him.

'I'll let him boss me around today.' Sarah smiled. The smile felt like a mask being pulled down over her face. She was having difficulty talking.

'You give him an inch, Sarah, he'll take a mile,' Nelson said from across the room. 'He's always been that way. That's how he got to be quarterback in high school. Not on his talent. Not with that chicken arm of his.'

The mood in the hospital room was better than it had been moments earlier. Even Dr Petito smiled at the Stefanovitch clan's amazingly wrongheaded but healthy defense mechanisms.

'I'm going to stand right here by the door,' Sarah said, as if she'd just thought of it herself.

'If I fall over, let me go,' Stefanovitch said in between deep breaths. He was propped against the edge of his bed now. Some pressure and weight were already being applied to his legs. There was so much going on inside his head that it was overwhelming.

Suddenly, with characteristic stubbornness, he pushed off hard from the hospital bed, almost as if that were the only way to make his family stop talking. 'I love all of you,' he whispered as he let go.

Stefanovitch took his first step in more than three years, with the help of a badly quivering aluminum walker. He'd only recently been fitted for the four-legged walker up in physical therapy. He figured it made him look about eighty years old.

He pushed the strange, awkward-looking walker one more step, the pain inscribed all over his face.

He took a third halting step. The pain and exhilaration seemed to be balancing a little better.

There was nothing but the noise of the clanking metal walker echoing inside the room. Not a sound came from Sarah or his family. Then Stefanovitch reached out one arm for Sarah.

*   *   *

Sarah couldn't have explained or described what it was like to hold him, to grab onto Stef at the end of his miracle walk. She didn't know which one of them was trembling more.

She wasn't sure where his body stopped, and hers began. Nelson and his father were right there to help, in case he actually did start to fall at the very end.

Stef didn't fall, though. His body shook very badly, but he didn't fall. He wouldn't let himself go down.

If he had had any energy left, he would have screamed out in joy. Instead, he whispered to Sarah, 'I would scream, only I can't make it happen. Not enough strength.'

The doctors in physical therapy had promised that in another six months he'd be able to use the walker competently. In sixteen to eighteen months, the chief therapist told Stef, he would walk with a severe limp, and the assistance of a bulky metal cane.

'In six months, I'll be dancing,' Stefanovitch said. No cane. No walker. No nothing. He made the promise to all of them, but especially to Sarah.

47

Isiah Parker
Harlem
Several Months Later

It was a cold and snow-blown evening, a few days into the new year. Isiah Parker finally left the Nineteenth Precinct station house around eight-thirty. To his surprise, he had returned to his detective duties with energy and dedication missing since before his brother's death.

He walked down Adam Clayton Powell Boulevard, listening to a pleasing cacophony of early evening traffic sounds. Certain physical things about the neighborhood made him think back to his youth. The aboveground railroad tracks. Billboards for the latest pomades and preachers. Pawnbroker shops. Men huddled for warmth around a trash-can fire.

Someone stepped out from behind the staircase of a brownstone a few doors down from the precinct house. Parker had been lost in his thoughts. He'd been careless.

'Turn around nice and easy,' he heard.

Parker turned slowly, a sense of fate already overtaking him.

What he saw couldn't have surprised him more.

Stefanovitch was standing there, leaning against a sturdy wooden cane. The walking cane had been carved by hand out in Pennsylvania.

'Your eyes are going to fall out of your head,' Stef said to Parker. 'Never seen a white guy up in Harlem before?'

'I'm just surprised at how ugly you are up on all fours.'

'You killed him, didn't you? The Grave Dancer. That

was you at the World Trade Center?' Stef asked. Then he smiled. 'I came all the way up here to shake your goddamn hand.'

Isiah Parker did better than that. He embraced John Stefanovitch, clasping his back tightly with both hands.

The two detectives stood there grinning in the shadows and winter cold of the Harlem street.

New York – Los Angeles – London

Hide and Seek

James Patterson

THE INTERNATIONAL BESTSELLER

First, there was the No 1 bestselling, page-turning *Along Came a Spider*. Next, the electrifying No 1 bestseller *Kiss the Girls*. Now, a breathtaking new novel of terror and suspense which proves, once again, that no one makes the pages turn faster than James Patterson.

Maggie Bradford is on trial for murder – in the celebrity trial of the decade. As one of the world's best-loved singer-songwriters, she seems to have it all. So how could she have murdered not just one, but two of her husbands?

Will Shepherd was Maggie's second husband. A magnificent athlete and film star, he was just as famous. But Will had dark, dangerous secrets that none of his fans could have imagined . . . that his own wife could never have dreamed of.

'James Patterson does everything but stick our finger in a light socket.'   *New York Times Book Review*

'It's interesting to note the point at which the word-of-mouth on a thriller writer becomes urgent recommendation. In Patterson's case, it began with *Along Came a Spider*. This latest will consolidate that esteem. *Hide and Seek* barrels along with an unforced drive. This well-paced novel could be the book that clinches Patterson's position.'

Publishing News

ISBN 0 00 649852 3

Black Market

James Patterson

From the author who would go on to create the superbly chilling international bestsellers *Along Came a Spider*, *Kiss the Girls*, *Jack and Jill*, *Hide and Seek*, *The Midnight Club* and *Cat and Mouse* comes an early work of astonishing pace and tension – a breathtaking novel of high finance, international terrorism and irresistible page-turning suspense.

The threat was absolute. At 5.05 p.m. Wall Street would be destroyed. No demands, no ransom, no negotiations. A multiple firebombing – orchestrated by a secret militia group – would wipe out the financial heart of America. Stop the world's financial system dead.

Faced with catastrophe on an unimaginable scale, Federal agent Archer Carroll and Wall Street lawyer Caitlin Dillon are pitched into a heart-stopping race against time, tracking the unknown enemy through a maze of intrigue, rumour and betrayal towards a truly shocking climax.

'The action is fast and furious.' *Wall Street Journal*

'A tough, twisting tale.' *New York Daily News*

'Among the best writers of crime stories ever.' *USA Today*

ISBN 0 00 649314 9

AVAILABLE
FROM HARPERCOLLINS

Along Came a Spider
Jack and Jill
Kiss the Girls
Hide and Seek
Black Market
The Midnight Club

Visit www.AuthorTracker.co.uk
for exclusive updates on James Patterson.

James Patterson first took the bestseller lists by storm
with his phenomenally successful international No 1